Death
on
The Argyle

Books by Anne Canadeo

Black Sheep Knitting Mysteries

While My Pretty One Knits

Knit, Purl, Die

A Stitch Before Dying

Till Death Do Us Purl

The Silence of the Llamas

A Dark and Stormy Knit

The Postman Always Purls Twice

Murder in Mohair

Black Sheep & Company Mysteries

Knit to Kill

Purls and Poison

Hounds of the Basket Stitch

Strangers on a Skein

Death on the Argyle

Death
on
The Argyle

Anne Canadeo

Kensington Publishing Corp.
www.kensingtonbooks.com

KENSINGTON BOOKS are published by

Kensington Publishing Corp.
119 West 40th Street
New York, NY 10018

Copyright © 2022 by Anne Canadeo

All Kensington titles, imprints, and distributed lines are available at special quantity discounts for bulk purchases for sales promotion, premiums, fund-raising, educational, or institutional use. Special book excerpts or customized printings can also be created to fit specific needs. For details, write or phone the office of the Kensington Special Sales Manager: Attn. Special Sales Department. Kensington Publishing Corp, 119 West 40th Street, New York, NY 10018. Phone: 1-800-221-2647.

Library of Congress Card Catalogue Number: 2022935881

ISBN: 978-1-4967-3241-5

First Kensington Hardcover Edition: September 2022

ISBN: 978-1-4967-3243-9 (ebook)

10 9 8 7 6 5 4 3 2 1

Printed in the United States of America

To the loyal readers and fans of the
Black Sheep & Company Mysteries, you are all
treasured members of this circle of friends.

"Sitting here with one's knitting, one just sees the facts."
—Agatha Christie, "The Blood-Stained Pavement,"
The Thirteen Problems

Death
on
The Argyle

Chapter 1

Lucy was late, as usual. She had no doubt that Maggie's presentation was well underway. At least the final stretch of pregnancy was some excuse for being the last to arrive.

With one hand bracing her impressive belly, she waddled up Main Street toward The Happy Hands Café. A chalkboard out front advertised the evening's events: a "stop and swap" scrapbooking session, beginners' quilting circle, and a speed chess tournament. Perfect pastimes for the soft, spring night.

Large letters above the list announced a workshop with Maggie Messina, owner of The Black Sheep & Company Knitting Shop. Lucy's good friend was giving a presentation called "The Art of Argyle." A pattern Maggie often called, "A perilous but rewarding journey."

So far Lucy had found the stitch only perilous. Frustrating was a more accurate description. After two or three attempts, resulting in hideous UFOs—unfinished objects—she'd pull apart the false starts and save the yarn for more rewarding projects. Maybe the stars and her knitting needles would align tonight, and she'd finally learn the secret. She could easily imagine a tiny argyle sweater and if she couldn't find a pattern, she was sure Maggie would figure one out for her.

Lucy stepped inside the eatery and looked around for her friends. The café was crowded. It had opened just a few months ago and quickly become a community hub, offering a homey setting where hobbyists could share their pursuits along with a menu of simple but delicious foods and desserts.

A newcomer to town, the café's owner Rebecca Hurley was not unknown to Lucy. The two women had been best friends in college but had fallen out of touch. Rebecca had to return home at the start of her junior year, and her family situation made it hard for her continue her studies. When Rebecca moved from her hometown, after her mother's death, she and Lucy lost contact.

Lucy had thought of her from time to time and even tried to find her on Facebook. As chance would have it, while waiting in the schoolyard for her stepdaughter, Dara, one blustery winter afternoon, Lucy spotted her old school chum in the crowd of parents and caregivers.

They were both surprised and pleased by their chance reunion and Dara's close friendship with Rebecca's stepdaughter, Sophie, made it even easier to rekindle the bond.

Lucy thought her old friend had done well. She was now an accomplished cook, though Luch had never seen Rebecca scramble an egg. And her "art major" background was clearly evident in the café's bright, eclectic décor.

Heading toward the dining area, a long glass case near the entrance displayed shelves of tempting confections and savory takeout dishes. Behind the counter, a big, brass espresso machine sputtered with fragrant steam. The rest of the café was filled with tables, with more seating on an outside deck covered by a green and white awning.

A bookstore had formerly occupied the spot, and tall wooden bookcases separated many of the tables, creating cozy meeting nooks for crafters. The wide shelves were now filled with bins, baskets, and boxes of crafting supplies, along with a library of how-to books on every possible amusement.

Lucy spotted Maggie at a table in the back of the room, holding up a pair of argyle socks. An impressive audience surrounded her. Some were knitting as they listened and others, taking notes.

Lucy's friend Suzanne turned and pointed to the chair beside her. She'd held the place with her huge handbag and quickly pulled it into her lap. Luckily, Suzanne and the rest of Lucy's knitting group sat at the back of the audience. It was always awkward to step over people on the way to a seat, and in her condition, the situation was positively comic.

As Lucy slipped into the empty spot, Suzanne leaned over and whispered, "Let's hope the baby doesn't inherit your DNA for being late, or you'll be pregnant for a *long* time, lady."

There was some truth to that, but Lucy wouldn't give Suzanne the satisfaction. "Let's listen to Maggie. We might learn something," she whispered back.

"I'm just here with the cheering squad. I have a better chance of hitting the lottery than learning to argyle. I can barely fringe a scarf."

Suzanne wasn't trying to be modest. For one thing, that particular trait was not in *her* DNA. She was indisputably the least able knitter in their group, but everyone admired her persistence. Suzanne insisted she knit purely for relaxation and the comradery of her BFFs, and Lucy couldn't imagine their weekly meetings without the sassy brunette.

What Suzanne lacked in stitching talent she more than made up for in business savvy and ran the most successful realty office in town.

Seated to Lucy's left, their friend Dana leaned closer and spoke in a hushed tone. "How do you feel, honey? I thought you might not want to come out tonight."

"I'm fine. It's just hard to get up off the couch lately once I sit down."

Dana squeezed her hand. "It won't be long. You have that glow. Did you try the meditation recording I sent?"

Lucy nodded, then admitted, "I fell asleep."

"You were tired. Rest is even more important for you right now." She smiled and turned back to face Maggie.

Dana was always thoughtful and nurturing, ideal traits for a psychologist. Or perhaps those qualities had led to her career. Either way, she'd been a big support during the ups and downs of Lucy's pregnancy, though each of her friends had helped in their own way.

Lucy finally focused on Maggie and realized the presentation was ending.

"If there are no more questions, I guess that's all I have to say. Thank you so much for coming. I hope everyone is inspired to try this classic stitch. I have information and patterns up front. Please drop by the shop anytime for help with your knitting glitches."

The audience answered with an enthusiastic round of applause. Suzanne sighed. "Maggie should charge for those knitting glitch consults. She'd make a fortune."

"She'd never do that." Lucy nearly laughed at the suggestion. "It's a good way to bring in new customers, and she loves fixing messed-up projects and putting knitters back on track. It's her mission."

"And a worthy one. She gives discouraged knitters hope," Dana noted with a smile. "Looks like the Yarn

Whisperer is swamped with fans. Let's find a table and order some dessert."

"Good plan. Those cupcakes up front are calling my name." Suzanne had earned the title of the Dessert Whisperer. Both her sweet tooth and baking ability were legendary.

Lucy and her friends settled at a table nearby and browsed the menu.

"Greetings, Black Sheep knitters. Welcome to Happy Hands." Lucy looked up to find her friend Rebecca, who was dressed in her usual outfit of jeans and a T-shirt, covered by a white kitchen apron. The bright yellow bandana tied across her forehead complemented her dark red hair.

"I'm sorry I missed Maggie's talk. I've been stuck in the kitchen all night. How did it go?"

"I missed most of it, too," Lucy admitted. "You'd better ask these loyal fans. Everyone, this is Rebecca. I'm glad you could finally meet."

Dana reached out to give Rebecca's hand a shake. "Lucy's told us so much about you, I feel as if we've already met. We love the café. It's so friendly and comfortable. And the theme is so clever."

"We may never knit at Maggie's shop again," Suzanne said, "but let's not tell her yet."

Rebecca smiled. "That's sweet of you to say. But from what I hear, highly unlikely."

"Do you knit?" Dana asked.

"When I have time. Which is next to never since I opened this place."

"When you have a few minutes to spare, you'll have to join us," Dana replied. "We meet at the shop every Thursday night, but you can usually find a few of us there practically any time. It's a very relaxing pit stop."

"I'd love that. I'll try to figure it out." Rebecca seemed

pleased by the invitation. Lucy was glad, but not surprised. She'd always thought her old friend would fit in perfectly with her knitting pals.

Rebecca pulled a pad and pencil from her apron. "Now, what can I bring you? My treat," she added. Before the women could protest, she said, "We have that six-layer chocolate cake you love, Lucy."

"I noticed. The baby kicks will keep me up all night . . . but it's worth it."

"Good call," Rebecca approved, marking the order on her pad. "I'll add a glass of milk to make it half-healthy?"

"I'll have the same," Suzanne said. "The milk will make me feel healthy, too."

Dana ordered for herself and Maggie a pot of mint tea and two carrot muffins. Once Rebecca left, Dana said, "She's lovely. How did you meet again, Lucy?"

"We were best friends in college until junior year. But Rebecca had to return home. Her mother was ill and there was no one else to take care of her. We tried to stay in touch, but you know how it goes. We were both moving around a lot in those days."

Images of the years between college and moving to Plum Harbor flitted through Lucy's mind. Single days after college, working as a graphic artist in advertising agencies in Boston. Promotions, new jobs, bigger apartments. A short, unhappy marriage overlapping all of that. Divorce and leaving office life to start her own business. Coming to Plum Harbor for the summer . . . and staying ever since.

"I went to pick up Dara at school one day and I found Rebecca there, waiting for her stepdaughter, Sophie. I guess it was around the end of February or early March? Rebecca and her family had just moved to Plum Harbor. It turned out that Sophie and Dara are in the same class and became best buddies."

"What a nice coincidence." Dana had taken her knitting out. She rarely missed a chance to make progress on her projects, and the café was the perfect atmosphere. "I bet the four of you have fun together."

"We do," Lucy agreed.

Dara was her husband Matt's daughter from his first marriage. Lucy couldn't have loved the little girl more if Dara was her own, but her status as an "extra" mom wasn't always easy. As Dara and Sophie had bonded over the past few months, Lucy and Rebecca found they still had a lot in common. Including the joys and challenges of step-motherhood.

Rebecca confided that she'd been unable to have children and was thankful every day that she had Sophie in her life. She was certainly as devoted to her stepdaughter as any birth mother would be. Even more so, Lucy thought.

Sophie adored her, too. Rebecca was the only mother the little girl had ever known. Sophie's mother had died in a car accident when Sophie was only a few months old.

Rebecca had met her husband Colin just a year after his wife's death. She'd told Lucy that he proposed a few weeks later and in the blink of an eye, Rebecca's life had gone from hopelessly single to instant family.

It was a heartwarming story, though Lucy guessed that marriage to Colin wasn't always easy. She didn't know him well but often sensed a certain tension between the couple, and noticed the guarded way Rebecca often spoke about him. Still, Rebecca never complained and no one's relationship was perfect, that was for sure.

"Dara and Sophie are lucky to have each other. Middle school can be rough, especially for girls," Dana said. "Solid friendships are so important at that age."

"High school is even worse." Suzanne spoke from experience with a daughter heading for college and twin boys about to enter ninth grade.

"Where would we be without our gal pals at any age?" Lucy asked.

"We would have much a smaller audience when we gave a presentation, for one thing." Maggie had snuck up without anyone noticing. She slung her tote bag over the back of an empty chair and sat down between Lucy and Suzanne.

Chapter 2

"You drew a good crowd. You didn't need us," Dana said. "And I'm all fired up to make Jack a new golf vest."

Maggie looked pleased. "I thought we could try argyle again for our next project, if anyone else is interested."

Suzanne gazed at the ceiling. "You all know how I feel."

Lucy almost laughed. "I'm game. Maybe a baby-size project will give me less chance to mess up. But Phoebe's not here and she should have a say, too."

Phoebe Myers, the youngest member of their group, was the assistant manager at Maggie's shop. She was also an aspiring knitwear designer and sold her unique creations online, at flea markets and fairs, and in the knitting shop.

"Where is our little Fiber Goddess?" Suzanne asked.

"With Harry, of course." Maggie picked up a menu. Harry McSweeney, a sculpture and ceramics artist, was Phoebe's on-and-off boyfriend. They'd broken up at one point but got back together last summer after Harry was the prime suspect in a murder investigation and Phoebe was the only champion of his innocence.

"He's making her dinner, and by all accounts is a very

good cook," Maggie reported. "Which reminds me, all that lecturing worked up an appetite."

"We ordered for you, too. No worries," Dana said. "Looks busy in here. It might be a while."

Lucy glanced back at the café's kitchen, where the action inside was partly visible through a narrow, pass-through window. A hectic scene, with cooks and waiters rushing in all directions at once.

"Guess I'll use the ladies' while we're waiting," Lucy announced in a weary tone. That was one thing she disliked about this stage of pregnancy; it was dangerous to stray too far from a restroom.

She headed back toward the sign and passed the kitchen. A curtain had been pushed aside, and the activity back stage was in full view. She saw Rebecca at a stainless-steel counter, head bowed as she focused on a task. Her husband, Colin, stood nearby, shouting over the din.

"Stop avoiding me, Rebecca. It won't change a thing. You're only delaying the inevitable."

Rebecca carefully ladled hot soup into a row of three white bowls and sprinkled chopped herbs on top. Lucy thought she noticed her friend's hand tremble.

"I'm sorry, Colin. You know this is our busiest time. Can't we please talk later, when I get home? And talk this out in a calm, reasonable way?"

Rebecca's expression was grim, but her tone gentle and patient, as if speaking to a child. Her husband was certainly acting like one, a spoiled little boy having a tantrum, Lucy thought.

Colin walked toward her, seething. Kitchen workers swiftly cleared a path, like startled rabbits hopping out of harm's way.

"I'm working on my novel tonight. You know *that*." He

paused and shook his head. "Why am I not surprised? You don't take my writing seriously; you never did and never will."

Rebecca didn't reply. She didn't even look at him. She stared down at the soup bowls, frozen with fear.

"If you don't go into your office right this minute, we'll have it out right here!" He pounded his fist on the counter. Rebecca jumped and sucked in a harsh breath as the bowls rattled and sloshed. One crashed to the floor.

Lucy jumped back. The sound of breaking glass, combined with Colin's angry outburst, was deeply disturbing.

An older man with thick white hair and a beard stepped between the couple. Lucy recognized Rebecca's father, Leo. He worked part time at the café as an extra hand in the kitchen, waiting tables, or whatever needed doing. Lucy was glad to see him tonight.

"Come on, Colin. Calm down. Whatever's going on, you two can talk it out at home, in private." His tone was conciliatory, his smoker's voice deep and rough. And his gaunt, stooped body not the least bit intimidating.

"Back off, Leo. I'll speak to my wife any way I like." Colin pushed Leo aside and made a move toward Rebecca.

But before he could get too far, a broad-shouldered man dressed in kitchen whites rested a heavy hand on Colin's shoulder.

Lucy had noticed him at the stove, Rebecca's cook, Nick Russo. His strong features were set in a forbidding expression, his square jaw covered by a five o'clock shadow. He stared down intently at his quarry from the shadow of a black baseball cap and looked as if he wanted to turn Colin upside down and shake him, like a stubborn bottle of ketchup. He looked strong enough to do it, too.

"You heard him. Leave her alone." Nick's voice was low, but Colin shouted back.

"Or what?"

The cook didn't answer. He fixed Colin with a cold stare until Rebecca's husband slunk back, laughing under his breath.

"So that's how it is. I get it." He turned back to his wife. "We do have things to talk about, Rebecca. I'm not leaving here until we have this out."

Rebecca's cheeks flushed, and she stared at the floor. Nick glanced at her, then returned to the stove. Leo had already begun to clean up the broken glass with a broom and dustpan. Colin turned away and headed to the dining area.

Lucy put her head down and pretended to be looking at her phone as he passed. She was relieved when he didn't recognize her, or notice she'd been eavesdropping. He was still in a lather and probably wouldn't have noticed Big Foot lingering in the shadows.

She watched him walk to the back of the café, to the table where Maggie had given her presentation. He spoke to the two women sitting there, then waited with an impatient expression. They glanced at each other, clearly surprised and displeased. One seemed frightened and urged the other to get up from her chair. As they picked up their cups and belongings and left, Lucy could only imagine what Colin had said.

Some of Maggie's handouts with instructions about the argyle stitch still sat in a neat pile on the table. Colin swiped them aside, then set up his laptop. Lucy couldn't see his expression, but guessed he was pleased to have chased off the interlopers. She'd often seen him sit at that table, in that exact spot, she realized, oblivious to everything going on around him as he typed in fits and stops on his laptop.

She knew that a lot of writers had funny quirks about where and when they could write. Rituals like sharpening a certain number of pencils or wearing earplugs. Colin clearly needed to be in his writing spot and must have considered the table permanently reserved, though the café's policy was first come, first served.

Lucy finally headed to the ladies' room, wondering what the confrontation had been about. Rebecca hadn't mentioned any serious problem with Colin. But his words had struck a grave note. Not just the typical marital bickering, about sharing household chores or forgetting to stop at the dry cleaner.

Lucy didn't want to jump to conclusions and hated to even consider it, but Colin sounded serious. She wondered what he wanted to "have out" with Rebecca so urgently.

"Just in time. I was about to steal your cake," Suzanne confessed. "Purely a selfless act on my part to protect your baby. This is potent stuff. You might go into early labor."

Lucy forced a smile. She glanced at the tempting dessert but couldn't take a bite.

"Hey, only kidding. Eat up, sweetie," Suzanne urged her. "You deserve a treat at this stage of the game."

Dana glanced at her with concern. "Do you feel all right? You look a little pale."

"I'm okay. Just not as hungry as I thought. I'll take this sugar bomb home to Matt. He'll love it." Lucy took a sip of milk, trying to calm down. "I hope Rebecca can come back and chat with us again."

"She never returned. A waitress brought the order out," Dana replied. "She's probably too busy."

Or too upset. Lucy had an impulse to tell her friends about the distressing scene she'd witnessed, then decided she didn't want to gossip about Rebecca. It would feel disloyal.

Maggie had finished her muffin and took a sip of tea. "Maybe we can catch her before we go. I want to thank her again for inviting me. These events always stir up business."

Lucy nodded but wasn't really listening. She saw Colin take a sip of coffee as he stared at his computer screen, then began to type at a furious pace. Rebecca had mentioned that he was writing a novel, but Lucy didn't know what it was about. He hadn't always been a writer, she recalled. That was a recent venture. He'd spent most of his professional life as a civil engineer, working for the county, and still looked the part, too, in his broadcloth, button-down shirt and baggy khakis. She knew it wasn't right to stick people in categories by the way they dressed, but in Colin's case, she couldn't help it. He looked like the boys in high school who joined the Mathletes Club.

Beneath that math-geek façade, Lucy had long suspected Colin was a difficult man with a cold, hard side. Now she knew for sure. He certainly wasn't a nice husband.

Lucy and her friends left the café without seeing Rebecca again. Alone in her car, she tapped out a text:

Sorry we didn't get to say good night. Everyone sends a big thank you for the desserts.

She paused, wondering if she should say more. A moment later, she added:

I'll be up for a while if you want to chat.

Lucy didn't know what else to say. "About your idiot husband" was what she really meant.

She added a heart emoji and sent the text. Maybe it was just as well that she didn't get involved. Rebecca and Colin could easily talk things out and be all lovey-dovey by tomorrow. That was certainly what Lucy hoped would happen.

Chapter 3

For most of her pregnancy, Lucy had kept up her daily routine of walking her dogs to the harbor every morning and stopping at Maggie's shop on her way home. As the weather grew warmer and her condition hit eight months, it was hard to make the trek to the village and back to her neighborhood near the beach. Instead, she drove to town with her dogs, parked at the harbor, and walked up to Maggie's shop. What she missed in exercise, she more than made up for in dishing the latest gossip with her friends.

She cruised down Main Street Wednesday morning and the harbor came into view. So did a police officer. He stood directing traffic around an ambulance and several squad cars, double-parked in front of The Happy Hands Café.

Lucy tried to see what was going on, then turned her gaze back to the road. Had there been accident? Was someone sick?

She parked, got out, and quickly stepped aside as Tink and Walley bounded to the sidewalk. For once, she didn't scold the big dogs for pulling her along.

The police had blocked the space around the café with yellow tape that said: POLICE LINE. DO NOT CROSS . . .

Not a good sign. A growing number of people stopped to see what was going on, including Emily Creeder, a reporter for the *Plum Harbor Times*. Lucy watched her trot behind a police officer who was clearly avoiding her questions. Emily was a friend, but Lucy knew there was no chance of catching her attention when she was on the trail of a breaking story.

Lucy waded into the group and soon found herself shoulder to shoulder with Edie Steiber, who owned the Schooner Diner down Main Street. Edie's family had lived in Plum Harbor for generations, and most people thought of her as the unofficial town mayor. An avid knitter and a good friend of Maggie's, Edie claimed that knitting for her numerous grandchildren and great-grandchildren kept the knitting shop in business.

"Hey, Edie, what's going on? Have you heard anything?" Lucy asked.

Edie turned, her big sunflower earrings bouncing from side to side. They matched her floral cotton dress, Lucy noticed. One of her warm-weather favorites.

"There was an accident in the café. A bad one. The ambulance has been sitting here awhile but they haven't brought anyone out. Not a good sign, if you ask me."

Lucy's heart skipped a beat. "I don't suppose you've heard who was hurt? Was it Rebecca Hurley?"

"The police aren't saying a word about who, what or where. You know how it goes," Edie replied.

She did know. The police wouldn't release any official information for a while. There would only be gossip. Frustrating but true.

She felt Edie touch her hand. "Maybe it's best if you don't hang around, Lucy. In your condition, I mean. These situations aren't pretty."

Lucy nodded but didn't intend to leave so quickly. Not until she knew if Rebecca was all right.

"Uh-oh, look who's coming out. Detective Reyes." Edie poked Lucy with her elbow. "Now I'm sure something nasty is up."

Lucy followed Edie's glance and saw the Essex County detective walk out of the café. She tugged off rubber gloves, her shoes covered by powder-blue paper booties.

Lucy felt another bolt of shock. Detective Reyes had been examining the café as a possible crime scene. Lucy hated to imagine why.

The detective joined a cluster of uniformed officers, and Lucy wondered if she should approach her. Lucy and her friends knew Marisol Reyes, in a way. Much to the dismay of the detective and her colleagues, the knitting group often found themselves involved in mysterious events around town. They gave the police a lot of help with their cases— even solutions, too. Though no one in the department would officially admit it. Ever.

Even if Detective Reyes took a moment to talk, Lucy knew she wouldn't reveal much.

A car pulled up. Lucy instantly recognized the dark blue Volvo SUV and was so relieved to see Rebecca behind the wheel, she felt light-headed.

Rebecca was all right. She hadn't been hurt in the café. But Rebecca owned the restaurant and of course had been summoned to the scene. She quickly got out of the car and ran to Detective Reyes.

The two huddled together, and Lucy's relief at seeing her friend unharmed quickly faded when Rebecca gasped and covered her face with her hands.

"No . . . not Colin," Lucy heard her say. "It can't be him. . . . Are you sure?" Rebecca's body shook as she began to sob.

Detective Reyes and another officer helped her to a nearby bench, where she collapsed in a heap.

Colin? Had Rebecca actually said that Colin was the

victim of the accident? Was he . . . dead? Lucy's head flooded with a thousand questions.

"Oh boy, looks like bad news. Poor thing," Edie murmured.

Lucy nodded, feeling numb. Then handed Edie the dog leashes. "Can you hold them a minute, Edie? Rebecca is my friend. I want to talk to her."

"Sure I can, but . . . hey, Lucy . . . you can't go over there," Edie called as Lucy ducked under the yellow tape.

Lucy ignored her and a few police officers who shouted as she made a beeline to Rebecca. A uniformed officer finally caught up and blocked her path. Rebecca sat a few feet away, crying with her shoulders hunched, her hands covering her eyes.

"This is a restricted area, ma'am. You need to be behind the tape."

"That's my friend. I just want to talk to her a minute. Ask Detective Reyes, she knows me."

Rebecca must have heard her voice. She lifted her head and called out. "Lucy . . . it's so awful. They say Colin is hurt . . . They say he's dead. I can't believe it . . ." Rebecca choked on the words and Lucy rushed to comfort her despite the shock she felt hearing that Colin had died in the accident. The officer made a move to stop her, but Detective Reyes waved him off.

"Ms. Binger is a friend?" she asked Rebecca.

Rebecca nodded. "Can she sit with me until my father comes?"

Detective Reyes nodded with a kind light in her eyes. "Of course. I'll get you some water."

The detective rose and Lucy took her place on the bench. She put her arms around Rebecca and hugged her close. "I'm so sorry. What a horrible shock. . . . What happened? Was it a heart attack or something?"

Rebecca's body shook with another sob. She wiped her

eyes with a tissue. "Worse than that. They said a bookcase fell on him. It must have happened late last night. He stayed at the café to work on his writing. A kitchen worker who came in early found him."

"Oh my goodness . . . how awful." Lucy swallowed hard. Rebeccca's explanation rattled her to the quick. The image of Colin's demise was horrific and she quickly brushed it aside, trying to calm herself so she could help Rebecca.

Rebecca nodded, her lovely face crumpled again as another wave of tears took hold. "How am I ever going to tell Sophie? The poor little thing. She'll be heartbroken . . ."

Lucy hugged her and Rebecca rested her head on Lucy's shoulder a moment, then sat back and took a deep breath.

"That will be the hardest part."

Lucy nodded, her expression grim. "If there's any way I can help you, any way at all, you just have to ask. You know that, right?"

Rebecca nodded and squeezed her hand. "Of course I do. Thanks for just being here."

Before Lucy could reply, a battered green van pulled up and Rebecca's father jumped out. "There's my dad." Lucy heard a note of relief in Rebecca's voice.

Leo made his way through the officers and trotted up to them. Rebecca rose and stepped into his embrace. "Oh, Dad . . . it's so awful. Colin is gone . . ."

"I know, honey. I can't believe it, either." Leo sounded stunned. He swallowed hard, his voice catching. He patted her back, his eyes filled with tears. "What did the police say? Do they know how it happened?"

"They haven't told me much so far. The detective said she would be back soon, to give me more information. And ask me some questions."

"Yes, of course. We'll just wait for her, then." He glanced at Lucy. "You're lucky you had your friend."

Rebecca nodded. "Yes, I am."

"Don't mention it," Lucy said quietly. She felt her presence was no longer needed. Rebecca had her father now.

Leo had left the family when Rebecca was very young, and they'd been estranged for a long time. But he'd come back into her life a few years ago, determined to make amends, to show he could be a good father and a good grandfather. As far as Lucy could see, he was fulfilling that promise and more.

Lucy stood up from the bench just as Detective Reyes came their way. "There's Detective Reyes. I'd better go. If you need anything at all, anytime, day or night, you'll call me, right?

Rebecca nodded, her eyes already puffy and red from crying. "I will, Lucy. I promise."

Chapter 4

"Lucy, you're pale as a sheet! Come, sit down."
Maggie looked alarmed as Lucy stumbled up the porch steps, her dogs in tow. Maggie dropped her knitting in her lap and led Lucy to a wicker chair. As Lucy flopped into the seat, her dogs laid down at her feet. Walley, the big brown Labrador, licked Lucy's hand, but she barely noticed.

"Do you feel faint or dizzy? Should I call Matt?"

Lucy shook her head. She wasn't sure how she'd made it to Maggie's shop, she'd felt so shaken by the scene at the café. It seemed as if she'd stepped into a bad dream. With Edie's help, she'd loaded the dogs into the car and Edie drove the short distance down Main Street.

"I have bad news. Terrible news," Lucy said quietly. "Rebecca's husband was in an accident. You know those tall, heavy bookcases in the café?" Maggie nodded, her eyes wide with curiosity. "It seems Colin was there last night, working on his writing probably. One tipped over and crushed him."

Maggie's mouth formed a small circle. She covered it with her hand. "Oh my word . . . Did he survive?"

Lucy shook her head. "He did not."

Maggie poured a glass of iced tea from a frosty pitcher that sat on a cart, then handed it to Lucy, along with two packets of sugar. "Stir that in. You need it for the shock."

Lucy did as she was told and sipped the sweet tea, though she wasn't sure it would help.

"How did you hear about it?" Maggie asked. "Did Rebecca call you?"

Lucy explained how she was headed to the parking lot at the harbor and spotted the commotion in front of the café. And how Detective Reyes allowed her to sit with Rebecca until Leo arrived.

"Detective Reyes was there? How did she seem?" Maggie had poured herself a glass of tea and sat across from Lucy. She'd been sorting out skeins of summer-weight yarn but put the task aside.

Lucy knew what her friend was asking. Was the detective in full-blown investigation mode, or just on the scene because someone had died alone in a freak accident?

"The café was cordoned off with yellow tape, and she came out wearing gloves and booties. But she didn't tell Rebecca that the police suspect foul play. Not yet anyway."

Maggie met her gaze. "Not yet? Why do you say that?"

Lucy shrugged. "I don't know. Don't pay any attention to me. I'm more than a little freaked out right now."

"Anyone would be."

Lucy sipped her tea. She wasn't sure what had made her say "not yet." She just had a feeling. One that gave her gooseflesh and seemed a premonition.

Her friends had been teasing her the last eight months, claiming that pregnancy spiked a woman's psychic powers. Lucy wasn't sure she believed in the old wives' tale, but she did feel strong hunches these days. Often accompanied by an eerie chill. Then again, being pregnant had sent her body's thermostat haywire.

"I know it's not right to speak ill of the dead, but Colin isn't a very nice person. *Wasn't* a nice person, I mean," Lucy corrected herself, adjusting to Colin's past tense. "To be fair. I never spent much time with him. We sometimes crossed paths at the café, or when Dara and Sophie had a playdate. He mostly ignored me, and when he acted friendly, it seemed fake and forced. At first, I thought he was shy, or just awkward socially. He struck me as sort of dorky and harmless. But I know for sure that if you scratched the surface, he could be difficult and demanding, and had an awful temper. Especially if he didn't get his way."

"You have good instincts about people, Lucy, and you're very observant. I don't doubt what you say is true. How was the marriage? Was Rebecca happy?"

Lucy wasn't sure how to answer. "If she was unhappy, she didn't complain. Not to me anyway," she replied, recalling a few passing remarks that weren't complimentary but didn't necessarily signal a bad relationship. "He'd been downsized from his job, in the county's Department of Public Works. She was supporting the family. I'm sure that caused some tension and I did see them argue. Well, more like him yelling at her about something, but she didn't fight back."

Maggie's expression turned thoughtful as she worked on a tangled length of yarn. "Did you see them argue often?"

"No, I didn't," Lucy quickly replied. "Though there was always tension between them. It's hard to describe. He often seemed to be . . . pecking at her, if you know what I mean. But she was very patient and tried to please him or, at the very least, solve whatever petty annoyance he was complaining about."

"I think I'm getting the picture," Maggie said quietly, with a note that let Lucy know the picture was not good.

"They did have a big argument last night, at the cafe. Remember when I went to the ladies' room while we were waiting for our order? I passed the kitchen and couldn't help seeing the whole thing."

Maggie cast her a knowing look, along with a small, wry smile. "Of course you couldn't."

"Everyone in the kitchen saw it, and I'm sure I wasn't the only customer, either," Lucy defended herself. "Colin wanted Rebecca to leave work and talk to him about something. He seemed to think it was very important, urgent even. He claimed she'd been avoiding him, but that wasn't going to change anything. She had to face it."

Maggie's head popped up, her interest snagged. "Face what?"

"I don't know. He didn't say."

"How did Rebecca react?"

"She just kept ladling soup, though I noticed her hand shake. She spoke to him very patiently but didn't stop working. Then he got even angrier and pounded the counter. A bowl of soup flew off and crashed on the floor."

Maggie sat back. "Sounds intense."

"It was. I thought he was about to . . . well, strike out at her."

"Maybe he has," Maggie said quietly.

Lucy had thought of that, too. She quickly brushed the awful image from her mind. "Rebecca's never told me anything like that. Maybe she wouldn't, right? Before it could get any worse, Rebecca's father, Leo, stepped up and tried to calm Colin down. When that didn't work, the café's cook, Nick Russo, confronted him. He's a lot bigger than Colin, too. Colin finally gave in and left the kitchen."

"Then what? Did he leave the café?"

"He went straight to his favorite table, shooed away a few customers, and set up his computer. I'd heard him tell

Rebecca that he planned to work on his writing all night. Even after the café closed, I presumed. I guess that's what he did and that's where they found him."

"You're probably right." Maggie's expression was grave, picturing the scene, Lucy guessed. "But just because he was unpleasant and a bit of a slacker, and yelled a lot, it doesn't mean there was foul play."

"No, it doesn't," Lucy reminded herself. Though for some reason, the more they talked about it, the more likely it seemed that Colin had died an unnatural death.

The yarn was smoothed out and Maggie placed the skein aside. "If he died under suspicious circumstances, I guess we'll hear soon. News like that travels fast in this town."

"Does it ever," Lucy agreed. She took a deep breath. The sweet, cold tea was taking effect and she was starting to feel herself again.

The heavy, soft warmth of her golden retriever's head resting on her foot helped, too. Tink always sensed when Lucy felt the slightest bit off. She was the perfect furry nurse.

"It's unfortunate that Rebecca and Colin argued so vehemently and publicly," Maggie said. "If it wasn't an accident, that could make things complicated for Rebecca."

Lucy knew what she meant. "The police always look at the nearest and dearest first. But if she has a solid alibi for the time of his death, there shouldn't be any issue."

"No, there shouldn't be," Maggie agreed.

"Either way, it is a nightmare. One that's just begun," Lucy said.

"What's a nightmare? What did I miss?" Phoebe stood in the doorway, a huge coffee mug in one hand, her knitting tote dangling from the other. "I hope you're all right, Lucy?"

Lucy was touched by her concern. "Perfectly fine. Just a little shaken up."

Phoebe stepped inside and the screen door slammed behind her. The day promised to be unseasonably warm for early May in New England, and Phoebe had dressed in a pink T-shirt and a long, gauzy skirt with an intricate pattern that included purple elephants.

"A man died in the Happy Hands Café last night," Maggie told her. "Crushed by a bookcase. He was the husband of Lucy's friend Rebecca Hurley. I'm sure you've heard us talk about her."

"The Happy Hands lady? Sure, I know who she is. How awful! I'm so sorry for your friend, Lucy. What a horrible thing to go through."

"It is horrible. Rebecca and Colin have a little girl, nine years old, the same age as Dara. She's Colin's child from his first marriage. The first thing Rebecca worried about was telling her. She'll be devastated."

Maggie made a little *tsk* sound and shook her head, as reading glasses slipped down her nose. "It's tragic for a child that young to lose a parent. I'm not going to offer some platitude about children being resilient, either. With time and support, she'll likely be okay, but it's an emotional wound she'll have to deal with her whole life."

"Unfortunately true. At least she has Rebecca and Leo. Rebecca adores her and the feeling is clearly mutual."

"That's something," Maggie agreed.

"It's a lot." Phoebe had taken a seat and was sipping from her mug. It said *Socks By Phoebe* in bright pink script. "I wasn't close to my dad when I lost my mom. He tried his best, but he just didn't get me like my mom did. At least I had my brother, Pete."

Lucy was sorry now that she'd brought up the sensitive topic. Phoebe had lost her mother to breast cancer when she was only eleven or so. Her father had quickly remarried, and she'd always felt on the outside of his new family. He lived in Arizona now and she saw him very rarely. But she was still close with her brother, who was in the navy.

"And you have all of us," Maggie reminded her. "Your Stitching Sisters."

Phoebe laughed. "I never heard you use that term before, Maggie, but it definitely fits."

Lucy thought so, too, when she thought of their knitting group. But Maggie and Phoebe's bond went far beyond stitching sisters, or even accolade and mentor. Maggie often called Phoebe her Fiber Daughter and meant it. No slight to her real daughter, Julie, who lived in the Midwest. Lucy had often thought the fit was mutual; Phoebe filled a void in Maggie's life as much as Maggie stood in for Phoebe's lost mother.

"Rebecca has no close family except for Leo. None that I've ever heard about," Lucy added. "She needs her friends now. I think I'll cook or bake something and drop it off at her house tonight."

"That's very thoughtful. If you want some company, I can come with you," Maggie said.

Lucy felt relieved to hear the offer. "Would you? Even though she's a good friend, that type of visit is so hard. If it's not too much trouble, I'd be grateful to have you there, Mag. Matt has late hours tonight, so I can't drag him along."

Lucy's husband, Matt, was a veterinarian with an office in town. They'd met almost five years ago, when Lucy had impulsively rescued Tink and the scraggly dog got sick before Lucy had even brought her home.

"I don't mind. I like Rebecca very much and want to help her if I can."

Since Rebecca lived near the village, Lucy offered to

pick Maggie up at the shop at six o'clock, her usual closing time. It was almost nine and time for Maggie and Phoebe
to start their workday.

Lucy had work waiting for her, too, in her home office.
The bigger her pregnant belly got, the harder it was to
concentrate on her projects: designing brochures, book
layouts, and various graphic art assignments.

Today it would be nearly impossible. She doubted she
could keep the news of Colin Hurley's death far from her
thoughts.

If it hadn't been an accident, Lucy wondered who in the
world would have taken his life.

Chapter 5

Lucy picked Maggie up at the shop at six, as they'd planned. Maggie placed a pan covered in tinfoil in the back seat, alongside Lucy's casserole dish, also covered with foil.

"When did you have time to cook?" Lucy glanced at her friend as she started up the car again.

"The shop was quiet, and Phoebe is more than capable of covering. It's just a quick recipe I found online. You toss some tomatoes with olive oil and herbs and roast them in the oven on very high heat. And you stick a block of feta cheese in the middle. That's the fun part." She glanced at Lucy and nodded. "When everything looks toasty, you mix the whole thing with pasta, fresh basil bits, and such. I like to add a little chopped onion and garlic to the oven at the end. And maybe a pinch of red pepper, for a kick."

Maggie's shop had been a small Victorian house before it had been turned into retail space. When Maggie took over, she found the kitchen mostly intact and kept it that way. She used most of the space as a storeroom, but the appliances came in handy on their meeting nights and whenever she wanted to serve sweet or savory snacks to her customers.

"Sounds delicious." Lucy felt hungry listening to the description. She'd been hungry all the time throughout her pregnancy, except for a brief period at the start, when she'd had some morning sickness.

"It seemed a good choice for this sort of call. I know it sounds a little ghoulish, but has anyone ever written a condolence call cookbook? A collection of comfort food recipes—casseroles and desserts that cook up quickly and travel well? I think there'd be a market for it."

The suggestion made Lucy grin, reminding her why she was grateful Maggie had offered to come along. "I'm pretty sure the field is clear, Mag. If you can't find a publisher, you can always go DIY."

"You think I'm joking, but I'm not. Well, a little, I guess." Maggie glanced back at Lucy's package. "What did you make?"

"Reliable old mac and cheese. It's a recipe Grandma Binger used to make for me and Ellen whenever we stayed over. You add evaporated milk and it comes out extra rich. I had everything in the house because I've been craving the stuff twenty-four/seven since I got pregnant."

"So I've heard. The recipe sounds yummy. Your grandma must have been a good cook," Maggie remarked.

"Not really, mac and cheese was her best dish. Along with her peanut butter cookies," Lucy said with a small laugh. "It's intimidating to cook for someone who owns a restaurant. Though I'm sure Rebecca will appreciate our efforts."

"I'm sure she will, too. Come to think, she's not actually the café's cook. It's that guy Nick, right? The one who faced Colin down last night during the argument?"

"That's right." Lucy turned off Main Street and followed Old Farm Lane. Rebecca did not live far from town, but the house was in a woodsy, secluded spot. The road was suddenly pitch-black and she turned the high beams on.

"I've been thinking of Rebecca all day," Lucy admitted. "And about what might evolve if Colin's death was due to foul play. The police will look at her closely. Especially after that argument."

"They have to check every angle. We know that by now, Lucy. I don't think there's any reason to worry. One step at a time," Maggie reminded her. "One condolence casserole at a time, you might say."

After another turn or two, they arrived at the Hurleys' house; a small, rustic-looking cottage covered by brown cedar shake shingles, with forest-green shutters, a brick-red door, and dark yellow trim. The house was set back from the road, surrounded by tall trees.

Neighbors were distant, their homes out of view after nightfall. Lucy had always found the cottage and its secluded location charming, but tonight it felt very isolated, despite all the lights on within.

She pulled into the curved driveway and the Jeep's wheels crunched over stones and pine needles. There were a few cars on the drive and she parked behind a small hatchback.

Lucy took her dish from the back seat and waited as Maggie did the same. "We aren't the only ones who had this idea," Lucy said.

"Obviously not. They haven't been in town long, but Rebecca must know a lot of people through the café. Colin must have had friends, too."

"Sure he did," Lucy replied automatically, though she wasn't sure at all.

The front door was open. Lucy walked in first, and

Maggie followed into a small foyer where sweaters and jackets sat piled on a bench. There was a living room to the left, a dining room to the right, and a kitchen down a short hall that led back from the front door. Visitors chatted quietly in every room, drinks in hand. It wasn't a party atmosphere, but not a completely somber one, either.

Somewhere in between, which was good for Rebecca, Lucy thought. She needed to be distracted and comforted tonight, to feel the support of people who cared about her.

They went into the kitchen to leave the food and Rebecca greeted them. "Lucy, Maggie . . . It was so sweet of you to come. And you even cooked? You shouldn't have gone to so much trouble."

"No trouble at all. We wanted to." Lucy hugged her, slanted to the side to accommodate for her belly. Rebecca returned the hug, fiercely for an instant, before she let go.

Rebecca stepped back and forced a smile. Her eyes were puffy and her nose red from too many tissues. Her long hair was pulled back in a tight low ponytail, her face bare of makeup, and her complexion pale as paper. She had on the same T-shirt and jeans she'd been wearing that morning. She looked as if she'd been through a hectic day. Probably one of the most grueling in her life, Lucy reflected.

"We just wanted to see how you're doing, Rebecca," Maggie said.

"Everyone's been so kind. I expected to be alone tonight. But people just keep coming by, bringing food and cakes." She glanced at the counter that was covered with offerings. "And wine. Can I pour you a glass?"

Lucy stepped over to a row of bottles and a pile of plastic cups that had been set out on the counter. "We can help ourselves," she said.

Lucy poured herself a glass of sparkling water, and Maggie splashed a bit of cabernet into a plastic cup.

"I hope the police aren't watching the house. They might get the wrong idea and think I'm having a party."

Gallows humor, Lucy thought. She also hoped the police weren't watching the house. She knew they could get the wrong idea about a lot of things right now.

"Why do you think they'd be watching?" Lucy asked. "Did Detective Reyes say something that bothered you? She must have had a million questions."

"Maybe a million and one. I lost count." Rebecca sipped a glass of white wine. "It wasn't anything specific, just her attitude. She's coming here tomorrow to speak to me again. I can't imagine what else there is to ask."

As an investigation evolved, there were always more questions. But Lucy didn't want to worry Rebecca about that now.

"What have the police told you so far? Do they have any reason to think it wasn't an accident?" Maggie said.

Rebecca's mouth formed a tight line. Lucy could see she was reluctant to reply. She moved a step closer and spoke in a quieter tone. "I don't think they've released the information to the press yet, but Detective Reyes told me it looks like the bolts that hold the bookcase to the floor had been tampered with. The hardware is old and rusty. She said it would be easy to think they had slipped out by accident, but the police are sure, for some reason, that someone loosened the screws, then slipped them back in place."

"So it looked as if the bookcase was stable but didn't need much of a push to fall over," Maggie said.

"That's right. Detective Reyes thinks that fact alone is enough to conclude that Colin's death was"—Rebecca paused, unable to continue for a moment—"not an accident."

Lucy also thought it was ample reason to draw that conclusion. Not to mention that *particular* table was Colin's favorite spot, and someone studying Colin's habits would have observed that Colin could be found there many nights, working into the small hours when no one would be around to witness a stealthy intruder, intent on murder.

"Oh, and they told me something more. My office was searched. Drawers pulled out of the desk, the file cabinet opened, and documents thrown around. There was some petty cash in the desk, a few hundred dollars we keep on hand for odds and ends. That was missing."

"So it might have been a robbery?" Maggie had picked off a grape from a platter of fruit and cheese.

"Possibly." Rebecca shrugged. "The police don't know much yet and frankly, I get the feeling that they aren't telling me half of what they've figured out."

Lucy guessed her assessment was right. Investigators played their cards close to their vest at this stage, even with a victim's family.

"Does the café have a security system? An alarm or video cameras?" Maggie had popped the grape in her mouth and took another.

"We have both. It reduces the insurance payments. For some reason the alarm didn't go off. The police took all the video recordings. I guess they'll tell me tomorrow what they see." Rebecca bit her lip, looking worried about that conversation. "They asked if I've fired anyone recently. But there are no disgruntled employees lurking around. And they asked if Colin had any disputes with friends or neighbors, or maybe a colleague from his old job."

"Did he?" Maggie asked bluntly.

"Not that I knew of." Rebecca shrugged and sipped her wine.

They must have asked about her marriage; if it was a happy one. Lucy wondered how Rebecca answered that question, but didn't feel it was appropriate or considerate to ask now. She also wondered if Rebecca had told the police about the blowup in the kitchen the night Colin died. If, for some reason, she had not, the information would surely reach them and make it seem as if she was trying to hide something.

And they would learn how Nick Russo had confronted Colin to protect Rebecca and stop the quarrel. She doubted the police would suspect the intervention led to Colin's death. But you never knew with these things.

"You must feel so overwhelmed." Lucy felt a wave of sympathy for her friend. "It's enough of a shock to lose Colin so suddenly, without a police investigation tossed in."

"It has been a shock. Part of me keeps expecting him to walk in any minute and pour himself a beer. And watch Sophie run over for a hug." Her words got shaky and she dabbed her eyes with a tissue. "It made me realize how we go through our routines every day, almost in a trance, expecting our lives will never change. But they do change. Suddenly, without warning. Not always for the better."

The insight was true and sobering. "How is Sophie?" Lucy asked. "She must find it impossible to believe Colin is gone."

Rebecca nodded, blinking back tears. "It was so hard to tell her. It was the worst moment of my life. She's old enough to understand on a logical level, but, of course, she still wishes it wasn't true and that somehow we'll wake up tomorrow and he'll be here."

Lucy understood that reaction. She felt that way herself

when she lost someone. She'd heard there were many stages of grief, and denial was one of the first responses.

Rebecca lifted her head and took a steadying breath. "The police helped me find a grief counselor. She came to the house this afternoon and spoke to us for a while and she'll come back tomorrow. Nothing can make Sophie's pain go away, but I think counseling will help her."

"I think so, too," Lucy said.

"It's wise to have all the support you can find. Especially a specialist who understands how children react to such a tragic loss," Maggie said.

"I'd do anything for Sophie. She's the most important thing to me in the world. I'm all she has now. And she's all that I have."

Her voice was quiet, her words heartfelt. Lucy reached out and touched Rebecca's hand.

"I'm sorry . . . I didn't mean to get so . . . dramatic," Rebecca apologized with a small laugh.

Maggie shook her head. "No apologies necessary. Not under these circumstances. Is there any way at all that we can help you in the coming days, Rebecca?"

"You're helping me now just by being here and listening to me vent about this . . . this nightmare. The café is closed until the police finish the investigation. They have no idea how long it will take. Sophie will be home from school at least a week. That's what the therapist recommends. She also said the sooner I can hold a memorial for Colin, the better. These rituals and customs provide a sense of closure, I guess. Even for a child."

"We can help you with that, when the time comes," Maggie said.

"I can help you with Sophie," Lucy offered. "Dara's company would be a good distraction."

"The best," Rebecca replied.

More visitors walked in and Rebecca glanced at the door. Lucy didn't want to monopolize her company.

"We'll say good night. Promise me you'll stay in touch?" Rebecca hugged her again. "I'll check in with you tomorrow. I promise. Thank you again, for everything." She hugged Maggie as well and walked with them to the door.

"No thanks necessary, dear," Maggie patted her arm. "Please drop by the shop if you need some company."

"I'll take you up on that," Rebecca replied.

While Rebecca greeted more visitors, Lucy and Maggie slipped out, into the dark night. The temperature had dropped and Lucy rubbed her arms for warmth. She clicked open the car and was about to open the driver's side door, when a roaring motor froze her in place.

She and Maggie turned to see a motorcycle speed up the driveway. It slowed a bit just before it passed, the engine finally sputtering to a halt. The driver parked the bike near the house and hopped off. Broad shoulders filled a leather jacket, and worn jeans hugged slim hips and long, lean legs.

Lucy had already guessed the rider's identity. Confirmed when he pulled off the helmet and smoothed his thick brown hair with his hand.

Lucy and Maggie climbed into the Jeep and fastened their belts. "Wait, let me guess," Maggie said. "Nick, the cook from the café?"

"You nailed it." Lucy started the engine and smiled briefly at her friend.

"He makes an entrance, doesn't he?" Maggie murmured.

Lucy agreed. "A real bad-boy type."

"I hate to label people based on superficial impressions. But in this case, I agree. The police asked Rebecca about disgruntled ex-employees, but she didn't mention them questioning her *present* employees," Maggie mused. "Of course, they will. Maybe they've already begun."

Lucy headed down the driveway toward the road, careful to steer around the awkwardly parked motorcycle.

"I'd say Nick, the bad-boy cook, is at the top of the list."

Chapter 6

Lucy pulled up to the knitting shop Thursday night and parked behind the line of cars that belonged to her friends. She was the last to arrive, as usual, and almost hadn't made it. After a long workday and a visit to her OB/GYN, she'd felt tired enough after dinner to go to bed. Or at least drift into a nap watching TV with Matt.

But the weekly comradery of her pals lured her like a siren song. While Matt cleaned the kitchen, she caught a second wind and headed to town.

A warm yellow light shone in the shop's front window, behind a row of big paper flowers and spring knitting projects hanging from a clothesline. The clever display made her smile and Lucy stepped inside, instantly cheered by the sound of familiar voices and laughter.

"There she is. We were losing hope," Suzanne greeted her.

Maggie ran to meet her and took her knitting bag, though it was quite light and no burden at all. "You look tired. Maybe you shouldn't have made the effort."

"I am a bit pooped," Lucy admitted. "But I couldn't resist." She sat in her usual seat at the big oak table in the back of the shop, where Maggie held group lessons, and where they shared dinner on knitting nights.

"Have you eaten yet? We saved you a plate," Dana said.

"I had a bite with Matt, thanks. But I won't refuse dessert." She gazed around hopefully.

"You're just in time. Phoebe baked for us. Something called Candy Shop Blondies. Sounds very . . . 1960s?"

Lucy laughed. "My teeth ache just hearing the name. But I won't complain."

"There's also some vanilla ice cream. To balance the palate." Maggie stepped over to the sideboard and set a container and an ice-cream scooper on the table, along with a pile of dessert dishes.

"Tell us about the checkup. How did it go?" Dana turned her chair to see Lucy clearly. Her friends had kept close watch on her doctor's appointments all through her pregnancy, often dispelling her concerns and fears about issues the doctor raised or symptoms that always turned out to be nothing.

"It wasn't very long. But that's a good sign, right? Everything looks fine. Right on schedule. I'm exactly four weeks from the due date. The doctor said the baby is getting bigger, almost six pounds," she added, feeling a little frisson of excitement.

"I guess Baby Binger-MacDougal is going to be a good-size, healthy baby." Maggie sounded excited, but as if she didn't want to make Lucy anxious.

"A bruiser," Suzanne murmured.

"Suzanne, was that necessary?" Maggie hushed her, along with a look. Lucy was grateful. She knew Suzanne was only teasing. but it still made her nervous.

"How do you feel?" Dana asked in a more serious tone.

"I know I'm supposed to get a huge jolt of energy about now, but I mostly feel as if I'm carrying around a giant bowling ball. And I haven't seen my toes in weeks."

"You ought to get a pedicure before the baby comes. A little self-care is a good thing and you'll never have time after. Not until the baby gets a driver's permit." Suzanne had just started a project and was only a few rows into it. Lucy guessed the light blue mohair, with its fluffy, feminine appeal was going to be a summer top for her daughter. It certainly wasn't argyle.

"Speaking of treats, here comes dessert," Maggie said quietly.

Phoebe could be heard coming down the stairs from her apartment. She paused just before the bottom step, then leapt into view, holding out a tray decorated with paper doilies.

"Ta-dah! Welcome to the candy shop! All your favorites—M&M's, Kit Kats, peanut butter cups, Baby Ruth bars."

Phoebe presented the tray to Dana first, and Lucy watched as Dana's commitment to healthy eating warred with her tendency to encourage creative efforts.

"Those blondies look . . . amazing. I'll just take a small bite. I'm so full from dinner."

"I'll try one," Suzanne said. "Nice touch with the gummy bears."

"That was the finishing touch, for decoration. I didn't want the bears to melt in the oven."

"Smart thinking," Suzanne nodded with approval as she chose a blondie.

The tray was passed around the table and Lucy took a small square. The confection looked strange but tasted delicious, and as Maggie had suggested, a dab of vanilla ice cream was the perfect counterpoint to the conglomeration of flavors.

"Have you heard from Rebecca?" Maggie glanced up from her knitting, an argyle project that looked like a man's vest in summer-weight yarn. Most likely for her husband, Charles, who wore Maggie's creations proudly. "I wonder how it's going with Detective Reyes."

"I texted her this afternoon, but she only sent a short note back, promising to call."

Dana fidgeted, shifting in her chair. She adjusted her glasses, then turned her work over and back again. Lucy noticed and could see that Maggie did, too.

"Come on, Dana. Spill it," Lucy prompted her.

"Your body language is *so* giving you away," Phoebe noted, drawing on one of Dana's favorite tools.

"Okay, you got me." Dana looked up from her knitting and grinned.

Dana's husband, Jack, had been a detective for Essex County before leaving the force to earn a law degree. He practiced in town and still had a lot of connections in the squad room. He often gave Dana the inside scoop on interesting cases, which she passed on to her friends, though she really wasn't supposed to.

"I haven't heard much more than you already know," Dana continued. "For some reason, the security cameras at the café, front and back, were knocked out of alignment and didn't catch much. Rebecca said she'd just had them serviced and the equipment should have been recording correctly. The police did find some video from a security camera at a shop down the street."

Dana checked the stitches on her work as she spoke. "They can see a car drive into the café parking lot and come out again a while later. The film quality is blurry and taken from a distance. They're not even sure yet of the car's make, or plate number."

"Don't they have high-tech ways of blowing up the images to see those details?" Suzanne asked. "That's what investigators on TV do."

"Sure, but not the investigators in Plum Harbor. They probably sent the tape to a special crime lab for deeper analysis." She picked up her needles and continued to stitch. "The police discovered straight off that the bolts that should have secured the bookcase to the floor had been loosened. No question that his murder was intentional. There was some cash stolen and an office ransacked, but they're not convinced it was a robbery gone wrong." Lucy had already learned those details of the crime scene from Rebecca last night, so she was not surprised. Maggie had heard them as well. "They've questioned the café staff and heard about the argument between Colin and Rebecca," Dana added. "Which isn't good news for her, I'm sorry to say."

"I was afraid of that." Lucy felt the candy shop blondie form a small brick in her stomach. "From what I heard, Colin wanted to have it out about some problem between them, and claimed Rebecca was avoiding him. I'm sure the police have asked Rebecca what their squabble was all about."

"What did Jack say?" Suzanne asked.

"I asked him, but he hadn't heard. No matter what it was about, the argument makes Rebecca's location at the time of the murder critically important. If she has a solid alibi, she's easily eliminated as a suspect."

"If not?" Lucy sighed. Dana looked down at her knitting again, reluctant to elaborate.

"I wanted to ask her last night," Lucy said. "But she was so upset about Colin and Sophie, I didn't have the heart."

"That's you all over, Lucy. You're so considerate." Phoebe met her gaze with a soft smile. "Some people I know definitely don't have that sort of restraint."

Had her gaze drifted to Suzanne? If so, Suzanne hadn't noticed, her eyes fixed on the front of the shop. "Maybe you can ask her right now," Suzanne suggested. "I think Rebecca just peeked through the window.

Chapter 7

"I was just passing and saw the lights on. Hope I'm not interrupting anything?" Rebecca had taken a few steps into the shop and paused.

"Just the usual stitching and chatting. Come on back and join us." Maggie rose to greet her unexpected guest, then guided her to an empty chair at the table.

"Can I get you something? A glass of wine? Or some coffee or tea?" Maggie offered.

"Tea would be perfect, thanks." Rebecca looked tired, Lucy thought, her complexion pale and dark shadows beneath her hazel eyes. Who wouldn't be exhausted by the challenges she faced on so many fronts right now?

"We were just indulging in the amazing dessert Phoebe made," Dana passed Rebecca the plate of Candy Shop Blondies.

"And wondering how you were doing," Lucy added honestly.

She hoped Rebecca didn't think that they'd been gossiping. They were concerned, that was different. Though she did feel a bit guilty now that Rebecca had appeared.

Rebecca met Lucy's gaze. "I'm sorry I didn't call you today. There's been so much going on. I've been giving Sophie as much attention as I can and the police . . ." She paused and caught a breath. Lucy had never seen her so stressed. She was always so calm and grounded, even in the midst of chaos at the café.

"The visit from Detective Reyes didn't go well?" Lucy asked.

"She came to the house, but not to talk. She asked to search Colin's home office and our bedroom. A few uniformed officers were with her. They went through the rooms and took away a lot of stuff in boxes. When they were done, she asked me to come to the station to answer more questions."

Lucy felt her chest tighten. "Did she show you a search warrant?"

"It wasn't like that. She asked if I'd allow them to look through his belongings to get a clearer picture of what was going on in his life and maybe get a lead on who had killed him. I had no reason to object."

"They would have returned with a search warrant anyway. By agreeing, it shows you have nothing to hide," Dana pointed out.

"That's what I thought, too. More or less," Rebecca replied.

"What happened at the station?" Maggie sounded concerned.

"They showed me some videotape from a security camera. I think it's set up at the hardware store down the street."

"We heard that they saw a car drive in and out of the café's parking lot," Maggie told her. "Dana's husband has connections on the police force, and he sometimes hears information about investigations," she explained.

"Oh, then you know about that. It's no problem for me," Rebecca admitted. "But that's not all they saw. I'm guessing your husband didn't hear that there was also a small amount of video from the security camera in the back of the café, taken early in the evening," she said to Dana. "It shows me and my cook, Nick, sharing what people call a . . . private moment?"

Dana shook her head. "He definitely did not."

"The police seemed very pleased with themselves when they showed me that clip. As if they'd solved the entire case with two minutes of blurry film. It was absolutely nothing. I was upset . . . about something." She paused. Lucy and her friends knew she meant her blowup with Colin, but she obviously wasn't ready to talk about it. "I went outside to clear my head," she continued. "I guess I was crying when Nick came out for a smoke. Or maybe I started crying when he asked if I was okay?"

She sighed and shook her head. Lucy could tell she felt embarrassed. "I'm not sure how it happened. He put his arms around me in a friendly gesture and I hugged him back. It was over in an instant and there was nothing else to it. Nothing like that has ever gone on between us before. Our relationship has been strictly professional. I swear."

Rebecca's voice rose on a frustrated note and Lucy could only imagine how she'd felt defending herself to the police.

"What do the police think?" Lucy asked, though she already knew the answer.

"That we're having an affair. What else would they think? From that totally false assumption, they're jumping to some crazy theory that we plotted together to get Colin out of the way."

Lucy felt her heart clench. This was not good. Not good at all. . . .

Maggie emerged from the kitchen with Rebecca's tea. She stood by her chair and handed down the steaming mug. "The police are going to test a lot of wild theories before this is through. I know it's easy to say and hard to do, but hang tight. Don't let them rattle you."

Rebecca held the mug in both hands and sighed. "I am rattled. To my bones. It's enough of a shock for your husband to die so suddenly, in such a freak way. Then to learn he's been murdered . . . And have the police point a finger at you?" She shook her head, curly strands of her dark red hair falling loose from her ponytail.

She lifted her head and took a sip of tea. "The problem is," she said quietly, "Colin and I had a huge argument just a few hours before he died. Right in the café kitchen. Plenty of witnesses."

"Yes, we know. I was on my way to the restroom and I saw it through the kitchen door," Lucy admitted. "I didn't mean to eavesdrop. It's just that . . ."

Rebecca dismissed her apology with a wave of her hand. "Lucy, I'm sure half the restaurant overheard that row. A lot of people told the police about it, too."

Rebecca paused, seeming reluctant to continue. Finally, she said, "It wasn't just an ordinary spat, either. We were arguing because Colin wanted a divorce. He'd sprung it on me out of the clear blue just a day or so before. He was going to move out and had all the paperwork drawn up to split our assets."

"That's outrageous," Dana said.

"I thought so, even for him. Colin could be very impulsive. We didn't have a happy marriage, but we had agreed to stay together for Sophie's sake, at least until she was in high school. A divorce is never easy for kids, but it's especially hard for children her age to handle."

Lucy was surprised to hear that admission. Then not so surprised. Her intuition had told her that Rebecca's marriage was not rock solid.

"So, he went back on his agreement. He didn't want to wait that long," Maggie said. "Was it another woman?"

"I don't know. Though I think there were other women, from time to time."

"This is concerning," Dana said quietly. "It gives you a motive in the eyes of the investigators. Was there money involved? Did you have joint assets?"

"Not much." Rebecca shook her head and Lucy felt relieved. "I've been mostly supporting the family for months, since Colin was downsized. He wanted to work on his writing instead of looking for another engineering job. The restaurant is doing well and we managed to make ends meet without his salary. He was given some severance pay and he told me that the novel he was working on was optioned by a film producer. Overall, he seemed to have money. He bought himself a fancy, custom-made bicycle soon after he was let go. I thought it was a luxury, but he claimed after working nine to five for so long he deserved it. He did contribute to bills, here and there. As far as assets, we rent the house and the cars are both leased. There's a joint bank account, but there's never much in it," she added with a shrug. "Colin had a life insurance policy, but it will just be enough to cover the funeral."

"Not exactly *Double Indemnity*, is it? That's something in your favor," Suzanne remarked.

Dana did not look convinced, Lucy noticed, and that made her nervous.

Dana put her knitting aside and met Rebecca's gaze. "I still think you need an attorney, Rebecca. I can help you find a good one if you don't know who to call."

"A lawyer? Really? But I haven't done anything wrong."

"Of course you haven't," Lucy said quickly. "But you need an attorney to deal with the police. You said it yourself. They're getting the wrong idea."

Rebecca looked glum and didn't reply.

"A full account of your activity on the night Colin died is important. I'm sure Detective Reyes asked you about that first thing," Dana said.

"There wasn't much to tell. I closed the restaurant at eleven, right after the cleanup was done. Sometimes I stay a little later to do paperwork or check the supplies. But I was beat."

"Colin was still there, writing?" Maggie asked.

"Right in his favorite spot. He listens to music with ear pods when he's on his computer, so I walked back to tell him I was leaving. I said if he still wanted to talk, I'd be at home."

"What did he say?" Lucy asked.

"He looked up a moment but didn't answer. He just kept typing and I felt . . . dismissed? I assumed he was still angry, but he got like that when he was writing. As if he was in a trance. He hated to be interrupted."

Rebecca sighed. "That's the last thing I said to him and the last time I saw him . . . alive, I mean." Her voice faltered. Lucy could see that reliving the details of that night was upsetting. Of course it would be, even if their marriage had not been a happy one.

"I'm sorry, Rebecca. We don't mean to grill you," Maggie said softly. "You've certainly had enough questions from Detective Reyes. If you'd rather not talk about this . . ."

Rebecca shook her head. "It's okay. I want to tell you everything. Maybe you'll see something I've missed. Something the police have missed, too."

"No guarantee, but we'll try," Maggie replied. "What happened at home? Was Sophie with you?"

"Sophie was at my house," Lucy said. "The girls were off from school Wednesday. A teacher's conference day or some such, so they were having a sleepover."

"I went home and sent Colin a few texts, telling him I was ready to talk. I hoped to persuade him to see a counselor with me. I was hoping we could work things out. Or even visit a mediator to work out a separation agreement, if that's what he really wanted. I certainly wasn't going to sign a pile of documents that ended our marriage without having any input."

"Of course not," Suzanna agreed. "Who in their right mind would?"

"In Massachusetts, couples can separate by signing an agreement which sorts out matters like child custody and a visiting schedule, the separation of any assets and debts, and any support payments due," Dana explained. "It's not the same as a 'legal separation.' The document doesn't have to be filed with the court, but it's helpful if the couple plans on divorcing. And, in this state one party in a relationship can file for a divorce, claiming 'Irretrievable Breakdown of Marriage,' whether or not the other agrees."

"I don't know anything about separation or divorce laws, but I'm starting to think Colin did his research," Rebecca said.

Lucy agreed. It sounded as if he'd planned to use those laws to his advantage, too. "So you were home alone, waiting for him to reply to your messages," Lucy said. "Did you see anyone, or speak to anyone on the phone?"

Rebecca shook her head. "It was late. But I was wide awake, feeling nervous, expecting another argument. The house was a mess, so I cleaned up and started a load of laundry. Colin didn't help with the housework, even though he was home every day."

What a gem. If they had gotten divorced, Rebecca would have been well rid of him, Lucy thought.

"I finally decided to go over to the café. Which was probably the biggest mistake of my life. But I knew I wouldn't sleep a wink unless I tried to talk to him." Rebecca sighed.

"I drove into town and parked behind the café. But I couldn't get my nerve up to go inside. I was afraid to be alone with him. Afraid he'd lose control of his temper and be impossible to reason with."

And possibly hurt her? Lucy wondered if she meant that but didn't want to say. "So, you just sat there?" Lucy asked, her pulse quickening.

"For a few minutes. I'm not sure how long," Rebecca continued. "I probably would have sat there all night, trying to make up my mind, but my father called. He'd gone up to Newburyport for an open mike night with his singing partner, Alfie, and called me from the road. He was having chest pains and was headed to an urgent care center. He asked me to meet him, so I just started the car and headed over there."

Lucy knew that Rebecca's father had a serious heart condition and was living on a knife's edge. Another heart attack could be his last, Rebecca had once confided.

"So you left to meet your dad." Dana sounded encouraged. "What time was that?"

"He called about . . . one or so? I hate to think about it, but Colin may have been already been dead while I was sitting in the parking lot." Rebecca covered her face with her hands a moment and took a breath to calm herself. "The thing is, I saw no reason to deny that it was my car in the video, even though the image is so blurry. I know that eventually they'll figure it out and that will really make me look guilty."

"You did the right thing, Rebecca," Lucy assured her. "The police have to prove that you went inside the restaurant."

"The time of Colin's death is important, too," Dana said. "It's usually a window of a few hours. Sorry to say, that may not help you."

"The medical examiner must have determined that by

now. That's one of the first things they do. Haven't the police told you what it is?" Lucy asked.

"No, they didn't," Rebecca said.

"Another reason you need an attorney," Suzanne murmured.

"The killer may have been in and out by the time you arrived. Or they may have been there while you were sitting your car," Lucy speculated. "Maybe they even knew Colin listened to music with earphones while he was writing and wouldn't hear someone creep in," Lucy suggested. "Either way, that made it easier to surprise him."

Rebecca nodded. "I think that's true. I also think it was someone who knew Colin's habits and routines."

"But it's possible that you were on your way to help your dad at the time of the murder. Your father's call could help you," Dana said, turning the conversation back to Rebecca's alibi.

"I made it to the urgent care center by half past one. I was driving fast and there was no traffic. Luckily, my dad was fine. His chest pain was just indigestion from too many nachos."

"Let's hope when Colin died you were miles away." Suzanne had taken her knitting out but had not made much progress, Lucy noticed. "There must have been people at the urgent care center who saw you there and could confirm your story."

"I never actually went inside. My dad met me in the parking lot," she recalled. "I think he was embarrassed about making such a fuss. But I'm sure there are security cameras at a place like that."

"Very likely. And working correctly, too," Maggie agreed.

"It might take a day or two to check out my story, but surely the police will realize I'm telling the truth?"

"It sounds like simple logic to us. But a detective intent

on making an arrest can twist things around until up is down and chocolate is vanilla. And you know you're innocent . . . but they insist that you're not." Suzanne was suddenly stitching the mohair at top speed. For her.

Fired up by recollections of being in the hot seat herself, Lucy guessed. Years ago, the feisty brunette had been accused of poisoning an office rival with a tainted diet shake. She was completely innocent, but somehow the investigation pinned her as the prime suspect. Her friends had not only supported her through a very public ordeal but also helped the police nab the real killer.

"The police must have asked you this, Rebecca. Maybe a few times by now. Can you think of anyone who would have gone to such lengths to harm your husband?" Maggie's tone was intent, more than curious.

Rebecca shook her head. "I really can't. But Colin and I led very separate lives. A 'don't ask, don't tell' sort of marriage. There's doubtlessly a lot I don't know about his private life. And maybe never will."

"Let's hope Detective Reyes drills down and finds a few leads that pull the focus off of you." Maggie pointed with her knitting needle. "Everyone has secrets. Even close couples might be surprised by what comes out in this sort of situation."

"The police must be looking at all of his contacts— friends and former coworkers. Not just you," Lucy assured her.

"That's what they *should* be doing. Let's hope they follow through." Dana put her work aside and slipped off her reading glasses. "I agree wholeheartedly with Maggie. Secrets will come out that will open new leads. But I still think you need to find a good attorney."

Dana's tone was soft but serious and Lucy shared her concern.

"I'll think about it. I promise," Rebecca replied.

Lucy couldn't tell if Rebecca was sincere or just being polite. She hoped it was the former and decided she would encourage Rebecca more, if she didn't take Dana's advice.

Rebecca's phone buzzed with a text and she glanced at the screen. "It's my dad. Sophie is asking for me. She's having trouble sleeping. I'd better go."

"Poor little thing." Maggie rose to walk Rebecca to the door. "I'm so sorry for what she's going through."

"I'd give anything to have Colin back just for her sake," Rebecca said. "That's why it's so crazy for the police to think I took his life. No matter how he treated me, I'd never do that to Sophie."

If anyone doubted Rebecca's innocence, Lucy thought that declaration would make them reconsider. But the police didn't operate that way. Words didn't matter much. It was facts that counted, and sometimes facts were made to fit where investigators wanted them to.

Lucy's friends were quiet after Rebecca left. Maggie returned to her seat and took up her project. Lucy had brought her knitting bag but hadn't taken her knitting out. The argyle pattern baby jacket was not going well. Lucy knew she was too tired and distracted to focus on the complicated stitch but tried anyway.

"It's very troubling," Maggie murmured. "It sounds like Rebecca went to the café for a totally innocent and logical reason and, unfortunately, arrived at exactly the wrong time. No wonder the police won't eliminate her from their list of suspects."

"I wish there was a list," Lucy said. "I'm worried she's the only person of interest right now."

"I'll be interested to hear the medical examiner's guess on the time of death." Dana's head was bowed over her work. "That might also hurt her, since it's usually the span of a few hours."

Lucy was having trouble following her pattern and put

the project aside. "I wish she knew more about Colin's friends and connections. Sounds as if the police took away a lot of his stuff. But there must be something left that offers a glimpse into his private life."

"She said he asked for the divorce 'out of the blue.' I think that's a good place to start," Suzanne suggested.

"You're right, Suzanne. Something must have flipped that switch. Another woman?" Maggie wondered aloud.

"I doubt it." Phoebe rolled her eyes. "He doesn't sound like a guy who jumps when a woman makes an ultimatum. Like, 'Leave your wife, or else.' Just the opposite, I'd say."

"Good read, Phoebe." Dana gazed over her the frame of reading glasses and smiled. "I doubt it was a woman, too."

"I think Colin had secrets and he was killed because of them," Lucy said bluntly. "I'm also afraid Rebecca may get blamed for this crime. But I'm going to do everything I can to make sure that doesn't happen."

"Whoa, Lucy . . . Unleash the kraken!" Suzanne called out, making everyone laugh.

"I think our kraken forgot that's she very pregnant." Maggie met Lucy's gaze. Her expression was stern but in a mocking way.

"What does being pregnant have to do with it? This is important. I can't sit home organizing onesies all day."

Her friends exchanged indulgent glances, but nobody argued with her. She was thankful for that.

Chapter 8

Lucy sat on the front steps of her porch and watched Matt tug weeds from the soft brown patch of garden that took up most of their front lawn. Every spring since they'd been together, they would prepare the soil for planting and start their vegetables and flowers right about now. This was the first time Matt was sowing the seeds without her, and she felt frustrated to be sidelined.

She loved to lose herself in a day of digging, raking, and pushing the wheelbarrow from one side of their property to the other. She loved the scent of dry leaves gathered up, like an old paper wrapper, and the scent of the fresh earth underneath. She loved finding the bright green shoots of their perennials, poking up courageously, and silently cheered to see them return, each plant like an old friend and happily looked forward to watching them grow and bloom in months to come. Her amazement at the process never failed.

She even loved the ache in her arms and legs when she finally staggered inside, straight into the shower, covered with dirt from head to toe. Under her fingernails, of course and even in her ears.

"Don't look so glum, sweetie. You're on the bench for a

good cause," Matt reminded in his good-natured way. "You'll be back in the game soon enough, Farmer Binger."

"I hope so. People can't stop telling me how I won't have time to breathe 'once the baby comes.' " She mimicked the singsong, well-intentioned warning.

Matt sat back on his heels and faced her. "You'll be able to do all the things you like to do. You'll just take the baby with you."

Lucy appreciated his confidence. She had at least three baby backpacks and two different strollers—gifts from the shower—and she intended to use all of them.

"All I'll say for now is, I hope our sprout likes to keep on the move. And it's way too nice out to sit and mope. I'm going to take Dara to the beach. We're meeting up with Rebecca and Sophie."

"Good idea." Matt had filled a bushel with weeds and dumped it in the wheelbarrow. "But if you have the slightest twinge, promise you'll call, right?"

She could tell he was trying to keep it light but couldn't hide the note of worry in his tone.

"I promise." She stood up and rubbed her back. It did bother her lately, too much weight in front, like carrying a bowling ball. "The worst that will happen to me today is being mistaken for a beached whale."

Matt laughed. He pulled off his hat to wipe his brow and smiled, reminding her how this whole thing started in the first place. "Cutest whale that ever washed up around here. That's for sure."

"Gee, thanks. I feel loads better." Her tone was mocking, but she couldn't help but laugh as she went inside to call Dara.

Lucy and Matt lived in a section of town known as the Marshes, a neighborhood adjacent to the public beach but not the least bit fancy. Most of the houses had been built as summer cottages, only to be winterized and expanded as the village grew and the properties turned over to year-round residents. Lucy's house had belonged to her aunt Claire, who had no children of her own and doted on Lucy and her older sister, Ellen. Every summer Lucy and Ellen would come to stay with her for several weeks, which worked out well with her mother's schedule. Isabel Binger was a college professor and archeologist and loved nothing better than to travel to some distant, rugged landscape in the summer and hunt for artifacts of lost civilizations.

Visits to Aunt Claire were almost like summer camp, and Lucy continued to stay close to her aunt and visited often as an adult. When Claire passed away, she left the cottage to both Lucy and her sister.

Lucy had moved to Plum Harbor from Boston over five years ago, after her first marriage dissolved and she chucked her nine-to-five job in an advertising agency to build her own business. The quaint town, not quite a tourist destination and not quite a suburb, seemed the perfect place to start over, and she soon realized that her decision to leave the city and the nine to five office grind had been the right one.

Ellen's taste had outgrown the cozy, unpretentious village. Her family preferred beach vacations at more exclusive, upscale resorts like Martha's Vineyard or Newport. When Lucy married Matt, Ellen was happy to sell the couple her share of the cottage—which Suzanne said could pass for Craftsman style if you squinted a bit.

It wasn't the grandest house in town, or even in the neighborhood. Many modest homes had been knocked down to build mini-mansions in the years since she'd moved there. Lucy thought those houses looked ridiculous on the postage-stamp-size properties. But her cottage was perfect for her and her family.

The cottage was walking distance from the beach, but Lucy and Dara had so much equipment to cart that they packed up Lucy's Jeep and drove. Rebecca and Sophie were already there and waved as they saw Lucy's SUV approach. Dara sprang out of the car as soon as Lucy had parked, and the two girls hugged a moment under Rebecca's umbrella.

Dara turned to Lucy. "Can we go down to the water? We won't go in."

"Sure. Just feet, and stay in sight," Lucy reminded her. The water in New England stayed chilly until July, and Lucy doubted that the girls would be tempted to go any farther than their knees, once they felt a wave or two.

Rebecca helped Lucy unload her beach chairs and umbrella. "Let me take this stuff. You shouldn't be carrying anything."

Lucy felt guilty but knew her friend was right. "Why does it always feel as if you need to take half the house for a few hours at the beach?"

"Maybe it's some obscure law of physics? I do the same thing," Rebecca confessed.

A few minutes later, the chairs were unfolded and the umbrella opened. Lucy and Rebecca walked down to the shoreline, where the two girls worked intently on a project in the border of smooth sand left by the outgoing tide.

"We're making a heart out of shells," Dara explained.

Sophie had just placed a white fan-shaped shell in the curving row they'd built so far. She looked up at Rebecca. "For Dad," she said solemnly.

Rebecca touched the top of her head and nodded. "Good idea. Would you like some help?"

"You can look for more shells. We need a lot." Dara handed Lucy a bucket. "We like this kind, only white . . . please," she added, remembering her manners.

"Will do," Lucy nodded, happy to have an assignment. "I'll point them out and Sophie's mom will bend over."

Rebecca laughed. "I thought of that but didn't want to say."

Lucy and Rebecca strolled along the shoreline, foaming waves lapped at their bare feet. A light breeze carried the salty scent of the water. It was a very fair day for early May. Lucy had brought along a light hoodie but found she didn't need it. Her beach dress blew in the breeze, and the sun beat down on her bare arms and legs.

"We won't stray too far, but I think they're fine," Rebecca said, glancing over her shoulder. "I'm happy to see Sophie so distracted, even if it is a project for Colin."

"Doing something so hands-on might help her express her feelings," Lucy said.

"That's just what the therapist told me."

They walked down the beach in silence. High tide had left a fringe of seaweed in their path, and Lucy spotted some interesting shells trapped in the strands.

"I'm glad you stopped by the shop Thursday night, Rebecca. Everyone was happy to see you. But I hope we weren't too . . . intense." Lucy knew that she and her friends had asked Rebecca too many questions, but then again, Rebecca had asked for their advice.

"Not at all. I wanted to tell you what was going on. And I've decided to take Dana up on her offer to recommend a lawyer."

Lucy was happy to hear that but was also concerned by Rebecca's tone. "Any reason you changed your mind?"

"I found out something at the bank yesterday morning

that will probably make the police suspect me even more. Or maybe I should say, I found something missing at the bank."

Lucy looked up at her. "Oh no . . . what is it?"

"Colin wasn't just ending our marriage. He was going to move out of the country and take Sophie with him."

Lucy was shocked. She took a deep breath to steady herself.

"Are you sure?"

"I was going through our safety deposit box, looking for his life insurance policy, and realized that both his passport and Sophie's were missing. The bank records show he'd opened the box on Monday. He must have taken the documents out then. I checked our credit card statements and sure enough, there are two airline tickets for this weekend, one-way to Costa Rica." Rebecca paused, her voice low and shaky. "If Colin was still alive, he and Sophie would be gone by now. Tucked away somewhere where I'd never find them."

Lucy touched Rebecca's shoulder. "What a heartless plan. But I think your assumptions are right."

Rebecca nodded, her chin trembling. "I'm sure the police will put the pieces together, too. Or maybe have already." She looked up and met Lucy's gaze. "This is going to make them think I did it. More than they already do. It's my own fault, when you think about it."

"Don't say that, Rebecca. How in the world can this be your fault?"

Before she could answer, Sophie ran toward them. "We need more shells, please. Did you find any for us?"

"Right here, sweetheart. This should keep you busy." Rebecca handed over the bounty, the bucket more than half-full.

"Good job," Sophie said, mimicking a teacher voice. She handed Rebecca an empty bucket and ran back down to the beach to Dara.

"I should have been stronger. I should have stood up for myself. I always gave in to him, just to keep the peace. I told him a thousand times that I wanted to legally adopt Sophie, but he always put me off. He said I was her real mother in every way and a piece of paper didn't matter. Well, it matters a lot in a courtroom. If a divorce had gone through, I had no legal rights to share custody, or even visit Sophie. I wouldn't have had any rights as a parent. He knew that, too. That's the hold he had over me. That's why I put up with his moods and foul temper and self-centered ways. That's why I stayed in the marriage. For Sophie. I thought if I could hang on until she was old enough to have a say in family court, Colin couldn't keep her away from me."

The plastic pail, a few shells rattling in the bottom, hung from Lucy's arm as she slung her other arm around her friend's shoulder. "What horrible pressure you've lived with all these years, Rebecca. I had no idea."

"I did my best to focus on the positives, for Sophie's sake. We had our family routines and outings. We even had fun together, when Colin wasn't in one of his sulks. But it was a bargain with the devil. I've been set free in one way, but I'm terrified Colin is still going to win. From whatever cold corner of eternity he ended up in."

A cold corner indeed. The more Lucy heard about the "real" Colin, the more she could imagine him in a frigid, dark place. Or a very hot one.

"I'm not going to lie. This does give you a stronger motive from the perspective of the police," Lucy said honestly. "But we know it wasn't you. The question is, who really killed Colin? Why was he in such a rush to leave the country? Did you ever get the feeling he was hiding something from you?"

"Sure I did, like . . . all the time." Rebecca shrugged. "I suspected he was seeing another woman, but I never confronted him. He was very touchy about his privacy. He'd even lock the door to his home office when he was out. I thought he was just overly protective of his space. Now I wonder about it. I've been so busy with the restaurant and caring for Sophie ever since we moved to Plum Harbor, it wouldn't have been difficult to slip something by me," she admitted.

"We're on the right track, but it's nothing you can bring to the police. Can you recall anything odd or suspicious that Colin did or mentioned to you? Even if it seemed normal at the time but seems suspicious now?"

Rebecca walked the shoreline, searching for shells in the lapping waves. "Not really," she began. Then she said, "There was something. But I'm not sure I should tell the police about it."

"If it would turn their attention to a new suspect, I think you definitely should."

"That's just it. I think it will but . . ." She shook her head, as if arguing with herself. "I'd have to throw someone I know to the wolves. Someone who trusts me."

Lucy tried not to jump to conclusions, but her pregnant-lady vibe knew who Rebecca was protecting.

"Let's start with what you remembered."

Rebecca stared at a shell at her feet, picked it up, and tossed it in the pail.

"Colin was an avid cyclist. He'd go for a long bike ride every morning out on Route 1A." Lucy often saw cyclists on the busy, narrow road and never liked passing them.

"One day last week," Rebecca continued, "he came

back to the café without the bike, looking awful. His biking outfit was dirty and torn, and there were bruises and cuts all over his body. At first, he told me that he'd fallen, and the bike had been damaged. But a stranger had given him a ride and told me the truth while Colin was in the bathroom, cleaning up. A big motorcycle had pulled up next to Colin and forced him off the road."

Lucy nearly gasped at the thought. "He's lucky he wasn't killed."

"Exactly. At the time, I thought it was just a really aggressive, reckless driver. You hear about road rage all the time. Or people driving under the influence. Now I wonder if the motorcyclist's true intention was to kill Colin, or at least cause serious injuries. Colin caught a lucky break. He was thrown off the bicycle into thick brush that blocked his fall. His bicycle skidded into traffic and was run over by a truck."

The image was frightening. "He didn't go to the hospital? Someone must have seen what happened and called nine-one-one."

"A few drivers stopped to help him, and an ambulance came, but he refused to get inside. The police came, too, and wrote up a report, but he wouldn't make a formal complaint. He insisted that the guy who sideswiped him could never be found and he wanted to forget it."

"This could be very important, Rebecca. I think it shows Colin had someone after him. Whatever the reason, it can't be good. You have to tell Detective Reyes so she can open a new line of investigation."

Rebecca stared out at the water and nodded. "I know I should, but . . ."

"But what?" Lucy didn't mean to sound sharp but knew she did. But she didn't understand why Rebecca was withholding this information. It suggested that someone was after Colin, seeking to hurt him, or worse.

"I just don't understand why you won't tell them, Rebecca," she said in a calmer tone. "It could help you a lot."

"Maybe," Rebecca agreed. "But it could hurt someone else."

Chapter 9

"It might get Nick Russo in trouble," Rebecca finally admitted. "He's the first one the police will suspect. His motorcycle is black, too. The same color as the one that sideswiped Colin. They already think something is going on between us. They might say the bike accident was a first attempt on Colin's life, and when that didn't work . . . Well, you know better than me how they jump to the wrong conclusions."

Lucy took a deep breath and let it out slowly, like her birthing coach had taught her. "A lot of people ride black motorcycles. That doesn't prove anything. Nick may have been nowhere near Route 1A that morning. Wasn't he at the café, working?"

"I checked the time sheets. He hadn't punched in yet and he takes the same road every day to work. Besides all that, Nick has a record. He served two years in prison. I'm sure the police know that about him by now, too."

Lucy was surprised by that admission. "That does complicate things. Why was he sent to jail, do you know?"

"A white-collar crime, nothing violent. He was an accountant for a manufacturing company, a family-owned business. He had an affair with the boss's daughter. The family was trying to sell the company and she persuaded Nick to plump up the profits and assets in their financial records to make it look as if the company was worth more."

A bad pun about "cooking the books" came to mind, but Lucy restrained herself. "But they got caught?" she said instead.

"The woman who'd engineered the scheme cut a deal with the prosecutors and claimed it had all been Nick's idea, so he was only one who ended up behind bars."

"That's rough. But he still went through with it." He had broken the law and he was a grown up. Lucy wasn't so willing to let the man off the hook.

"He takes full responsibility for his part, which is one of the reasons I hired him after he told me the story. People make mistakes. We all do. It shouldn't define a person for the rest of their life if they accept the blame and face the consequences."

Lucy agreed with that, though she didn't think the police saw it quite the same way.

"And prison wasn't an entire waste of time for him. He'd always loved to cook and learned how to run a commercial kitchen while he was there. He's very good at it." Rebecca paused. "I know he's not to blame for Colin's death, and I'd hate to save myself by turning the focus on him. It doesn't seem fair."

"This puts you in a tough spot. But you can't worry so much about protecting Nick Russo. If he's as innocent as you think, he'll be fine."

Rebecca glanced at her but didn't seem persuaded.

"Don't take my word for it. Ask your attorney what to do. You're going to call Dana for a referral, right?"

"Yes, I am." Rebecca dropped a few more shells in the bucket. "Can you give me her number? I have a feeling

Detective Reyes is going to bring me back to the police station for more questions any minute."

Unfortunately, Lucy had that feeling, too.

When they returned to the girls, Dara and Sophie were excited to show off their creation. The two had carefully arranged the white shells on a smooth stretch of sand in the shape of a huge heart, and the word *Dad* had been spelled out inside with white stones. Lucy felt her heart clutch at the sight.

"Do you think Daddy can see it, Mom? I mean, from wherever he is now?" Sophie turned and gazed at the clear blue sky.

Rebecca nodded, unable to speak. Lucy expected her to burst into tears. But she forced a smile and hugged Sophie tight. "I'm sure he can, and he loves it. And he's so proud of you."

Feeling hot from their hard work, the girls shrugged off their T-shirts and shorts and waded into the water to cool off. Dara was a strong swimmer and the waves were gentle today. But Rebecca went into the water with them anyway, and Lucy tucked up her dress and trudged in up to her knees.

The water felt chilly and gave her goose bumps, but a few splashes on her neck, face, and arms felt bracing and woke her up. It woke up the baby, too, she noticed, feeling fluttery kicks deep within. She waddled back to the blanket, seeking a chair and the shade.

A few minutes later, Rebecca brought the girls up to the blanket and doled out the sandwiches and drinks she'd brought in a cooler. Lucy offered cookies and fruit.

The girls laid together on a beach towel, playing a card game, while Rebecca gathered up the trash from lunch. "There's so much food at the café. I hope the police will let me rescue some. I can use it for Colin's memorial."

"Have you made any plans?" Lucy had been leafing through a mother-to-be magazine. All the articles made her feel nervous and unprepared and she put it aside.

"I've set a date for next Saturday. I'm going to hold it at our house. It's hard to say how many people might come. I've sent word to his old office and cycling club. And to the woman who ran his writing group, Judith Esterhauzy. Ever hear of her? She writes mysteries as J.D. Bailey."

"Can't say that I have . . . and why do so many mystery writers use initials instead of their first name?"

"That's a mystery to me, too. Anyway, Judith saw a story about Colin on the news and called to offer condolences. I'm not sure if she or any of the others will come, but I wanted to let them know."

"I thought struggling writers were loyal to each other. Hemingway and Fitzgerald? Ezra Pound and James Joyce?"

Rebecca rolled her eyes. "Colin's work was hardly at that level—though he fancied himself a genius." She opened her water container and took a sip. "He loved the group at first. Everyone was so supportive, he said. But there was some sort of falling-out. I'm not exactly sure what happened. He never gave me the whole story. Even if he had, he probably wouldn't have told me the truth."

Lucy's curiosity was piqued. "Was Colin the one who caused the rift?"

"I can't say for certain, but I'm pretty sure he did. I heard that there was a big scene in the café. I'd left early that night, and missed it, so I don't know how it started or what went on." Rebecca brushed sand off her knee. "To be fair, I have to say that it must be hard to straddle the line between giving your fellow writers honest, helpful criticism and hurting their feelings or even insulting them. I think it requires a level of tact Colin didn't possess."

"So maybe he insulted someone's writing and the others took sides?"

Rebecca nodded. "Possibly."

Rebecca was right; artists of any kind, knitters included, were sensitive to even well-intended critiques. Add to that, not all critiques were well intended.

Could Colin's death be traced back to a spat in a writing group? The idea seemed laughable, like the plot of a cozy mystery. But the story made her curious, and local author, Judith Esterhauzy, also known as J.D. Bailey, couldn't be too hard to find.

Chapter 10

The weather was hot and muggy Monday morning. Low gray clouds threatened rain. Lucy took the dogs for a short walk around her neighborhood but texted Maggie so she wouldn't worry. Maggie had been with her husband, Charles, on their sailboat all weekend and was looking forward to starting the week with Lucy's usual visit.

Too bad for me. But seems the wiser course.

Drop by if you're driving around town. I'm curious to hear what's up with Rebecca . . . I must confess.

Lucy was eager to tell her, too, and glad to see the weather clear quickly. A light shower refreshed the newly sown garden, and the sun was out in its all glory by noon, when she left for the knitting shop.

One of Maggie's classes, Spring Fling, was just letting out when she arrived, and Lucy wove around the exiting students as she made her way up the brick path.

She found Dana and Phoebe on the porch. "How's it going, Lucy?" Phoebe was watering the flower boxes, filled with an array of huge pansies—butter yellow, apricot, violet, brick red, dark blue salvia, and trailing vines. Lucy envied the way Maggie managed to keep the pansies blooming far past the early spring, their happy time.

"I'm still able to do everything I want to. Well, most things. Just moving a lot slower."

"Sounds about right." Dana patted the cushions on a wicker chair. "Have a seat, put your feet up." She brought over a small wicker hassock. "This is a tricky time, mom-to-be. You can hold water and get edema, and that won't be good."

Lucy didn't think she was at risk but did as she was told. It did feel good to sit so comfortably, even though she felt a little silly in such a pose in the middle of the day.

Phoebe punched up the cushion behind her head. "I'll get you some water. You need to stay hydrated."

"I appreciate the attention, guys. But I think you're overdoing it just a bit."

Phoebe returned with the drink. "Enjoy it while you can. We won't even know you're in the room once Baby Binger-MacDougal arrives. Will we, Dana?"

Dana shook her head in agreement, her solemn expression breaking into a grin. "You'll be mama non grata. Take my word for it."

"Mama non . . . what?" Maggie stepped out from the shop, a tape measure around her neck. Her gaze settled on Lucy. "You look relaxed."

"I'm getting the royal treatment." Lucy turned to Dana. "Before I drift off into an unscheduled nap, did Rebecca ever get in touch? I gave her your number on Saturday. She was ready to talk to a lawyer."

"No worries, she's set. Helen Forbes agreed to represent her. I think the police won't be so eager to drag Rebecca down to the station now unless it's absolutely necessary."

"I hope so. Rebecca expected Detective Reyes to call her back in. It looks like Colin was going to leave the country and take Sophie with him. Their passports are missing from a safety deposit box, and she found charges for airline tickets on a credit card. One-way to Costa Rica. She only put the pieces together on Friday, but you know how the police are. They'll suspect she knew all along, and it gives her even more reason to have killed him."

Her friends looked disturbed to hear of Colin's plan and her conclusions. "Sounds like Colin was on the run," Dana said. "I've heard that Costa Rica is one of those places where cash can buy a lot of happiness and secrecy. A person could easily hide away there, beyond the reach of law enforcement here, and dangerous enemies. I hope the police notice that. Someone must have been after him for some reason?"

"Seems so," Lucy replied. "Rebecca told me that Colin had a bad accident on his bike just last week. He walked away with a few cuts and bruises, but it could have been fatal. At the time, it seemed like a case of road rage or reckless driving. But now Rebecca thinks it was intentional."

Lucy had purposely been vague and hoped her friends didn't ask for more details. Rebecca hadn't asked her to keep the incident confidential, but Lucy thought the less said the better, especially anything about Nick Russo.

"That's big, if you ask me." Phoebe turned from her task and a few sprinkles from the watering can sprayed her friends. "No wonder he was skipping town."

"I think it could be big, too and I hope the police follow up on the lead," Dana put aside her knitting and took a few bites from a container of salad. Lucy spotted greens, quinoa, blueberries, and chicken.

Blueberries? Lucy tried to imagine how the combination tasted.

"I'm not sure if the police know about that yet." Lucy sipped her water, a ploy to avoid Dana's gaze, though she guessed her astute friend would still sense she was hiding something. "Rebecca planned to ask her lawyer what to do. She's probably told Helen about the incident by now."

Lucy hoped that was true, no matter what Rebecca felt she owed the fine-looking cook.

"It's not much, but hopefully enough to draw the investigation away from Rebecca." Maggie had opened a carton and was removing skeins of yarn, a soft shade of yellow that reminded Lucy of the lemon chiffon pie her aunt Claire used to make.

The memory made her hungry. And nostalgic. She was so weepy lately, she decided not to look at the yarn. She didn't want to cry.

"I heard another story about Colin that was interesting." Lucy sat up and set her glass aside. "He was in a writing group that met at the café. Until there was a falling-out and he was either kicked out or left. Maybe a bit of both. The group packed up their tent and left the Happy Hands, too. He wouldn't give Rebecca the details but seems he was at the center of some rift between the members."

Dana picked up her knitting again. Jack's new argyle vest was more than half done and Lucy felt an envious pang, thinking of her infant-size argyle effort, barely started.

Maggie placed the last skein in the pile and looked at Lucy. "I doubt he was killed by a rival writer, but when you think of it, using a bookcase as a weapon fits that theory perfectly."

"Too well," Lucy said. "Wouldn't a writer be smarter and not so obvious? Anyway, I doubt someone from the group would go that far, no matter what the dispute. But it's worth looking into. The group is run by a writer named Judith Esterhauzy. She writes mysteries as J.D. Bailey."

"Why do mystery writers use all those initials and pseudonyms?" Phoebe asked. "To be more mysterious?"

"I was wondering the same thing," Lucy admitted.

"No mystery for me. Judith taught English at the high

school when I was in the art department. I think Bailey is her maiden name. I did hear she'd left teaching for a writing career and was doing well. I suppose you could ask her about the initial thing when you meet. Assuming that's your plan?"

"It is. I looked her up online. She has a website, of course. She runs the writing group at a coffeehouse in Hamilton now. She told me to come by tomorrow night if I want to chat about Colin."

"Good work, Lucy. I wish I could tag along, but I see clients Tuesday nights." Dana frowned over her work and looked disappointed.

"I'm teaching my "1-2-3 Knit-A-Bikini!" workshop tomorrow night. Sorry," Phoebe apologized.

Lucy couldn't imagine wearing any sort of knitted swimsuit. Wouldn't it feel itchy? But Phoebe's creations sold out online, and the workshop was very popular.

Maggie had opened another box but lifted her head before sifting through the contents. "I'm happy to ride shotgun if you want company. I'd like to see Judith, and an extra pair of eyes and ears might be helpful. I'm not sure you should travel alone right now in your state, Lucy. Even to Hamilton."

The reminder was delivered with love and concern, but Lucy still balked. "I've read all the books and blogs and seen all the videos. There are a few signs and symptoms before the grand finale and I don't feel any of them."

"Yet," Dana added, giving her a look. "You'd be surprised how fast those last-minute warnings can come."

"Did you ever order a three-course meal and the waiter brings everything out at once?" Maggie asked in a playful tone. "The last stretch can be just like that."

"I hate when that happens, though you can't really blame the waitstaff. It's more of a problem in the kitchen," Phoebe noted.

"I hate it, too." Lucy hoped her pregnancy wouldn't wind up that way, like bad service at a restaurant. But you never knew. Even her doctor couldn't say for sure what was going on in the kitchen right now.

"If you really want to come, Mag, please do. As long as you're not trying to babysit."

"I'll be babysitting . . . but not you, exactly." She leaned over and gently patted Lucy's tummy.

Dana laughed and gathered her work, along with her salad container. Her lunch break was over. "Good luck tomorrow night. Let me know if you find out anything juicy about Colin."

"Of course we will. I'll issue an all-points news blast," Lucy promised.

As Dana headed up Main Street, Lucy took her knitting from her tote. She must have sighed out loud as she looked the project over. Maggie's gaze was on her when she looked up.

"What's going on with your baby argyle?"

"It's a miniature mess. Maybe it's a bad time to attempt such a complicated stitch. My focus isn't so great these days."

Maggie stretched out her hand and Lucy passed the lump of needles and yarn, which was supposed to end up as a hooded baby jacket with an argyle yoke. That's what she intended it to be, eventually, though she had only fumbled her way through a few rows so far.

"Unfortunately, this pattern tossed you in the deep end," Maggie murmured.

"Thanks for the sympathy, but even if you fix the snarled up parts, I'll just mess it up again," Lucy replied with a sigh.

Maggie was already concentrating on the puzzle and didn't seem to hear her. She did love to decipher messed-up knitting. Like an ace decoder at Bletchley Park during World War II.

"There's not much here . . . but it is a gnarly mess," she agreed. "Maybe you should put this aside until the baby comes. Though I can't see how you'll be able to focus any better then."

Lucy guessed that was true. "Aren't I supposed to be flooded with all those calming, zen-like hormones about now?"

"It's not the same for everyone. Just do you, Lucy. Pregnant Lucy, I mean." Maggie offered her wise smile, which always made Lucy feel better.

"Thanks, good advice. That's about all I can do." She returned the smile and stuffed the project in her knitting bag. She had to pick up Dara soon and make a stop at the organic market on the way.

"See you tomorrow night. I'll text to make plans," Lucy said as she lifted her bulky body from the deep chair.

Maggie answered with a thumbs-up. "I am curious to hear what Judith has to say about Colin. For all we know, he could have been a completely different person with his friends and fellow writers than he was with Rebecca."

"Must say I never thought of that. Mostly because I doubt it."

Lucy waved goodbye as she headed for her car. She was also curious to hear what someone, besides Rebecca, had to say about Colin Hurley.

Chapter 11

The Beautiful Bean in Hamilton was everything a gourmet coffeehouse should be: a sanctuary devoted to coffee beans and coffee lovers, with a low ceiling and subdued lighting, decorated in a warm mustard color with brick-red and chocolate trim. Vintage-era posters and photos filled the walls, and the scent of freshly ground coffee hung in the air like a rich perfume.

Maggie and Lucy ordered at the counter, where a massive grinder growled and a coffee machine sputtered. Maggie ordered a double espresso, and Lucy would have loved a latte but settled for a mug of steamed milk sans the espresso shot. She did ask for a dollop of caramel syrup as a consolation prize. They'd just picked up their cups when Maggie spotted her former colleague Judith at a large table in the back of the shop.

"There she is." Maggie quickly stirred a packet of sugar into her demitasse cup, and Lucy led the way to their quarry.

The writer had her laptop open but was reading printed pages and marking notes. Her smooth brown hair, threaded with silver, was parted in the middle and pulled back in a short ponytail, the stray bits held in place with bobby pins. The style wasn't all that flattering to her round face, though Lucy had the distinct impression the teacher turned author had little interest and even less patience for fussing with her appearance.

Square black glasses balanced on her thin nose, above a small mouth, pinched in an expression of complete concentration. A mug of black coffee sat beside a pile of pages, separated by paper clips.

Lucy guessed her age to be early sixties or so, about the same as Maggie. Though Judith had more crinkles and wrinkles than Lucy's friend. Especially when she looked up and smiled.

"Maggie Messina—as I live and breathe. Good to see you." Maggie's appearance wasn't a complete surprise. Lucy had emailed to let Judith know Maggie was coming and looked forward to seeing her. Still, it had been years since the two had rubbed shoulders in the faculty room at Plum Harbor High. Judith rose to greet her old friend and took Maggie's hand in both of her own.

"Good to see you, too, Judith," Maggie greeted her.

"Thanks for giving us a few minutes of your time. I'm Lucy Binger."

"Lucy, of course. Forgive my manners," Judith apologized. "Please sit down. I was just going over some writing from the workshop," she explained, pushing the papers aside.

She met Maggie's gaze and smiled again. "So we both jumped ship early. Hasn't hurt either of us, has it?"

"To the contrary. You look wonderful, and you've enjoyed some real success in your second act. Congratulations on your books. I haven't read them yet, but I just reserved the newest title at the library. *Middle Age Can Be Murder*?"

Judith laughed off the compliment, her blue eyes sparkling. Her plain features, far more attractive when she smiled, Lucy thought.

"I've published a few mysteries. It's a not a big deal. I was a dedicated fan and wanted to try my hand. Almost every high school English teacher is a closet novelist. You must know that. It's been fun, but Stephen King is sleeping soundly," she reported with a laugh.

"I'm impressed by any published author," Lucy said. "And you run a writing group, right?"

"I've run the group for a few years. It's not so easy to stop teaching altogether." Her voice trailed off with a self-conscious grin.

"I know exactly what you mean," Maggie sympathized. "I went from teaching art projects to knitting projects. Why fight it?"

"I guess you'd say I'm more the group leader than a teacher," Judith explained. "I'm further along professionally than most of the members, but we all have an equal say and critique each other's work. I do step in to steer the discussion if it's headed in a negative direction. But we try to treat each other with respect, published or not, and do our best to support all efforts."

"That brings us to the reason we sought you out," Lucy explained. "We heard that Colin Hurley was part of your group but left after a disagreement. We were wondering what the conflict was about."

Judith sat back and set her glasses on the table. "The disagreement was between Colin and a writer named Graham Paxton. Colin was working on a novel, a macho sort of thriller. Ordinary Joe protagonist up against powerful forces and triumphs, against all odds. Wins the heart of a beautiful babe, to boot, of course."

"How original." Maggie's tone was dry as toast.

"Isn't it? But who can fault him? The formula sells. The problem was . . . well, I hate to make blanket pronouncements on anyone's creative work. We've all heard stories about books that are rejected by a hundred publishers and go on to be bestsellers. But," Judith paused, searching for the right words, "I never thought he'd get anywhere with that pile of typing."

Ouch, that one stung, Lucy thought. "What did the rest of the writers think?"

"Colin sent everyone a file of the manuscript, but we never got to discuss it. We were just about to start when Graham Paxton walked in. He was incensed and accused Colin of stealing ideas from a project he'd passed around the group a few months prior. Of course Colin denied it. Before I knew what was going on, fists were flying. And some of the other members took sides."

"Oh dear . . . what a scene," Maggie said.

"It was dreadful. A few members ran off, playing it safe. While the bolder and brawnier ones broke up the boxing match."

"Did Colin ever come back?" Lucy asked.

"Even if he wanted to return, the others voted him out. I sent him a short message expressing their wishes. Of course, we couldn't meet at his wife's café after that, though it is a charming place."

"Understandably," Lucy said.

"Was Graham Paxton booted out, too?" Maggie asked.

"The group had more sympathy for him. A lot of members agreed that Colin pilfered Graham's ideas and also threw the first punch. I let Graham know he was welcome back but he'd more or less outgrown us, even before the incident. He never returned, either."

"Shortly before his death, Colin claimed a producer optioned his novel to turn into a movie. Did you know that?" Lucy watched Judith's expression carefully.

She looked truly shocked, then smiled self-consciously and shrugged. "Stranger things have happened. As I said before, we've all heard those stories. Who's to judge?"

"Do you think any of the writers in your group heard that news?" Lucy asked.

"If they did, I'm sure I would have heard, too. If there's one thing this group likes to do, it's gossip about each other. They're sweet as pie on the surface, but underneath, they're ambitious and competitive. And envious."

"Do you think Paxton could have heard somehow anyway?"

Judith had just said it was unlikely that anyone in the group knew when she didn't. But Lucy had to ask.

"I can't really say. I suppose Colin could have let him know, just to brag and rub salt in the wound. Then again, he might have been afraid that Graham would claim Colin owed him something. I'm sure Colin didn't want to share his payday. Not that Graham needs it. He's doing very well. He has several books out and one just hit a bestseller list."

Maggie stirred her coffee with a short silver spoon. "How are the others taking that news?"

"They claim to be happy for him. I'm sure there's some private wailing and gnashing of teeth. 'If he can do it, we can,' they tell me. Can lightning strike the same writing group twice? That's the question."

"You never know," Maggie offered hopefully.

Lucy forced a smile. She felt confused. As she suspected, Colin had crossed another writer in his group and had probably jilted Paxton out of his fair share of the option payment he'd received.

But, on the other hand, Paxton had moved on to bigger and better things. Even if he knew about the slight, maybe he took it in stride and didn't feel the need to chase after Colin.

"That's the whole story," Judith said. "May I ask why the infighting of a little writing group interests you?"

"Colin's wife, Rebecca, is the focus of the investigation into Colin's death. We're absolutely positive she's innocent," Lucy said. "We're looking for information that will lead the police in a new direction."

"I see." Judith nodded and fiddled with a pen. "Well, hope this helps."

Lucy felt sure that it wouldn't but didn't want to be rude. "Thanks for your time. If anything, it's an interesting window into Colin's personality."

"It is," Maggie agreed.

"Would you happen to have a file of Colin's manuscript you could send me?" Lucy asked. "I'm interested to read it."

Judith thought for a moment. "No, I'm sorry. I don't keep projects from the group very long on my computer. I'll take a look," she offered. "But I suspect it's gone."

Lucy was sorry to hear that. "Thanks for trying."

"Before we go, one last question. It's sort of silly," Lucy admitted. "Why do so many mystery writers use initials instead of their first names?"

"Good question and I don't think there's any one answer to it. I know why I do it. For one thing, Esterhauzy is a mouthful, which is why the kids at school called me Mrs. E. And it's a small town and I like my privacy. It helps me fly under the radar, you might say. I never know when a story I hear in the news, or even a real-life event someone tells me, might end up in my writing. Of course, I disguise those situations in my stories. But I must admit, sometimes they slip out of my subconscious and onto the page undisguised, and I don't even realize it. I guess the pen name gives me a little protection?"

She winked and Maggie laughed. "A little, I suppose. But I suspect, not always enough."

Maggie rose and picked up her empty cup. Lucy did the

same. "Thanks again for your time," Lucy said. "I'm going to look for your books."

"It was a pleasure to meet you, Lucy. And I really enjoyed catching up with you, Maggie. The next time I need a break from writing, I'll grab my knitting bag and stop by your shop."

"I'd love that. Come by anytime and we'll continue the conversation."

The coffeehouse was much busier as they walked out. They didn't speak until they reached Maggie's car.

"That was an interesting story about Colin. But not surprising," Maggie said as she slipped into the driver's seat.

"Not surprising at all," Lucy agreed. She worked hard to pull the seat belt over her belly, nearly spraining her arm. She sat back and sighed.

"You seem disappointed."

"I am," she admitted. "I guess I hoped to hear that Colin had cheated someone who was far more desperate. Who felt that Colin had stolen his last chance at success, and he or she had nothing to lose by confronting him."

"That scenario is a bit dramatic, but I'll chalk it up to baby hormones. Maybe Colin did steal Paxton's ideas, and Paxton heard that the novel was optioned, even if Judith and the group have not. And Paxton may have asked Colin for his share, but Colin blew him off."

"All of that could have happened," Lucy agreed. "But Paxton sounds too successful and professional to confront Colin face-to-face. And push a bookcase on top of him, no less. I think he would have hired a lawyer and brought Colin to court."

Maggie nodded, her thick, short curls—a mixture of brown and silver—bounced around her face. "We don't even know how much money was involved. How much do authors get if a novel is optioned for a screenplay?"

"I have no idea. I should have asked Judith. I guess I can look it up."

"We did learn something. Colin did not take criticism well. Sounds like a bit of a narcissist, though we'll have to ask Dana to confirm the diagnosis."

"You think?" Lucy turned and laughed. "I don't know how Rebecca managed to live with him all those years."

"I think 'managed' is the operative word. She had strategies to keep the peace," Maggie observed quietly, "and kept telling herself she could hang on until Sophie was older. Which was a fragile illusion."

"Well said." Lucy had never been able to put into words what she'd observed between Rebecca and Colin quite that way. Maybe she'd been too close to the situation.

"I guess my theory was a dead end," Lucy said honestly. "But I am curious now to read Colin's novel. I wonder if Rebecca can find a copy."

Maggie smiled. "Judith seemed to think it was dreadful. What did she call it?"

"A pile of typing. I think there's a Truman Capote quote in there somewhere."

"I think it's a polite way of avoiding a much ruder description. Why do you want to read it?"

Lucy shrugged. "Even Rebecca can't tell us much about what he was really thinking and feeling . . . and hiding. Maybe his writing will."

"When I was a teacher, there were always a lot of signs around the school, reminding kids that, 'Reading opens up new worlds.' "

"I'll be satisfied if Colin's manuscript just opens a new can of worms. The police have Colin's phone and laptop, what was left of it." Lucy stifled a wince at the thought. "And they took tons of papers out of his home office. But maybe Rebecca can find an extra copy of the manuscript somewhere. If she knows his username and password, I could find the document in the cloud."

Maggie perked up at the suggestion. "What is the cloud, exactly? I think of it like something Emerson called The Over-Soul . . . and Jung called the Collective Unconscious. Is it like that, except in a high-tech way?"

Lucy laughed. "It's more a like a big, virtual attic, where you've dumped so many boxes of stuff, you can't remember what's in any of them."

"I get it. Sort of," Maggie murmured. "Do you think the police are searching Colin's virtual attic by now?"

"I hope so," Lucy said sincerely. "My prego-lady goose bumps insist he was hiding a skeleton or two up there."

Maggie glanced at her. "I think your pregnant-lady goose bumps are right."

Chapter 12

A big orange sun was slipping behind a bed of gray blue clouds as Lucy stumbled out of Maggie's car and walked toward her house. She loved the way the sun set so late in the summer and wished the day could last as long all year-round. Matt was still working in the garden, watering the rows that had already sprouted small, green leafy tufts.

He turned to greet her, careful to keep the hose aimed in the right direction. "You look beat, honey. Did you go out to dinner with Maggie?"

Lucy had been intentionally vague in the text she'd sent to her husband that afternoon, noting that she would be out when he got home and he should get his own dinner.

"Not exactly. We just met for coffee. I had a latte . . . without the espresso."

"You must be hungry. I ordered some takeout. There are leftovers."

Lucy was cheered by the news. She felt faint with hunger, but the thought of fixing anything more complicated than cheese and crackers was overwhelming.

"Why did you go out for coffee at this hour? Did Maggie need to have a heart-to-heart?"

Lucy held fast to the banister and pulled herself up the porch steps. Tink had been dozing on the porch but jumped to greet her and gently licked her hand.

"Nothing like that. We went to The Beautiful Bean to talk to a writer who knew Colin. We thought she could tell us something that would help Rebecca get the police off her tail."

Matt shut the water off and shook his head. She could tell he didn't like that explanation.

"I know you want to help Rebecca, but honestly, you've done enough. You helped her find a lawyer and you spent time with her and Sophie on Saturday. You can't be running all over, skipping dinner and exhausting yourself. Don't you get it? You could have a baby any minute. In the middle of . . . who knows where."

Lucy was annoyed but couldn't argue with his scolding. She did feel wiped out and deflated. The journey to Hamilton had been a waste of time. No denying it.

Still, she stood at the top of the steps and stuck out her belly for full effect. "I won't have the baby in the middle of 'who knows where.' I'll be right in the hospital, like we planned. My little red tote bag is packed and ready to go."

He dropped the hose and walked toward her shaking his head, and she realized that he wasn't being difficult just because she hadn't been home for dinner. He was genuinely worried.

"I'm sorry. I don't mean to worry you. I feel perfectly fine."

"I hope so," he said.

Matt walked up a few steps, and she slipped her arms around his shoulders and kissed his forehead. "If it makes you happy, I promise to stick close to home until the baby comes. No more goose chases. Wild or otherwise, okay?"

"That does make me happy." He put his arms around her and returned her kiss.

"So . . . what sort of takeout did you get?" Lucy couldn't help breaking the sweet mood. She suddenly felt so hungry she thought she might faint. Matt would really be upset if that happened. . . .

"Chicken parm. Spaghetti on the side."

Lucy did a fist pump. "Yes . . ."

"I thought mac and cheese was the baby's favorite?" Matt slung his arm around her shoulder and led her into the house, Tink following close behind.

"It is, but I can't eat it every day. I don't want to spoil our baby that quickly," she teased him.

Wednesday morning, Lucy slept late. Matt had drawn the bedroom curtains and shut the door on his way downstairs. Lulled by the air conditioner's hum, she missed her alarm and woke to find it was nearly ten. She found a text on her phone from her husband. He'd walked the dogs and would call her later, when he had a break between appointments.

Obviously, he had assumed she would not walk into town this morning, and it was already too warm and muggy for the trek. Lucy dropped a few ice cubes in her mug, which was mostly milk and a few tablespoons of decaffeinated coffee that she allowed herself each morning during her pregnancy. It was impossible for her to go without any coffee at all. Normally, she drank about a pot of the stuff before noon.

She checked her to-do list and decided to spend the day catching up on office work and the last of her baby prep schedule, which included preparing meals for the freezer.

She was feeling very virtuous and organized, dumping

chopped onion bits and cans of beans and other ingredients for chili in the slow cooker, and boiling up pasta for
baked ziti when Maggie called in the afternoon.

"Just checking in. Feeling okay?"

Lucy knew she meant, "I was wondering why you didn't
stop by this morning."

"I promised Matt I'd stick close to home. He was annoyed when I got back from Hamilton last night and hadn't
even eaten dinner."

"Understandably," Maggie replied. "What are you up
to? Feathering the nest?"

"Feathering the freezer. So we don't have to eat a lot of
takeout. That gets tired fast."

"And expensive. *And* it's not very healthy. Whatever
you eat, the baby will be eating, too," she reminded her.
"I'll donate a few meals when the time comes."

"Thanks, Mag. Matt will appreciate that. He'd never
admit it, but I think he likes your cooking better than
mine." Lucy's tone was joking, though she knew it was
true.

"Don't be silly. Dads can cook, too. There should be a
cookbook for fathers-to-be. I'm going to look for it online
and give it to him as a baby gift."

"If there isn't one, you can write it. Right after the collection of condolence casseroles," she teased.

"Good idea. And tell Matt I said he's right. You need to
stick close to home and take care of yourself. Don't stay
on your feet too long in the kitchen. Read a book, take a
nap. It's not a crime. Maybe you should skip knitting night
this week. We'll miss you, but we understand."

Lucy expected the first two suggestions but was shocked
by the last. "Of course I'm coming tomorrow night. I'll be
bored to tears by then. Besides, I'm sure the four of you

can handle a little emergency baby delivery, until the EMTs get there."

"Don't even joke about it." Maggie's tone was deadly serious.

Lucy laughed. She heard a customer in the background, asking a question. "The buttons are in that cabinet in the back, sorted by size and materials. I'll be right with you," Maggie promised her.

Then to Lucy she said, "Stay in touch and stay out of trouble."

"Will do," Lucy promised as she ended the call.

Staying out of trouble was exactly what Lucy intended to do. After cooking, she answered a few emails, fixed herself a healthy lunch, and sat on the sofa, studying the latest edition of *What to Expect the First Year*.

She'd practically memorized *What to Expect When You're Expecting* and felt ready to look ahead. " 'Kick through the goal, Lu!' " her father had always advised during her soccer-playing years. Good advice, too.

But looking *too* far ahead, to potty training and other toddler milestones, made her more nervous about the baby's arrival. She put the books aside and opened her laptop.

She'd just about given up her theory that Graham Paxton had murdered Colin at the café. For one thing, she'd quickly researched the typical payment for an option on a novel. With Colin's newbie status and since the novel was unpublished, it seemed likely that the payment was less than ten thousand dollars. Half of that, or whatever deal was struck between the two men, hardly seemed worth cold-blooded, premeditated murder.

Paxton's website came up quickly. It looked sharp and professional. The author photo showed a man in his early fifties, sitting on a rock in a woodsy setting, gazing at the camera with a calm expression and slightly amused smile.

His brand said, steady, strong, philosophical but also "man of action." From his gray buzz cut and strong jaw to the camouflage vest over a black T-shirt—arms crossed to display bulked-up biceps and a huge watch with a zillion extra buttons that could probably track nuclear subs.

More photos on the bio page showed him signing books for fans, speaking on panels, paddling through rapids and . . . riding a motorcycle? Lucy paused to enlarge the small square. A black motorcycle, too, she noticed, peering closer.

She bookmarked the site and sent a link to her email so she could show her friends tomorrow, on knitting night.

His book titles reinforced the former military, or military wannabe image: *Ten Second Warning*, *Off the Grid*, and *Doomsday Strategy*. Still, he smiled warmly for the camera, a big black Labrador at his side. Anyone who likes dogs can't be all bad, she thought. If that was actually his dog and a not a canine for hire, brought in for the photo shoot?

There was the usual bio and praising review quotes and a page that listed events and appearances. Lucy noticed he was promoting his newly published novel, *Doomsday Strategy*, with a series of book signings and interviews.

She scanned the dates, surprised to see a signing at a bookstore in Boston that had taken place the night of Colin's murder.

The coincidence quickened her heartbeat and made her reconsider. Paxton was successful, and money was most likely not an issue. But maybe there was some other issue between the two men? Some deeper, less obvious grievance that could have driven Paxton to murder Colin?

Pondering possibilities, Lucy put the laptop aside and dozed off. Tink and Walley were curled up nearby, very pleased to have a daytime snoozing partner.

The cell phone woke her. Lucy felt confused a moment, her head foggy with midday sleep. She expected it to be another check-in call from Matt, but the name LEO appeared on the screen.

She answered in a drowsy voice, fumbling to sit up. "Hi, Leo, what's up?"

"Lucy, thank goodness you answered. I didn't know who else to call."

Lucy felt alarmed at his tone but tried to stay calm as she awkwardly sat up. "What's the matter? What's going on?"

"The police were just here. They took Rebecca to the station for more questions . . ." Leo paused, wheezing as if he'd just run a marathon.

"Not good," Lucy agreed quickly. "Did you call her attorney?"

"I did," Leo managed. "She was at a meeting but promised to get there soon. I just hate thinking of Rebecca alone with those cops, being badgered and bullied." Leo sounded so despondent, Lucy thought he might cry. "It would make me feel a heck of a lot better if I went to the station. Even if I can't see her. Could you pick up Sophie after school and keep her awhile? I'm so upset. I don't think the kid should see me in this state."

"Don't worry, Leo. It's going to be all right," Lucy summoned up far more confidence in her tone than she actually felt. "Helen Forbes is an excellent attorney. She won't let anyone bully Rebecca. I'll watch Sophie for as long as you need. No problem. Please calm down and take care of yourself. You won't be any good to Rebecca if you get sick," she reminded him.

"You're right. I've got to get a grip," he replied in an apologetic tone. "I just feel so frustrated by this whole mess. That Colin, causing problems for Rebecca even now. I should be protecting my daughter, but there's nothing I can do."

From the bits and pieces Rebecca had disclosed about her father, Lucy knew he'd been through a lot during his life, traveling around the country, patching together a living from his music and odd jobs. He'd left Rebecca and her mother when Rebecca was ten years old, and there had been little contact between them for years, even when her mother died while she was in the middle of college.

But he came back into her life about two years ago, determined to make amends and be a true father to her again. And a grandfather to Sophie. Rebecca had confessed that it wasn't easy at first. There was so much emotional baggage to unpack, her hurts and disappointments and even anger at his absence. But she also knew that with her father's health issues, she didn't have years to work on their relationship. Somehow, they figured out how to resolve and accept the past and forge a new bond, and Leo seemed determined every day to prove himself a supportive and loving parent.

Rebecca deserved a lot of credit, too, Lucy thought, for giving her father a second chance. Lucy guessed that Leo was alarmed to see the happiness and peace he'd found with his estranged daughter and her family suddenly shattered by Colin's death, and poor Rebecca the target of the murder investigation.

"I'd better get over to the school," Lucy said, noticing the time. "Please let me know what's happening?"

"I will, Lucy. You're a great gal. Rebecca loves you and I can see why. And could you please come up with some excuse for Sophie about why you had to pick her up instead of me or Rebecca?" he added before ending the call.

"I don't want her worrying about her mom, poor little thing."

"I understand." Lucy said goodbye and hung up.

Lucy and Matt tried to be as open and honest with Dara as they could, even about difficult topics and situations. But she could understand Leo's impulse to shield Sophie from further distress. The little girl had just lost her father and didn't need to worry that the police would take away her mother, too.

Chapter 13

Lucy was the first to arrive at the shop Thursday night and found Maggie setting up the sideboard with plates, flatware, and napkins. Appetizing scents wafted out of the kitchen and Lucy wondered what was cooking.

"You look rested and ready," Maggie greeted her.

"I am," Lucy agreed. "Let me help you set up."

"You just sit." Maggie rested her hand on Lucy's shoulder and guided her to a chair. "I'll bring you a glass of mineral water. You need to stay hydrated."

Lucy sat back but felt fidgety. "If I was any more hydrated, I'd float away," she called out. Maggie was back in the storeroom and didn't reply.

When she returned, Lucy sipped her water as Maggie finished preparing for the meeting.

"How's the baby argyle coming along? You must have had time to work on it the last few days."

Lucy was afraid Maggie would ask about the project and knew she couldn't hide the truth for long. "It's not going well, I'm afraid. I'm starting to feel discouraged."

"I'm sorry to hear that. It's such a sweet little pattern." Lucy could tell from her tone that Maggie was about to launch into a pep talk. Luckily, Suzanne arrived.

"Lucy, I'm so glad you're here. I heard you were

grounded." She dropped her tote on her favorite seat and poured herself a glass of wine.

"My jailer has a soft touch. He lets me out now and then, on a very short leash."

"Glad your leash reaches the shop." Suzanne crunched down a pita chip covered with hummus, then stared at the part left in her hand. "Maggie must have made this. It's so good. Not like that beige paste they sell in the supermarket."

Lucy had already enjoyed several dips into the hummus bowl. "It is good. She could put the recipe in her condolence cookbook."

Suzanne looked puzzled. "Her what?"

Lucy grinned and shook her head. "Never mind. Just a little joke. You had to be there."

Dana came in next and greeted Lucy with a hug. "Maggie said you were sticking close to home. How are you feeling? Any Braxton Hicks?"

Lucy had not experienced false labor pains and hoped she skipped that predelivery symptom. Wasn't it going to be alarming enough to have real labor pains?

"Not a twinge. I had a few things to do at home. Feathering my nest."

"It's good to feel prepared. It will keep you calm." Dana poured herself a glass of wine and refilled Lucy's glass of sparkling water.

Phoebe had run up to her apartment take care of her cat, Van Gogh. She bounced back down the steps to catch the conversation.

"So, are you ready, Lucy?" she asked.

"I never had a baby before, it's hard to judge."

Maggie had come out of the kitchen again holding a platter of empanadas. Hot mitts covered both hands. "Women have been having babies for a long time. Our culture makes it much more complicated than it actually is."

"I keep telling myself that," Lucy replied. "But all the baby magazines and catalogs tell me the complete opposite. I think those people are up nights, figuring out how to scare new parents—and devising a lot of gadgets that will give us a false sense of security."

"It's a marketing scheme all right, but sounds like you're wise to the game," Suzanne said.

"So why do I keep falling for it?"

Suzanne laughed and placed an empanada on a dish. "These look yummy, Mag. What's inside?" She placed the dish in front of Lucy and went back for some salad.

"I roast a lot of vegetables, add some grated cheddar, anything that melts nicely. Then bake it inside a little pocket of dough. I also made a meat filling, with chopped beef, onions, and spices. That's a homemade two-ingredient dough, just flour and water. But you can use pizza dough or even use store-bought pastry dough if you like."

"If this tastes half as good as it looks and smells, the recipe is the next to feather my freezer," Lucy said. "I did love the empanadas they served at Rebecca's café."

"Speaking of Rebecca, any news on that front?" Suzanne glanced at Lucy and then at Dana.

"There is, but nothing good, sorry to say," Lucy replied between mouthfuls. "Detective Reyes brought Rebecca to the station yesterday for more questioning. They've set Colin's time of death as somewhere between midnight and two."

"That's a wide window and, unfortunately, Rebecca's car was seen at the café inside that time frame," Maggie noted.

"It looks bad," Suzanne said bluntly. She forked up a bite of food from her plate. "She's just not catching any breaks, is she?"

"Not one," Lucy agreed. "There's more. The police found a cyber account wallet on Colin's phone. He had some type of cryptocurrency account. You know, like Bitcoin. But it was another type, maybe Monero, or one called Quantum."

"At the risk of exposing my tech ignorance, I can't understand how that works," Maggie confessed. "How can money be virtual?"

"I never understood that, either, so I did some research. It was created by someone called Nashimoto, but that may have been a pseudonym for an individual or a group. Anyway, the creator stepped back into the shadows because the idea of cyber currency is to be free of any centralized source or administering organization. And from what I've read, the main reason it has value is because people say it does," Lucy announced bluntly. "At one time, every U.S. dollar was backed by gold, but that's not true anymore. A twenty-dollar bill has value because you can go to the store and buy twenty dollars' worth of groceries. And the grocer can go the gas pump and get twenty dollars' worth of gas, right? So even real money only has value because we assign value to it."

"I'm sort of getting it . . . go on," Maggie encouraged her.

"Another reason is that there will only be a limited amount of the currency. Bitcoin, for example, will only produce a certain number of coins. So it gains value because the supply is limited and the demand is growing. Also, because people are willing to buy cyber coin for 'real' currency. When someone wants to cash in cyber currency, it's more or less auctioned off to the highest bidder."

"Sounds like the stock market," Suzanne observed.

"It is like the stock market, in a way, which is why some people hold it, or trade it, as a moneymaking investment," Lucy explained. "Though it doesn't represent shares in anything real, like a company. Another reason it has value is because it can be used to purchase real goods. But often on the dark web or in shady deals. One of the objections to recognizing virtual currency is that the transactions are not transparent and can be used to evade taxes and other legal guardrails. Drug dealers use it to hide their exchanges and payoffs, and other shady operators love it, too."

Dana glanced at Lucy. "That's mostly what I've heard about it, granted, from Jack, who tends to look at everything from a legal perspective. Isn't it true that you can hide your identity completely as an account holder and everything is done with electronic wallets and passwords?"

"That's exactly right." Lucy nodded. "And it's impossible to get into an account without the password. Even account holders who lose or forget passwords are sunk. Some of them end up shut out of millions of dollars. There's no centralized bank or organization like PayPal who can help you get back into the account. It's all computers talking to computers. I read an article about a guy who has billions trapped in a cyber money wallet and he's just waiting for some technological breakthrough to help him open it."

"Billions? Really? That would drive me crazy," Phoebe shook her head and added a classic eye roll.

Suzanne had been quietly enjoying her empanada and patted her mouth with a napkin. "Okay, so nobody knows yet what's in Colin's account. But just the fact that he has one shows he was hiding money. Money he didn't receive in his civil servant's salary, or even his severance pay."

"Not necessarily," Lucy replied. "He could have been an investor. The value of Bitcoin has boomed over the last ten years. A lot people who bought small amounts have made amazing profits."

"All right, maybe he was playing the virtual money market," Suzanne conceded, "but I hope Detective Reyes will also consider that the money in that account came from another source. Most likely, one that's illegal and needs to be hidden."

"No matter how he got it, he was definitely hiding it," Lucy agreed. "Rebecca was basically supporting the family. She thought his only income was a small severance payment and then there was that movie option money. But he still wasn't contributing much to the family finances. Meanwhile, he may have had a ton of money hidden away."

"That guy could have written the creepy husband playbook." Suzanne pointed in the air with a knitting needle. "Worms have a higher moral code."

"Excuse me, I'd rather you didn't insult worms. You'd be surprised at how much they feel." Phoebe sounded indignant. "They're always put down as the lowest of the low when, ecologically, they're amazing. They're soil superheroes."

"I love finding big, juicy worms in my garden. They make the dirt so rich and healthy," Maggie said.

"Ugh . . . I'm eating, for goodness sakes." Suzanne shivered. "Can we get back to the investigation of Colin's murder, please?" Suzanne was clearly peeved about the detour into helpful garden creatures. And they hadn't even mentioned ladybugs yet.

"What did you say Colin did for a living? Before he decided to be a grouchy, undiscovered genius, I mean?" Dana asked.

"He worked for the Essex County Department of Public Works, as a senior engineer." Lucy wanted another bite of empanada but hated the bloated feeling she got lately when she overate, like a balloon about to pop. She took her knitting out instead.

"He probably earned a decent salary and got good benefits. But I doubt it was enough to save much. Rebecca told us that his unpublished novel had been optioned by a producer," Maggie reminded the group. "Were you able to figure out how much money that would have paid?" she asked Lucy.

"Not as much as you'd think, according to all the writer blogs and Q&A forums I found online," Lucy reported. "Since he was totally unknown and the book wasn't published, it was likely only a few thousand dollars."

"Hardly enough to require a secret cyber stash. It had to come from somewhere else. Somewhere connected to the reason he was murdered," Suzanne said.

"The police must realize that by now, too," Maggie remarked. "I don't understand why they're drilling down on Rebecca and not exploring this new lead; i.e., why did a civil servant need a secret cryptocurrency account?"

Dana rose and began collecting the dinner plates. "Unfortunately, from what Jack heard, the hidden account also supports Rebecca's motivation to want her husband dead before he could divorce her."

"So typical I could cry," Suzanne exclaimed. "Or punch something." Lucy guessed the conversation had triggered memories of her own harrowing ordeal with law enforcement. "They twist everything around to fit their pretzel-shaped theories."

"Another twist I forgot to mention," Lucy cut in, "Colin died without a will. Rebecca urged him to draw one up, for Sophie's sake, but he always avoided it."

"What does that mean, exactly? His estate goes into probate, is that it?" Maggie asked.

"All assets are frozen until a judge determines who should inherit his money and property. In the state of Massachusetts, his wife is legally entitled to half if there's no will specifying other wishes. Rebecca said if she does inherit anything, it will go into a trust fund for Sophie."

Suzanne shook her head. "I'm sorry, Lucy, but all these little bits of evidence—circumstantial, mind you—are piling up like my credit card bills come the first of the month."

"Suzanne? You promised us you'd quit that QVC habit," Maggie admonished.

Suzanne shrugged. "I might need another intervention. My point is, Rebecca and Helen better counter Detective Reyes's narrative soon, or they'll be doing it in a courtroom."

The dire prediction gave Lucy a chill. It was a dark perspective but an accurate one.

"We need to figure out where Colin got his cyber coin," Lucy proposed. "Even if the police are on it, I don't trust them to put the dots together in Rebecca's favor."

"Good point." Dana cleared off the rest of the table. "As long as you don't leave the house to find the dots. We don't want Matt mad at us."

Lucy rolled her eyes. "Don't worry, I'll take the heat. It's hard for him to stay mad at me in this state for long. He already knows I'm going to the memorial at Rebecca's house on Saturday. Rebecca invited Colin's former coworkers. I'll chat them up. People dislike speaking ill of the dead, but frankly, they usually can't help gossiping a little."

"Sad but true," Suzanne agreed.

"I'll also nose around the internet and see what I can find. A perfect way to pass the time while *breaking in my new nursing rocker*." She gazed at Dana, hoping she was satisfied.

"That sounds very cautious and cozy. Matt will never know what you're up to," Maggie said.

"Exactly," Lucy agreed. "I did a little virtual snooping yesterday, between stocking the freezer and taking a nap. I checked out Graham Paxton's website."

"Should we know that name?" Dana had taken out her

knitting. Jack's golf vest was almost done. She was working on the back and had just reached the ribbed armholes. Lucy practically sighed aloud, admiring the smooth, even stitches.

"Is he a hot new movie star? I speed-read the celebrity magazines on the supermarket checkout line, but it's hard to keep up." Suzanne stood at the oak server and tugged the lid off one of her huge plastic cake holders. She had a full collection of various sizes. Lucy recognized the special cupcake carrier.

"He writes geopolitical thrillers. You know, the world erupts in violence and the president ends up circling the Earth in a space station or some sort of super-sonic, stealth jet that the average citizen doesn't even know exists?"

"Actually, I don't know that type of story and can't say I want to." Phoebe looked horrified listening to the skimpy summary.

"It's a very popular genre," Maggie countered. "Popular in the movies, too. Colin was writing a novel in a similar vein, and Paxton was in his writing group. They had a falling-out when Colin showed the group his novel in progress and Paxton accused him of stealing ideas."

Suzanne approached the table with a platter of cupcakes, decorated with pink and yellow icing and little flowers; the dessert looked like an edible bouquet. "So you think Paxton heard that his stolen ideas were going to be made into a movie?"

"We're not sure, but it's certainly possible," Lucy said. "By the way, those cupcakes are beautiful."

"They look too pretty to eat," Dana agreed. "But I will anyway," she added with an impish grin.

"I will, too." Phoebe reached out and selected a yellow cupcake with a swirling orange flower on top. "But I'll take a picture first, for my Instagram account."

"Thanks, Pheeb, I'm honored," Suzanne said in an unusually modest tone.

Maggie selected a pink cupcake with purple flower and set it on a napkin near her place. "No one in the writing group, including Judith, had heard of Colin's triumph," she said, returning to a more important topic, "so he must have kept it secret from them, hoping it wouldn't get back to Paxton."

"But maybe it did," Phoebe cut in, "and he asked Colin for his share, but Colin brushed him off, so he got all crazy and obsessed about it, because this was his big break and he'd worked so hard on his novel, but never got any credit or recognition," she said in a stream of consciousness rush. "They argued and Colin laughed at him, probably in a cruel way," she added. "And Paxton lost it and ended up killing Colin. You know how nutty artists can get."

"Present company excluded, of course," Maggie said, giving her a look.

"Of course," Phoebe conceded. She took a deep breath. "Sorry, that sounded a little over the top, right?"

"I had the same theory, but you really know how to pitch it, Pheebs," Lucy confessed. "The problem is, it doesn't quite fit Paxton. He's fairly successful. He's published three or four books and according to Judith Esterhauzy, his newest just hit some bestseller list."

"So even if he'd heard about it, Colin's double cross was not a big deal," Dana said.

"As I mentioned before, the option payment Colin received couldn't have been much. Probably just a few thousand dollars," Lucy reminded her friends.

"If he even got one," Suzanne countered. "That man sounds like an incorrigible liar. We know he had a secret stash of cash. He probably fabricated that movie offer to account for having some spending money, more than Rebecca was able to spare from their tight family budget."

"I think you've hit on something, Suzanne. He probably did make that up. The lie would have helped him cover up his source of secret income and was also a fantasy that reinforced the new persona he aspired to, that of a talented and successful writer," Dana said. "Albeit, unrecognized by those who knew him best. Rebecca and even his writing group."

"A prophet is never recognized in his own village," Maggie said solemnly.

Was she thinking of herself, Lucy wondered? In Lucy's book she was the wise woman of all things fiber related and definitely given her due by this village.

"The guy was a legend in his own mind. It's scary." Suzanne turned to Lucy. "So you're eliminating Graham Paxton?"

"I guess so." Lucy knew she sounded conflicted. "His website did list a book signing in Boston on Tuesday night, the same night Colin died, which gives him some alibi. But he could have snuck into town afterward and driven back to Boston again. It's only a two-hour ride, even less late at night when there's no traffic. Oh, and he rides a motorcycle. A black one, too. At least, he had his picture taken sitting on one for his website."

"What does that have to do with anything?" Suzanne asked.

"Remember I told you that a few days before Colin died, a reckless driver tried to push Colin off the road while he was riding his bike? Well, the aggressive driver was on a black motorcycle. So, both tidbits struck me as odd coincidences."

Maggie shrugged, carefully picking up stitches in Suzanne's powder-blue mohair project, as if performing surgery. "I don't think we should give either much weight."

"I'm not sure," Lucy said, sticking the small detail on

the note board in her brain. "Let's see if Paxton shows up at the memorial. That could be interesting."

"That's what I hate about going to a memorial for someone who passed under suspicious circumstances," Phoebe said. "I can't help wondering if the killer is standing right next to me at the buffet table." She cringed. "Chatting me up about the guacamole."

"If any likely suspects corner you at the appetizers, call me over right away," Lucy teased.

Phoebe made a face. "I'll keep 'em chewing, no worries."

Of course Colin's killer wouldn't reveal themselves that easily, even if he or she did attend the memorial. But it seemed to Lucy that the guilty party had known Colin well; so well that their absence from the event might seem odd or suspicious.

She had been teased for months about her pregnant-lady intuition, but on Saturday, Lucy planned to put her hormonal radar on its highest setting.

Chapter 14

Rebecca's rustic cottage looked cheerful and inviting in the dappled sunlight as Lucy drove up Friday morning. Lucy's thoughts returned to the night she and Maggie visited to offer sympathy and support. It seemed so long ago, though only nine days had passed since Colin had been found dead in the café.

A white van was parked in the driveway, the Happy Hands Café logo painted on the side. Lucy recognized two bus boys, carrying chairs. At least Rebecca had help with the heavy lifting. She saw Rebecca's father, Leo, directing them, but with his weak heart, he couldn't do much more than that.

Lucy walked to the front door with an armload of flowers balanced on her belly. Rebecca had politely refused her offer to make a dish or dessert for the gathering, or even to help set up, so Lucy picked up fresh-cut flowers at the farmers' market on her way over. There could never be too many flowers tomorrow, that was for sure.

Rebecca had held up a brave front on Wednesday night, when she'd told Lucy all about her visit to the police station, but Lucy could tell she was worried. Her friend certainly had enough to think about today, so Lucy decided she wouldn't mention the investigation.

She dropped the heavy brass knocker twice and heard soft, quick steps approach. Rebecca pulled open the door and greeted her, looking surprised and pleased.

"Lucy—is it you behind all those flowers?" Rebecca greeted her.

"I'd have trouble hiding behind a greenhouse these days," Lucy countered. "I thought you could use these for the tables tomorrow. Or wherever you want to put them."

"That was so thoughtful. They're beautiful. I didn't have a chance to think about flowers yet."

Rebecca took the bouquets and led Lucy back toward the kitchen. Passing the dining room, she recognized bus boys from the café as they rearranged the furniture to make room for extra chairs and a long buffet table.

"Looks like we'll have clear weather, so we're setting up chairs on the lawn in back. A minister from the church near the village green will say a few words and lead a prayer. Colin wasn't religious, goodness knows. But I don't think he'd object. I guess it will make me feel better," Rebecca admitted.

Lucy didn't comment, though she did think how often the rituals held to bid a loved one farewell were designed more for the survivors than the one who was gone. Colin was getting a very nice send-off, Lucy thought. Better than he deserved. He darn well shouldn't object from wherever he sat.

She followed Rebecca into the kitchen, led by appetizing scents, soft jazzy music, and the sound of chopping on a wooden block.

It was Nick Russo, wielding a long silver knife as he deftly sliced a pile of ripe tomatoes. There was a kitchen worker there as well. Pots and pans covered the big, six-burner stove.

"Watch that sauce. Don't let it boil," she heard Nick say.

Lucy hadn't expected to see him here. Though it seemed logical he'd help cook for the large gathering.

"I think you and Nick have met?" Rebecca asked.

He wiped his hands on the apron tied around his slim waist and smiled, his dark, brooding features transformed by twinkling eyes, deep dimples, and straight white teeth. "It's Lucy, right?"

"That's right. Smells great in here. What are you making?"

"Whatever the boss tells me to." Nick tilted his head toward Rebecca, the corner of his mouth lifting in a smile.

Rebecca laughed. "The menu is more of an improvisation. And a negotiation." She glanced at the cook. "We have to work with the ingredients we have on hand. We're a little light on appetizers, but there's a ton of guacamole."

Lucy recalled Phoebe's concern. She'd have to warn her little friend to steer clear of the chips and dips.

"There was a lot of food in the café cold box. At least the police let me retrieve it—escorted of course," Rebecca explained. "I know it's too much for tomorrow, but we'll donate the leftovers to a soup kitchen in town."

"Good idea, how generous," Lucy said.

"I can't take the credit. Nick thought of that," Rebecca replied.

If he'd heard her compliment, he didn't show it. He stood at the stove, his back turned toward them while his large hand sprinkled fresh herbs under pot lids like a sorcerer spreading magic dust.

He looked tough—and he had even spent time behind bars—but he did seem to have a softer, thoughtful side. An attractive combination, Lucy thought. She did sense chemistry between Rebecca and the charismatic cook. But she also believed Rebecca when she'd sworn there was nothing romantic going on between them, despite what the surveillance video from Tuesday night suggested.

Maybe there was nothing going on at that time, Lucy reflected, but now that Colin was gone, something could evolve. Or maybe, already had?

"When will the police let you back in the café? Did they say?"

"No word yet. The place is a mess. I've been paying the staff, but with the restaurant closed, I don't know how long that can last. There's no insurance coverage for this situation," she added with a grim smile.

Lucy didn't know what to say. She'd been so focused on the emotional side of Colin's murder, she hadn't thought of the financial impact.

"I have a cleaning company lined up to come in when the police leave," Rebecca added. "They specialize in crime scenes." She looked away as she explained. Lucy could tell the subject upset her. "Honestly, I'm not sure I'll be able to go back in and start over again. I'll be thinking of poor Colin too much and how . . . Well, it will be very hard to reopen and carry on as usual after what happened. I'm wondering if customers would even come back, all things considered."

"I hadn't thought of that," Lucy admitted quietly. She sympathized with Rebecca but still felt it would be very unfair if Rebecca gave up her business. It would seem to Lucy just another way that Colin had cheated her.

"Maybe you can find a new space," she suggested. "When you're ready, I mean."

"Maybe." Rebecca smiled and nodded as she picked up a tray from the counter that held a set of shears and a collection of glass vases.

"If you grab the flowers, we'll arrange them on the table outside," she said, heading for the back door.

Lucy was glad to be assigned a task and followed with the flowers. As she walked out she heard Nick humming in a deep baritone following the tune on the radio; Billie Holiday, her sultry voice crooning the lyrics to "More Than You Know."

On the flagstone patio, Rebecca set the tray on a wrought iron table covered by a large umbrella and Lucy put the flowers down beside it.

"Confession," Rebecca whispered.

Lucy braced herself. "Yes?"

"I failed flower arranging in restaurant school. What if I trim the stems and leaves and you figure out where to stick them?"

"Deal . . . And I have something to tell you. Remember you mentioned that Colin had trouble in his writers' workshop? I decided to look into it and spoke with the woman who runs the group."

"Judith Esterhauzy?"

Lucy nodded. "Maggie and I saw her at The Beautiful Bean in Hamilton, where the group meets now. She told me there was a falling-out between Colin and another author who accused Colin of stealing his ideas. The argument escalated quickly and they threw a few punches. The rest of the group got involved, too."

Rebecca sighed, her gaze fixed on the flowers. "So that's what the fracas was about. I'd never guess such an intellectual group could get so rowdy."

"Colin probably never told the guy he got the film option. The other author may have felt entitled to a share."

Rebecca's mouth was set in a hard line as she snipped the flower stems. "Do you think this other writer was angry enough to kill Colin over that?"

Lucy shook her head. "When I looked up the average

amount an unknown writer would get for that sort of deal, it doesn't seem enough to justify murder."

Rebecca seemed surprised. "Colin never told me the exact amount, but he acted as if it was substantial."

"Even so, this other writer is reasonably successful. He has a few books out, and the newest is a best-seller. If he had an issue with Colin, he would have pursued legal action. Not snuck into the café and attacked him."

Rebecca nodded. "That seems logical."

"The thing is . . . probably just a huge coincidence . . . I noticed that he also drives a black motorcycle." Lucy met Rebecca's glance as she handed over a floppy-headed peony.

"I don't know what to make of that." Rebecca shook her head and sighed.

"Neither do I. As I said, it probably doesn't mean anything."

Rebecca glanced at her. She seemed nervous and snipped the flower stems quickly and a bit too short, Lucy thought.

"Since you brought it up, I might as well tell you, I had a driving incident this morning, right after I took Sophie to school. A motorcycle was tailgating me. It started to make me nervous. Then it drove up the yellow line, right beside me. I thought he was trying to pass, so I slowed down, but he just hung around, right next to my window, for the longest time, driving so close, squeezing into my lane and revving the engine. It was hard for me to keep the steering wheel straight and not swerve off the road. And the sound of it, Lucy." Rebecca shuddered. "He finally drove off, but I was so rattled I pulled onto the shoulder and had to sit there awhile to calm down."

"That's awful! Thank goodness Sophie wasn't in the car."

"That was my first thought, too." Rebecca's hand shook

for a moment as she worked the shears. She set them down and took a breath. "It probably lasted only a minute or two but it felt like much longer. And it was probably just a nasty driver showing off. But it does seem like a weird coincidence, when you think of what happened to Colin, and on that same road."

"I don't think it was a coincidence. I think it was a warning."

"A warning? About what?" Rebecca paused, looking puzzled.

"Maybe someone thinks you know more about Colin's private affairs than you actually do. Where that stash of cyber cash came from, for one thing. And they don't want you to tell the police."

"Believe me, if I knew anything about Colin's secret bank account or what he may have been up to, I'd go straight to Detective Reyes. The problem is, I don't have a clue," she said glumly.

"Did you tell the detective what happened to Colin when he was bike riding?" Lucy hated to press her, but she needed to know.

"I did, just yesterday. When I talked it over with my attorney, we decided I'd warn Nick first. He was very supportive and told me not to worry about him. He also agreed that the incident could help clear me as a suspect." She plucked extra leaves off a bunch of chrysanthemums. "If the police believe me. They seemed skeptical, but they promised to check the traffic incident reports on that road on the day in question. An ambulance was called and there would be record of that, too. But there's no evidence of this morning's incident except for my word. The police will think I'm making it up to prove my point."

Lucy had the same concern but stayed positive. "There

are cameras on that road. They can look for your car and the motorcycle on video if you can remember where and when it happened. Meanwhile, they'll need to take both reports seriously and look in new directions for Colin's killer. When they do make an arrest and go to trial . . . and it won't be you, believe me," she quickly added, "the police have to show they didn't ignore any possible evidence or lines of inquiry."

"I hope that's true, Lucy." Rebecca sounded distressed. She handed Lucy the last of the flowers and squeezed her hand. "You're a true friend. I won't forget this."

"Sticking flowers in a vase? Don't mention it," Lucy teased. She stepped back to admire her handiwork and propped up a few drooping blooms. "And I'm not sure I did a very good job."

"I mean all of your support since Colin died and this mess with the police began. Helping me find a lawyer, you and Maggie going out of your way to speak to Judith Esterhauzy, all of your good advice."

Lucy was touched. "We've seen what can happen when a murder investigation gets pointed in the wrong direction. Speaking of Judith, she tried to find a copy of Colin's manuscript for me. But she'd deleted the file. Do you think he left an extra hard copy in his office, or maybe on a stick drive or device somewhere?"

"I'm not sure. I'll check around the house and let you know. Do you really want to read it? You must have better things to do these days." She glanced a Lucy's burgeoning belly but didn't say more.

"It will distract me while the clock is ticking down. Three weeks to go, as of yesterday," she noted. "The novel was so important to Colin. I'm curious to see why."

Before Rebecca could reply, Nick called to them from the back door. "There's some warm quiche that needs a taste test, if anyone's hungry for lunch."

Lucy doubted his cooking needed their review, but the clever invitation and buttery scent easily lured them back into the kitchen.

She'd keep her eyes and ears open tomorrow. As Phoebe had reminded everyone, the killer might be among the guests who came to honor Colin's passing.

Chapter 15

Lucy found a long line of cars parked at Rebecca's house, more than she expected. Dana and Maggie had come together from town and parked just ahead of her. She met them on the driveway.

"Looks like a respectable showing," Maggie remarked.

"I was worried we'd be the only ones here. Along with Rebecca, Leo, and Sophie, I mean." She didn't add Nick Russo's name to the list aloud, but certainly did silently.

"I guess Colin had more friends than we gave him credit for." Dana checked her lipstick and hair in a tiny mirror in her purse and clicked it closed.

"Or his acquaintances are curious?" Maggie asked.

"People come to these events for all sorts of reasons, some prurient," Dana agreed. "Not just to mourn or offer the loved ones sympathy and support."

"No matter why they're here, I'm encouraged," Lucy whispered as they approached the gate to the backyard. "The larger the crowd, the more chance of finding out what Colin was hiding from Rebecca."

"Go for it," Maggie replied. "In your condition, no one will ever suspect you."

"Definitely," Dana chimed in. "You look so vulnerable. You inspire instant trust."

Lucy knew they were teasing, but partly serious, too. "I didn't notice that card in my hand. But you have a point."

"Use it while you can," Maggie quietly advised. She held open the gate and allowed Lucy to pass through first.

Chairs were set up in rows over the lawn, facing a space in front of two apple trees, where a white candle and a vase of flowers had been placed on a small table. The minister would stand there to speak, she guessed.

Another table to the right held framed photos of Colin and to the left, she saw two wooden stools, a microphone, and a small amplifier. Two shiny wooden folk guitars sat in open cases nearby.

Rebecca stood up front, with Sophie clinging to her hand as she greeted guests. Lucy was so accustomed to seeing her dressed in jeans and a T-shirt—and the ever-present kitchen apron—she almost didn't recognize her friend. Her navy-blue dress was suitably sedate and sophisticated. Her dark red hair was gathered in a low, coiling bun, and her lovely features, large eyes and full mouth, were accented by just the right touch of makeup and small pearl earrings.

She hardly recognized Leo, either. His long, scraggly hair was combed back smoothly, his beard neatly trimmed. He wore a black sports coat over a stark white shirt, buttoned at the neck, where a bolo tie and silver and turquoise clasp hung. His dark blue jeans looked new, too.

He stood with a man about the same age, who Lucy recognized as Leo's singing partner, Alfie. He was also dressed and groomed with care in a gray linen sports coat over blue jeans.

The musical partners were cut from the same cloth, she thought, tie-dye circa 1969, and looked so similar they might have been brothers. They probably considered themselves "soul brothers," as people would say back in the day. They called their musical duo "The Rude Dudes," which she thought was a clever name and fit them well.

"Let's take seats near the back," Maggie suggested. "Suzanne just sent a text, she's running late."

Lucy liked that plan. She wanted to look the gathering over surreptitiously. She took the aisle seat and settled in and glanced at a program that had been left on each chair. She felt the poke of a sharp elbow and Maggie leaned closer to whisper. "Rebecca's cook sure cleans up well."

Lucy waited a moment or so, then slowly glanced back. She could have easily mistaken Nick Russo for a high-level, corporate executive, the cool but intense type, with a lot on his mind. He was cleanly shaven with a fresh haircut, wearing a charcoal-gray pinstripe suit, a burgundy silk tie, and tailored white shirt. A leftover outfit from his past life, as the CFO of a big company? No matter, he still wore it well.

He didn't acknowledge Lucy as he passed, his gaze fixed on Rebecca and Sophie, who still stood up front. But he didn't join them. A few coworkers from the café were already seated and waved him over.

A few moments later, the minister appeared and waited with a patient expression as the last guests to arrive found seats. His feathery hair was as white as his starched collar, his face pink and soft as a baby's.

"I'm Reverend Philip Filcher, from First Church. Thank you all for coming today to honor Colin Hurley's life and mourn his passing," he began in a soft but sonorous voice.

Lucy knew from Rebecca that the minister had not known Colin personally, only what Rebecca had told him about her husband. As Lucy listened to the eulogy, she wondered if that was as obvious to everyone else as it was to her.

"From his career in public service, using his mathematical gifts as an engineer for the community's safety, to his pursuit of creative writing, Colin was clearly a man of many talents and interests. A renaissance man, you might even say. An active man who loved long, challenging journeys with his cycling club and even practiced martial arts at a local dojo. An attentive father to dear Sophie," the minister added, glancing at the little girl. "And a husband who supported his wife Rebecca's professional endeavors."

Suzanne leaned over and whispered, "I hope somebody gives me a positive spin like that when I check out. As for the last line, more like she supported him, wouldn't you say?"

Lucy didn't answer, fixing her expression in a serious look. Silently, she agreed with Suzanne. She felt as if she'd wandered into the wrong service. The minister was painting an admirable, but somewhat inaccurate portrait. It was not the Colin Hurley she'd known. But everyone has their faults, and no one is as good or as reprehensible as they might seem to the world at large. It would do little good for Reverend Filcher to dwell on the negatives today.

"We've gathered here today to share our memories and honor a life cut short by tragedy. May our memories of Colin be a blessing and may his soul rest in peace."

The minister opened a small black prayer book and read a Scripture passage.

When the prayer was done, he closed the prayer book and very solemnly said, "To close our service, The Rude Dudes will play 'Amazing Grace.' "

Leo and his musical partner were sitting on the stools behind the microphone, guitars ready for action. After a moment of silence, they began to strum and sing.

"I've always loved this song," Dana murmured. "It's sad but somehow so uplifting."

Lucy loved it, too, and thought that was a good way to describe it.

As the hymn came to an end, The Rude Dudes bowed their heads and crooned the final lyrics in deep, harmonizing baritones. Leo struck one last sonorous chord that echoed in the soft summer air.

"Thank you all for coming," the minister said, raising his soft white hands. "May you go in peace into this beautiful day."

The group sat quietly a moment, as people will do after such a service. Then began to stir and leave their seats. Lucy felt as if she'd just woken from a nap, though she hadn't been sitting there very long.

"Short and sweet. Just the way a memorial should be." Suzanne checked the time on her phone. "Colin Hurley, RIP."

Lucy led the way out of their row. "The minister obviously didn't know him from Adam, if you'll excuse the pun," she whispered to her friends.

"Maybe that was just as well," Maggie reflected quietly.

Most of the guests had wandered toward the patio and house. A few already held frosty glasses in hand.

"I could do with a bite to eat before I head back to the real-estate wars," Suzanne said, heading toward the patio.

Maggie and Dana followed, but Lucy lingered. "I'm going to check in with Rebecca. I'll catch up with you later."

Rebecca had not made much progress from the spot where she and Sophie had sat during the ceremony, the front row of seats that now stood empty. A group of guests circled her, waiting to offer their sympathy.

Lucy drifted to the table of photos.

She picked up a framed photo of Colin when he was a little boy, maybe eight or nine years old? Red-cheeked, covered with snow, he sat on a sled and smiled up at the camera with a big shaggy dog standing nearby. There were other photos from school days, a Little League team, fooling around with high school friends and a few scenes of his college days. One with his first wife in a hospital room, holding newborn Sophie. More recent photos with Rebecca and Sophie at the beach, birthday parties and Disneyland.

She suddenly felt guilty for thinking so badly of him. He didn't look as if he'd been such a cold, self-interested person his entire life. At least, not in the photographs. She wondered what had happened to him. Had the death of his first wife so soon after Sophie's birth embittered him?

She considered asking Rebecca, though this was certainly not the time.

Lucy saw her turn and greeted Rebecca with a hug. "Thank you for coming," Rebecca said.

"It was a very nice service," Lucy said, not knowing what else to offer.

"I thought so, too," Rebecca agreed. "I didn't expect such a large turnout. But it's comforting to see so many people pay their respects. Even if I hardly know half of them," she confided in a whisper.

Lucy had a feeling it was one of those occasions that would pass for Rebecca in a blur of faces and names. More of Colin's acquaintances waited to speak with her, and Lucy stepped away. She made her way across the patio and into the house.

The kitchen was almost as chaotic as the café's. Nick had his suit jacket off and wore his fancy tie slung over one shoulder. A black kitchen apron covered his expensive shirt, the sleeves rolled to his elbows. He still looked darkly dashing, Lucy thought. Maybe even more than usual.

The dining room was crowded with guests who circled the buffet table like hungry seagulls. The room's small air conditioner was no match for the hot day, and the air felt close and heavy.

Lucy didn't feel up to working her way into the line. She wandered into the living room instead, which was a bit less crowded and slightly cooler owing to a whirring ceiling fan.

"Would you like a seat, dear?" An older woman jumped up from an armchair and offered Lucy the spot. Almost a head shorter than Lucy, she was very spry and stronger than she looked, Lucy realized, as the woman took hold of her arm. "You look a little peaked, you ought to sit a minute."

Her black hair was the shade of shoe polish, contrasting with her scarlet lipstick on a carefully outlined, rosebud-size mouth. Dark eyes sparkled under two swoops of pencil that signified eyebrows. Something about the woman reminded Lucy of the Red Queen in *Alice in Wonderland*. But a far friendlier version.

Lucy sighed. She did feel a little light-headed. "I would like to sit, thank you," she said, settling her bulky body in the chair.

"I'll get you a glass of water. Don't budge." The little woman wagged her finger and sounded like a school nurse.

It felt odd to be waited on a by a perfect stranger, but she did need to cool off and clear her head, and when you were pregnant, strangers of all kinds offered aid. Whether they were letting her jump the line in the bank or giving her a cart in the supermarket, there were certainly perks to the condition.

The Red Queen was back a few moments later with a tall glass of sparkling water. "It's cool, but I didn't add ice. The baby will do a tap dance."

Lucy laughed. "That is what it feels like, sometimes."

"Boy or a girl?"

"We want to be surprised." Lucy watched her reaction.

So many people looked confused or even disappointed that she didn't have an answer to their question.

The Red Queen looked pleased and cocked her head to the side. "How nice. That's just how it ought to be. Is it your first?"

Lucy nodded. "Is it that obvious?"

She smiled. "A little."

Lucy smiled at her honesty. "I'm sorry, I didn't even ask your name."

"Hazel Huebner. And you?"

"Lucy Binger. How did you know Colin?"

"I worked with him at the Department of Public Works. It's awful the way he died. I could hardly believe such a thing had happened when I saw the news. And now they say he was murdered?"

"The police found proof that it wasn't an accident," Lucy replied.

"What a tragedy. A young man with so much ahead of him." She sighed and leaned closer. "Right after he came into that big inheritance, too. Of course, he didn't want to slave away nine to five anymore with the rest of the cubicle crowd. He didn't have to. We all got that and wished him well. Most of us anyway," she clarified. "But now . . . well, it doesn't seem fair."

"Not one bit," Lucy agreed, quickly putting the pieces together. Colin quit his job and told everyone at his office that he'd inherited family money. But he'd told Rebecca his position had been eliminated due to budget cuts.

"What sort of work do you do, Hazel? Are you an engineer, too?"

"Dear me, no. Though plenty of women are in the field now. Not so much in my day," she noted. "I'm the department secretary. Over twenty-five years," she said proudly. "I know where the bones are buried." She chuckled at her joke. "I thought I'd see a few more folks from the office here. Besides Ahmed and Charlie. We came together. I'm sure Mr. Wexler would have come to pay his respects too, if he still lived in the area. Colin was one of his favorites. I sent him an email with the sad news. He was very upset," Hazel reported.

"Another colleague, you mean?" Lucy asked.

"Oh, of course you don't know who I'm talking about. How could you? George Wexler was Colin's boss. My boss, too. He was our department head for years, but he retired not too long ago. Moved down to Mexico," she added. "He came up for a visit not too long ago, to see his new granddaughter. But he doesn't come back much that I know of. Then again, can you blame him? He's living the good life down there, from what I hear."

Lucy's curiosity was piqued and she wanted to dig deeper. Before she could ask another question, Hazel quietly gasped. "Kiera? For goodness' sake. What's *she* doing here?"

She turned back to Lucy, her red mouth puckered, as if she'd meant to hold the last thought, but it had popped out.

Lucy was intrigued and scanned the room. Who had inspired the Red Queen's reaction?

Chapter 16

Lucy followed Hazel's gaze to the far side of the room, where an attractive woman stood by the French doors that opened to the patio. She was dressed in black from head to toe, her form-fitting dress and patent leather heels simultaneously somber and sultry. With her blond hair in a low bun, a small, retro-style hat, shaped like a black velvet wing, stretched from ear to ear. A short veil spilled down over her eyes. A fascinator, Lucy thought the type of hat was called. The effect was intriguing.

She met Hazel's disapproving stare with a cool expression, then strolled outside as graceful as a swan gliding over a placid lake.

"The woman in the hat?" Lucy asked bluntly. "Is she a coworker, too?"

Hazel's gaze lingered on the doorway before she turned back to Lucy. "She was. I haven't seen her for months." Her tone insinuated she hadn't wanted to, either.

Lucy wanted to find out the mystery woman's last name, but Hazel came to her feet and hooked her purse over a thick arm.

"Can I fix you a plate of food, Lucy?"

Lucy smiled. "I'm fine. You've been too kind already. Thanks for coming to my rescue."

"I have three daughters and nine grandkids, with number ten on the way. I know the mom-to-be distress signals. It won't be long now," she predicted cheerfully.

Lucy placed a hand on her tummy. "I hope you're right. I am *so* ready."

"Good luck. Take care of yourself and that baby," the Red Queen advised as she headed for the dining room.

Lucy sipped the rest of her water, enjoying the breeze from the swirling fan. She wondered if her friends were looking for her. She didn't see them anywhere.

Was it worth trying to catch up with the woman in black, or was she gone, in a puff of smoke? Hazel Huebner had reacted as if she'd spotted a skunk at a garden party.

Lucy was curious to know why.

She placed her empty glass on a side table and hauled herself out of the comfortable chair, feeling she could have just as easily closed her eyes and taken a nap there. Her head spun a moment when she stood up and she decided a bit of food would be a good thing. The dining room was almost empty now, and there was a bounty of dishes to choose from.

Lucy picked up a plate and began to cruise, finding herself on the appetizer end of the display. She resisted a tray of cheese puffs and slipped a few carrot sticks on her plate, followed by a deviled egg with a tiny flag of crisp bacon planted in the middle.

"This stuff is top notch," a deep voice advised. The recommendation was muffled by the sound of crunching chips.

Lucy turned and glanced at the man beside her as he spooned another helping of guacamole on his dish. The black T-shirt under a denim jacket was a casual look for a memorial, she thought, but definitely made a statement. Then she took in his tanned skin and even teeth, a cosmetically bright shade of white. His crew-cut silver hair and small blue eyes.

Suddenly, she got it. Hovering over the guacamole, no less. Wait until she told Phoebe, who fervently believed there was no such thing as a coincidence.

"Aren't you Graham Paxton, the writer?"

His expression brightened, pleased by the recognition, though her tone was more accusatory than enthusiastic.

"That's me. Are you familiar with my books?"

Lucy smiled. "Oh yes . . . I love that action . . . stuff." She paused, hoping he wouldn't quiz her on specifics. "How did you know Colin?"

Of course, she knew the answer, but wanted to hear his version of the relationship.

"Colin was a writer, too. Well, aspired to be, I guess you'd say. He never published, as far as I know. We met in a critique group. I was further along than most of the others. You know, coaching them. I like to give back," he offered with faux humility. He shrugged and stabbed a slice of smoked salmon with his plastic fork, as if harpooning a fish. "And the comradery is good for the soul. Writing can be a lonely business." He sighed with well-practiced sincerity.

"I can imagine." Lucy summoned up a sympathetic tone. She didn't see a wedding ring and wondered if that line helped him pick up women. "I heard that Colin was writing a novel. His wife said the book was optioned for a movie. Poor guy, a lot of good that big break did him."

Lucy was practically positive Colin had never received an option and had only told Rebecca that to account for his ample pocket change, which he was channeling from his cyber account, she now guessed. But she wanted to know for sure if the fabrication had reached Paxton, perhaps on the local writers' grapevine.

A bite of salmon stuck in the author's throat and he covered his mouth with a cocktail napkin. He squinted at her, tiny lines crinkling his tan skin. "I've never heard that. Are you sure?"

He was either an accomplished actor or was hearing this news for the first time.

"Oh, I'm certain. I thought that sort of thing happens all the time. Is it so unusual?"

"In Colin's case, it would be." He paused a moment, choosing his words. "It's not kind to say, especially today, but Colin's writing was quite amateurish, and his stories were . . . well, corny and clichéd would be the kindest way to put it. Except for the ideas he appropriated from other sources," he added in a stronger tone.

Lucy wondered if he'd elaborate on that point, but he seemed to pull back, focusing on his food again. "If the project had attracted any interest of that kind, I doubt he got much out of the deal." He shrugged. "Tragic the way he died. Now there's an interesting plot."

"I'd read that book," Lucy quickly replied. And skip to the end to find out who really killed him, she added silently.

"I'm not a mystery writer, alas. But my new thriller was just published, *Doomsday Strategy,*" he said smoothly, shifting into marketing mode. "Let me know what you think after you read it. You can contact me on Facebook, and all that."

Lucy nodded. She had thoroughly investigated the author on all the social media platforms. "Wait until I tell my friends that I just met Graham Paxton. They won't believe it."

At least that much was true.

"You're sweet." Basking in her flattery, he wore the same expression as Walley, her chocolate Lab, getting a belly rub.

"There they are now." Lucy spotted Maggie and Dana in the kitchen. She waved to them, then turned back to Paxton. "It's been so nice speaking with you."

"Likewise, Lucy." He flashed a smile and winked. An incoming platter of sliced sirloin and mushrooms caught his eye and he followed it to the far side of the table.

Though reportedly doing well in his career, Paxton clearly appreciated a free meal, she noticed.

Lucy wasn't very hungry but knew she needed to eat something. She'd just chosen a chicken dish and a spoonful of pasta salad when Maggie and Dana caught up with her.

"You've been on the move for a pregnant lady," Dana greeted her.

"Just circulating. I've had some interesting conversations," she added with a tantalizing grin.

Maggie's expression brightened. "Really? I can hardly wait to hear more."

Lucy was eager to give her friends a full report but knew this was not the right time or place. She took a last bite of food and set her plate on the sideboard. "I'm ready to go, if you are. I just want to say goodbye to Rebecca."

"We've already seen her," Dana said. "I guess we'll leave ahead of you."

Lucy said goodbye to her friends and looked around for Rebecca. She found her in the kitchen, arranging desserts on a table with coffee and tea.

"I just want to say goodbye. I'm sure it's been a hard day, but you did a great job. The gathering was lovely." More than Colin deserved, she almost added.

Rebecca hugged her. "It was so good to have you here. It meant a lot to me. It was nice of your friends to come, too."

"They wanted to be here for you and Sophie. If you need any help with her this week, or anything at all, just call me."

Rebecca nodded, and glanced at Lucy's tummy. "Only if you call me if *you* need help with Dara . . . Or a ride to the hospital?"

"Deal . . . though I hope it doesn't come to that." Lucy smiled at the gentle teasing.

"Oh, wait . . . I almost forgot." Rebecca opened a drawer near the sink and began sifting through it. "Where is that bag? I know I put it in here . . ."

It was the type of drawer where odds and ends wind up—pens, pencils, rubber bands, extra keys that don't fit any locks, expired coupons, stray postage stamps that have lost their glue, scraps of recipes torn from the news-paper, and so much more. Lucy had a drawer like that at home, too. Didn't everybody?

Rebecca seemed about to give up, when she pulled out a plastic sandwich bag and handed it to Lucy with a tri-umphant smile. "I found this in a fanny pack Colin wore when he went cycling. It was in the shed, near his bike equipment, and giving off an awful smell," she explained. "I found a rotten banana, some bike tools, and this."

Lucy saw a small red thumb drive in the bag, the type used to store computer information. There was a label on the bag and Rebecca read it for her.

"The label says, SINK HOLE–DRAFT 3. That was the title of Colin's novel. You said you want to read it?"

"I absolutely want to read it." Even more now than she had before. "That was a lucky find, thanks," Lucy took the little bag and slipped it in her purse.

"I'll be interested to hear what you think," Rebecca said.

They shared a final hug and Lucy headed out the back door.

At the edge of the patio, she spotted Judith Esterhauzy in a shady corner chatting with Graham Paxton. His back was turned, and Lucy couldn't see his expression, but the conversation was clearly animated and a private one.

Was he checking up on Lucy's story about Colin's option? It was possible.

She walked carefully on the stone-covered driveway to her car. Sunlight beat down, the air shimmering with heat. She blinked and paused, overcome by the oddest feeling.

Not exactly dizziness, more of a gooseflesh shiver on her bare skin, crawling up her neck and her scalp. She took a deep breath as a sharp, clear insight rose in her foggy brain, like a silver fish leaping above the waves for the blink of an eye.

The key to Colin's murder lay somewhere in his manuscript. Lucy was suddenly sure of it.

Chapter 17

It was frustrating to wait until Monday to relate all she'd learned at the memorial to her friends. Lucy felt bored on Sunday. More than bored, like a beached whale.

Especially since Matt still had even discouraged her from sitting on the porch to keep him company while he worked in the garden on Sunday, which turned out to be even hotter than the day before.

The knitting shop wasn't open on Sunday in the summer. It hadn't been since Maggie and Charles had started living together and, of course, after their marriage last fall. Charles was an avid sailor and Maggie was bitten by the bug, too, at least once she had adapted her knitting style to the high seas, figuring out how to keep her stitches smooth, even when the waves bounced the boat around. Lucy got seasick imagining it. Especially these days.

Lucy took out her knitting, which should have been a good distraction, but she wasn't able to focus. Maybe if she hadn't been working on a baby sweater? Her progress on the tiny argyle was pitiful. At the rate she was going, it would probably be done when their child was ready for kindergarten. Perhaps she could convert it to a slipper or sock?

Her mother called midday, her usual time to check in.

Lucy had given up on the knitting and was practicing swaddling, using a stuffed monkey from the baby's room and a flannel baby blanket. She placed it at a diagonal to the monkey, flipped up the bottom first and then each side, and wrapped the fabric as close as she could. Sometimes she even managed to get a little hood out of the top corner.

She had her cell phone timer going and was trying to beat her best time when MOM flashed on the screen.

"Hi, sweetheart, what are you up to?" her mother greeted her.

"Swaddling," Lucy replied. "Newborns like to be wrapped up tight. I want to make sure I can do this in the middle of the night."

Her mother laughed. "Sounds as if you're well prepared. As always."

Ever since she was a little girl, Lucy tended to overprepare, overstudying for tests, packing too many clothes for trips, buying too many canned goods for the pantry. Perhaps because her mother was just the opposite, the adventurous type who tossed a few things in a duffel and never worried if she needed to do without or improvise. Which was often the case during her many travels.

Isabel Binger had been a very attentive mother, in her way. But she was dedicated to her work as well. Lucy had never felt slighted and was proud of her mother, a well-known professor and archeologist. She taught at the University of Massachusetts in Amherst and visited Plum Harbor frequently. But during the summer, or any break in the college schedule for that matter, she eagerly headed off to work at some distant, dusty archaeological dig, her true passion.

Her trips usually took her to obscure, exotic locations, like a desert in the Middle East, or the Australian outback, or the rugged hilltops of Turkey. Mindful of Lucy's pregnancy, Isabel had confined her travels this summer, just a flight—or two—away in Colorado, at a recently discovered dig just outside of Durango, where the Ancestral Puebloan people lived over 1,200 years ago.

Lucy found their conversation predictable but comforting. Lucy related the other baby preparations that had taken up her week, and her mother excitedly described a bone fragment she'd uncovered at the dig.

"How do you feel, dear? Any signs yet?"

"Nothing unusual, Mom. The doctor says it will be a while."

"My knapsack is packed. Make sure Matt sends a text as soon as the baby is on the way. Maybe I should come back this week?"

Lucy thought the offer was sweet. But she knew her mother would stay for a while once the baby had arrived. There was really nothing for her to do right now but sit and wait.

"No need to cut your trip short, Mom. Everyone says first babies are notoriously late. I'm getting plenty of attention between Matt and my friends."

Too much, at times, Lucy thought as Matt marched by, silently asking if she'd taken her vitamins yet. She nodded and waved him off.

"It was the reverse for me. Your sister Ellen arrived right on schedule. You, on the other hand, took your sweet time. I think you were born more than a week past the due date."

"I'm still notoriously late for appointments," she admitted. "I'm seeing the doctor again this week. I'll let you know what she says."

"Please do," her mother insisted. "Take good care of yourself, Lucy. I'll be there very soon. I love you and can't wait to see you, sweetheart."

"I love you too, Mom," Lucy replied, suddenly wistful and weepy.

When she hung up, Matt sat beside her on the couch and put his arm around her shoulder. "Miss your mom?"

"A little." She stared down at her tummy and rubbed it over her T-shirt. "I guess that's only normal. She offered to come back this week, but I don't want her to end her trip early. The baby might not be here for a while."

"That's true." Matt placed his hand on her belly, too. "If only that little critter could give us a clue." He leaned over and whispered to the baby bump, "Hey in there, it's your dad. We can't wait to see you. Any ETA?"

Lucy laughed and Matt shushed her. "Quiet. I'm trying to hear the baby's answer."

She played along, simmering down. Finally, he sighed, kissed her tummy, and sat up again. "Our child wants to surprise us."

"I thought so. The first of many, I expect."

He smiled and squeezed her hand. "Brace yourself, it's going to be a long, exciting ride. I guess we should relax and try to enjoy the wait?"

"We probably should. But the relaxing part is hard," she admitted.

Monday brought cooler weather, cool enough for Lucy to drive the dogs to the village green and walk up Main Street to the knitting shop.

Maggie waved from the porch as she approached. "I was hoping you'd drop by. The shop is so quiet. The start of summer doldrums, I guess. I'm just taking a lunch break."

Lucy took a seat and pulled a plastic water bowl from her tote bag, then filled it for the dogs.

"Eager to hear what I found out at the memorial?"

"I nearly called you last night when we got in, but I didn't want to wake you." Maggie offered Lucy a bottle of water from the table set up with cold beverages for her customers.

"I was snoring like a drunken sailor, Matt says, right after we finished dinner. While he cleaned up the kitchen, I set up on the sofa with my laptop and started Colin's novel. But I only managed to get through a few pages," she admitted. A combination of pregnancy demanding an early bedtime and Colin's writing, which she'd found both overwrought and boring. Though, to be fair, so far she hadn't given the book a chance.

"You must have needed the sleep. You've been doing too much. You could have been running off to the hospital yesterday and I'd be stuck out at sea."

Maggie sounded genuinely distressed by the possibility, and Lucy was touched by her concern. Though her horror-stricken expression nearly made Lucy laugh.

"I wasn't running anywhere, believe me. Matt would hardly let me get off the couch."

"He just loves you."

She sighed and rolled her eyes. "While I was stranded, I had plenty of time to do some digging. And thinking." Lucy wasn't sure where to start. "First, guess who I met up with at the memorial? Graham Paxton," she said before Maggie could reply.

"The writer who had the dustup with Colin?"

"His version was more like, Colin was an amateurish author except for the ideas he *appropriated* from the work of others. But yes."

Maggie looked about to ask another question, then held her hand up. "Wait . . . here comes Suzanne. She'll want to hear the whole thing."

As Suzanne came up the walk, Maggie called to her.

"Hurry along, Lucy has a lot to report. She met Graham Paxton at the memorial."

"The guy we think Colin plagiarized from who just happens to drive a black motorcycle?" Suzanne scurried up the path on her platform heeled mules. She looked professional and cool in white pants and a sleeveless top with a draped neckline, the perfect shade of orange to complement her dark hair.

"Yes, and yes. But my theory is considerably revised," Lucy noted.

"He's off our suspect list?" Suzanne asked.

"Let's say I'm putting him to the side for now. Even though we did meet at the guacamole bowl."

Maggie leaned forward and spoke in a hushed tone. "Please don't tell Phoebe. We won't hear the end of it."

Lucy could see the wisdom in that request. Phoebe would be convinced her prediction had come true and Lucy had brushed shoulders . . . and tortilla chips . . . with the killer. She was notoriously superstitious, a trait her friends tried to discourage. She'd also had a run-in last summer at the farmers' market with a killer who was hiding in plain sight, and Lucy's anecdote about Paxton, however amusing it seemed to the others, would surely trigger memories of that experience.

"I was sort of looking forward to it. I mean, as a joke? But I get your point."

"She'll get some perspective someday and take these things lightly. But not quite yet," Maggie said. "It's a credit to Phoebe that she went back to the market this summer at all. She worked so hard there this weekend, I told her to sleep in. I'll catch her up on the high points later."

"With careful edits," Suzanne suggested.

"That's right." Maggie turned to Lucy. "Getting back to Mr. Paxton?"

Lucy related the conversation and how she'd played the role of gushing fan. "I could tell from his reaction he hadn't heard about the option on Colin's book, which I'm convinced now was just another lie to cover up Colin's mysterious, likely illicit stream of income."

"So, even though there was no Hollywood deal, you were wondering if Paxton may have heard the tall tale and believed it." Suzanne had taken a paper bag from her tote and pulled out a wrap sandwich. "And, therefore, had motive to get on his motorcycle and push Colin off the road. Or creep into the café and tip the bookcase?"

"That's right. But I never got that vibe. He was surprised, but after insulting Colin's writing a bit, in a subtle way," she added, "he brushed it off."

"So we scratch Graham Paxton off the list of possible assailants," Maggie noted, "and the driver of the black motorcycle, too, I suppose."

"That's another reason it can't be him. I can understand why he might have harassed Colin on his bike, but why bother Rebecca and nearly cause her to have an accident?"

"But it was clever of you to recognize him. He must have walked right past me," Maggie admitted.

"Me too . . . but I only had eyes for Nick Russo." Suzanne winked and sipped her tall, iced coffee drink. Lucy had gone nine months caffeine free completely and the scent of coffee so close and yet so far was driving her crazy. "Did you see the way he looked in that suit? He could rattle my pots anytime," she added slyly.

"Suzanne? What would Kevin say if he heard that?" Maggie's tone was scolding, but she was laughing, too. And blushing a little.

"We all think he's hot. Not a question," Lucy agreed. "The police have their eye on him, too, but for different reasons. I can see why he may have tailed Colin on his motorcycle, but again, not Rebecca."

"What do you think?" Maggie met Lucy's gaze. "I mean if Rebecca wasn't so convinced of his innocence?"

Lucy felt put on the spot. "I believed what she said about him, so I haven't given it a lot of thought."

"But the police probably think they were either having an affair and planned Colin's demise together," Suzanne said, "or Nick is wildly but silently in love with Rebecca and took it upon himself to do away with the obstacle to the object of his affections. Or maybe he even thought he was protecting her, like a knight in shining armor—and an apron—since Colin was such a twit."

Lucy stared at her. "It seems somebody here has given the question some thought."

"Come on, Lucy. Don't tell me all that hasn't occurred to you?"

"Some of it," Lucy conceded. "But that was before the memorial. And before I met Hazel Huebner and saw the woman in black."

Maggie and Suzanne stared each other. Maggie was the first to speak. "The . . . who?"

Chapter 18

Lucy quickly related her conversation with Hazel Huebner. "So it seems Colin was lying in all directions, telling his coworkers he'd come into family money and telling Rebecca he was laid off. But aside from that, Hazel was doing a head count of Colin's former coworkers, when she spotted this extremely attractive woman dressed in black. She'd just come in from the patio. Hazel said something like, 'What's she doing here? Some nerve . . .' Or something like that."

"Interesting." Maggie mulled over the story. "Did you get a good look?"

"Not really. She spotted Hazel and left. She definitely didn't want to reminisce about good times at the water cooler."

"I noticed her." Suzanne was using the straw to scoop up the creamy foam on top of her drink. "Chic outfit. Great hat. Nice figure, too, and not afraid to flaunt it."

"That's just about my summary. Hazel said she used to work in the building department, too, but had left a while ago."

"I wonder what her relationship with Colin was," Maggie mused.

"Come on, Mag. You just heard us describe her. A classic tall, thin, blonde. They must have been having an affair," Suzanne said.

"Not necessarily," Maggie countered. "Though it would account for her slipping in and out on Saturday, if she didn't want Rebecca to recognize her."

"I wondered about that, too," Lucy said.

"I bet if you could track her down, you'd learn a lot." Suzanne put her iced coffee aside and checked her phone. "But how can you find her? Did this Hazel mention a name?"

"Just a first name, but I had plenty of time this weekend to work on it." Lucy picked up the notebook computer Maggie used for her classes and office tasks.

"I did a little searching and surfing. The county has a surprising amount of information about their employees online. I also cross-referenced LinkedIn and other professional and social sites." She typed for a few moments, then showed her friends the screen.

"Kiera Nesbit, certified civil engineer with several years of experience in the Essex County Department of Public Works. I didn't recognize her from this picture but"— Lucy typed into the search bar again and brought up Kiera's page on a social media site—"if you look on Facebook or Instagram, I definitely think it's the same person. Here's a picture of her at a party. Looks like a wedding where the guests are in formal dress. Same hat, wouldn't you say?"

"Her photo on the county website looks like a mug shot," Suzanne murmured. "But I do think that's the woman I saw at the memorial. Did you find any photos of her with Colin?"

"Not so far. But she teaches a class twice a week, Sunset Tai Chi, at Crane's Beach in Ipswich."

"I doubt a tai chi teacher worth her Himalayan salt will let you anywhere near that class in your condition. It's probably an insurance issue." Suzanne took a bite of her sandwich, taking care that the mayo didn't squirt on her outfit.

"Why not? It's not martial arts. It's more like . . . very slow ballet. Pregnant women do yoga."

"A special version, the way my mom does it, sitting in a chair," Suzanne insisted. "Your Silent Swallow is going to lead to an ambulance siren."

"I don't need to take the class. I just want to speak to her."

"Stalk her, you mean?" Maggie had started gathering supplies for a class and glanced up from a folder filled with handouts.

"*Meet* her," Lucy replied. "It's always best to talk face-to-face in these situations. You know that."

"People can so easily hang up. Or not pick up a call from a strange number at all," Maggie said.

"Exactly." She cast Maggie a hopeful look. "Crane's Beach is beautiful at sunset. I bet you haven't been there in ages."

"Oh dear . . . I knew the conversation was heading that way." Maggie sighed, then fixed her face in a stern expression. "You know how to rope me into these things, don't you?"

"What do you mean?" Lucy honestly didn't understand the accusation.

"I worry about you running around alone Ms. Eight Months and counting. I know it won't do any good to tell you not to go. But I might spill the beans to Matt. That would clip your wings."

Lucy was shocked by the threat. "You're kidding, right?"

"I'm not sure." Maggie sat mulling over the question.

"Oh boy . . . play nice, ladies. I've got to go." Suzanne had scooped up her sandwich, half-eaten, and stuffed it back in the paper bag.

She glanced at Lucy as she headed for the stairs. "I think it will be fine if you keep a close watch on her, Mag. And she doesn't chase the poor woman over the sand dunes, or something crazy like that."

"I couldn't chase a turtle right now and you know it. I'll simply observe and tune in to the peaceful vibe," Lucy insisted.

"When is this class?" Maggie asked quietly.

"Tonight, at half past six. I need to drop Dara off at her mom's house around six." Matt and his ex-wife, Jen, had a joint custody arrangement, and Dara stayed with each parent half of the week. Their relationship was very amicable, fortunately for all involved. "I can pick you up right after that," Lucy said eagerly.

Maggie sighed—her surrendering sigh, Lucy was glad to hear. "All right, I'll let Charles know I'll be home late. What story are you cooking up for your poor husband?"

Maggie's question made her feel guilty about deceiving him, and Lucy nearly called her on the ploy. "The only thing I'm cooking up for Matt is dinner. The office is open late. I'll be home well before him."

"You've thought of everything."

"Not quite," Lucy replied honestly. Such as, what would she do if Kiera Nesbit flat out refused to speak to them? "But I think we'll learn something worth the bother of tracking her down. If Kiera and Colin were just coworkers and office friends, why did she fly in under the radar at the memorial? If they were more than that, I bet she knows what Colin was up to. A lot more than Rebecca does."

"That makes sense, but even if that's so, I doubt she'll tell us anything."

"We won't know unless we try. You must have some Eleanor Roosevelt quote stashed in your knitting bag that applies here?"

"How about, *Nothing has ever been achieved by the person who says, 'It can't be done'?*" Maggie offered. "And this time, that person might be me. I do know this is the last field trip until the baby comes. Will you promise me that, please?"

Lucy was touched by Maggie's concern. "I promise, honest."

"And not like you promised Matt," Maggie cut in, peering behind Lucy's back. "Fingers out front. I need to make sure they aren't crossed."

Lucy laughed, her hands in full view as she wiggled her digits. "Happy now?"

Maggie seemed satisfied a moment, then took one of Lucy's hands in her own. "No wedding ring? Are you trying to pick up men at the supermarket again?"

"Don't I get one last fling? I thought I read that somewhere in the expectant mom handbook," Lucy joked.

"Must be a revised edition. That's not what it said in the one I used. But I recall a warning about swollen fingers, ankles, and such. You're holding water."

"My rings always get tight in the summer. It's the humidity." Lucy's wedding rings hadn't fit for a while. She blamed it on baby weight. "I ate too much salty food this weekend."

"That will do it." Maggie handed Lucy another water bottle. "I know it sounds counterintuitive, but you need to drink a lot to flush out the bloat. It's not good for the baby."

"Flush being the main result. I'm definitely getting my ten thousand steps these days, walking back and forth to the bathroom."

Maggie smiled, then counted out sets of number five needles from a big collection she stored in a neat, square basket. "You'll be in good shape after the big day. That little one will keep you hopping."

"I keep hearing that. Though from what I've seen and read, it seems to me newborns mostly sleep, eat, and dirty their diapers. Then start all over again. There's a bit of burping and gurgling in between, I guess."

"That is the drill at first. Somehow, it's exhausting. I'm not exactly sure why. When Julia first came home," Maggie added, mentioning her daughter who was now grown and lived in the Midwest, "I remember hovering over her crib or baby seat, even while she slept, barely allowing myself to blink. It was as if I expected her to disappear." Maggie shrugged and laughed. "Maybe after all the waiting, I couldn't believe she was really there."

"I totally get that." Lucy easily imagined she would act the same way. At first, at least.

Maggie made a neat pile of the needles, then counted the balls of yarn in a big basket that sat on the wicker table. The yarn was a lightweight fiber, silk blended with bamboo, Lucy guessed. The popsicle colors—lemon yellow, peach, lime green—were perfect choices for summer knitting projects.

Lucy guessed it was almost one and the class would start soon.

"I have to touch base with a client before Dara gets home." She came to her feet and so did the dogs, stretching and yawning as she untangled their leashes.

"I need to get back to work as well." Maggie came to

her feet and picked up the basket. "I think it's too warm to hold the class out here. We'll focus better in the AC. You ought to get somewhere cool, too."

"I will," Lucy promised. She did feel the heat a bit, despite the shade from the porch. Her phone buzzed with a text and she picked it up. "I bet it's Matt checking up on me," she said to Maggie.

"Does he check in often?"

"Only every ten . . . or five? . . . minutes," Lucy said lightly as she glanced at the screen.

But the message wasn't from Matt. It was from Rebecca. Lucy opened it and read:

EMERGENCY. Can you call me?

Lucy quickly called Rebecca's number, feeling her pulse race. Rebecca picked up on the first ring.

"What happened? Are you all right?" Lucy greeted her.

"Someone broke into my house while I was out doing errands. My father walked in on the intruder and was struck over the head. I found him in the kitchen. He had tape over his mouth and his hands and legs were tied. I nearly fainted at the sight," she confessed. "But he seems all right, thank goodness. I called 911 and an ambulance took him to Essex Hospital. I'm on my way over there now."

"That's awful! How frightening. Was it a robbery?"

Lucy could see that the conversation had attracted Maggie's attention. She stood quietly by with an expression of concern.

"I thought so at first. But nothing's been stolen. They even left my laptop and the TV. But Colin's office looks like a tornado ripped through it. They must have been looking for something." That made sense to Lucy. "The police are still at my house," Rebecca continued.

"Detective Reyes wants me go to the station to make a statement as soon as I'm able."

Another statement, Lucy thought. But didn't interrupt.

"Could you pick up Sophie at school and bring her back to your house? I'm not sure how long I'll be at the police station, and then I'll need to take care of my dad. I hope he doesn't have to stay at the hospital."

"Of course I'll take care of Sophie. No problem. Will Helen be with you when you speak to the police?" Lucy said, mentioning Rebecca's attorney.

"Yes, she'll meet me there later, after I've taken care of my father."

Lucy felt relieved. Even under these circumstances, she thought Rebecca still had to be on guard with Detective Reyes. "Keep me posted and give your Dad a hug from me."

As Lucy ended the call and put her phone away, Maggie said, "Was that Rebecca? What happened?"

"Someone broke into her house. Sounds like they were looking for something in Colin's office. Or just trying to scare her. Leo has been staying over ever since Rebecca had that run-in on the road with the motorcycle. He walked into the kitchen and was struck unconscious by the intruder. They gagged and blindfolded him, and tied him up to a chair. Rebecca thinks he'll be fine but I could tell she's still worried about him and unhinged by the whole thing. How much stress can a person stand?" Lucy felt alarmed but also angry. "I hope the police are finally going to see that she had nothing to do with Colin's death and the person who killed him is out there, harassing Rebecca now. Doesn't this prove it?"

"It does to me. But Detective Reyes is the one who must be convinced. She does get tunnel vision now and then."

Lucy let out a frustrated breath. "I hope Kiera Nesbit can point us to the *right* tunnel. It's totally crazy and so unfair that Rebecca is still a suspect, while she, Sophie, and Leo are obviously in danger."

Maggie's grim expression silently confirmed Lucy's fear.

Chapter 19

"Did Rebecca say anything more about the break-in when you saw her?" Maggie sat beside Lucy in the Jeep as they drove down Route 1A toward the village of Ipswich and Crane's Beach.

"She didn't want to talk about it in front of Sophie. But she let me know in Mom-speak that she managed to clean up in between getting Leo home and talking to the police."

"She's super woman, that one." Maggie's tone was admiring and not at all ironic.

"She didn't want Sophie to have any idea of what had happened. It's enough that the little girl just lost her father. Leo has a bump and a horrible headache, but nothing worse. Rebecca was relieved that his blood pressure and other vitals were fine, too."

"He's lucky. Sounds as if it could have been a lot worse. Did he get a look at the person who attacked him?" Maggie asked.

"They came up behind him and covered his eyes while he was unconscious. He didn't see a thing until Rebecca found him."

"That sounds terrifying. I guess there's no alarm system or security cameras?" Maggie asked.

"None of that. It's a rental. The owner claims the neighborhood is safe. He's never had a problem. He'll have an alarm installed but wouldn't go for security cameras. Too expensive, he said. But Nick Russo insisted that Rebecca needed them and he ordered a few. Rebecca doesn't have a clue about those things and neither does Leo, but Nick is good with high tech gadgets, and he will set them up for her. The police promised to keep an eye on the house, too."

"As in stationing a car outside to protect them?"

"I don't think they'll go that far. Just some extra drive-by patrols. Though, they might have been watching Rebecca since Colin died and watching the house to see who was coming and going."

"Too bad they weren't snooping this morning." Maggie had taken out a tube of sunblock and smeared some on her arms and face. The sun was so low, Lucy doubted it could do much damage, but she admired Maggie's vigilance.

"Ironic, isn't it?"

Maggie paused with her smearing. "Perhaps. Or, someone was watching the house, and knew when Rebecca was out and when the police patrol wasn't nearby."

"I thought of that, too. I guess they didn't expect to find her father there. All this stress can't be good for him. He has a weak heart. Rebecca says there's no cure short of a transplant and he's not a candidate. He can't stop smoking, either," she added.

"Rebecca mentioned his heart problem to me. But I didn't know it was that serious."

Maggie slipped her sunglasses on and fluffed her hair with her fingers. "I hate to be pessimistic, but I doubt the police will catch the intruder."

"They said they're going door to door to ask the neighbors for information, but I also doubt they'll find the creep who did it. I think it's more important to figure out what they were looking for."

They had come to the village of Ipswich and drove past the village green and over a small stone bridge. Less than a mile farther on, Lucy turned off the main route. "I like to go the back way. It's a pretty ride."

"Yes, it is. I remember. We used to take Julia to an orchard around here to pick apples, or peaches. Whatever fruit was in season. There were farm animals to pet, too. A gigantic black and white hog, I recall. And they sold treats in a big barn, fresh donuts and cider. Homemade ice cream. A lot of the flavors were made with the fresh fruit, like peach and strawberry . . ."

"Stop, you're making me hungry." Lucy's stomach growled. It was doing that a lot lately. She had an appetite for ten instead of one and a half.

"Sorry . . . Maybe you should have stayed home and had dinner at a decent hour, instead of this jaunt," Maggie murmured. "You don't want your blood sugar dipping down."

"I had a snack. I'm fine," Lucy insisted.

They drove past miles of open land, filled with marsh grass, golden in the low rays of the sun. A few houses could be seen along the road and in the distance. Lucy envied the view.

Signs announced the turnoff to Crane's Beach. Lucy thought it was the best beach around. To find a better one you'd need to drive hours, to Cape Cod. The beaches in Plum Harbor were pretty, but the shoreline was rocky and the waves not nearly as dramatic. The sand at Crane's was silky, and the shoreline stretched as far as you could see.

The parking lot was practically empty. She easily found a space near the bathhouse and food stall. As they got out the scent of grilled hot dogs was almost overpowering, but Lucy did her best to ignore it.

She hadn't bothered with a bathing suit. She knew she wasn't going to swim and just wore a sports bra with spandex shorts, covered by a huge orange maternity top that would have served as a mini dress in her younger days. Her hair was pulled back in a clip and she pulled a Red Sox cap over her head.

She'd brought a tote bag with a towel and a water bottle but hadn't bothered with a chair.

"Let's do it," Lucy summoned a gung-ho tone.

Maggie tugged at the straps of Lucy's tote. "You lead the way. I'll be the Sherpa."

"Don't be silly. It's practically empty."

"Good, that makes it easier for me." Maggie's stern expression slammed a lid on further argument, and Lucy handed over the bag.

"I'm not an invalid, I'm just pregnant," she muttered.

Maggie ignored her. She'd also brought a bag and one dangled from each arm as they started off on the boardwalk that led to wooden stairs and down to the sand.

"The class can't be hard to find," Maggie said. "It's a quarter to seven. I hope it doesn't last any more than an hour. Any idea what you're going to say to her?"

"Not exactly," Lucy admitted. "I'll just wing it, I guess."

Lucy had silently rehearsed a few scripts, but none felt quite right.

Maggie shook her head, marching after Lucy. There were more people on the beach than Lucy had expected, families and couples, young and old, savoring the last hour or two of a beautiful day. But no group who looked like a tai chi class.

Maggie stopped walking and dropped the bags. She whisked her brow with a shirt sleeve. "I don't see them, do you?"

Lucy shook her head and gazed around; one hand flat to shield the glaring sun that hovered just above the horizon.

"Wait—look." Maggie pointed. "Way up there, past the volleyball players."

Lucy gazed up the shoreline. In the far distance, she did see a group of people who all stood in the same pose, knees slightly bent, with one hand pointing forward and the other slowly sweeping back.

"Yes, that must be the class. They'll be breaking up soon," she said, glancing at her watch. "We'd better get over there."

Lucy set off at double time, pressing a hand to her bouncing belly. Maggie was right behind her, leaning forward as she trudged through the sand.

"Why do they meet all the way down here?" Lucy muttered, breathlessly.

"For privacy? Those poses look challenging . . . and awkward. I just saw one senior tip over," she noted with concern. "That silver-haired lady in the pink sweats?"

Lucy had noticed, too. "She's getting up. No harm done."

"Can you lose the flip-flops? They're spraying me with sand," Maggie admitted. "I'll dump our bags by those rocks to lighten my load. No one will bother them."

"Good idea." Lucy slipped off the rubber slides and left them by the tote bags. They headed down the beach again, moving faster.

They had to swing wide when they passed a beach volleyball game. The players were so intense they didn't seem to notice Lucy and Maggie walking by. Lucy hustled as the ball sailed her way. Just in time to escape being trampled. Wouldn't Matt love to hear how that happened?

The tai chi group was swooping into a new pose, with

arms slowly circling up and legs squatting, palms meeting in a prayerful, peaceful meditation.

"It's a little like Zen ballet, wouldn't you say?" Lucy had taken a few dance classes when she was a girl. The phase hadn't lasted long.

"Let's hope they hold a good thought for a few more minutes," Maggie huffed. "If we don't get there soon, our target might disappear up those stairs. I'm sorry, Lucy, but I'm not chasing her."

A wooden staircase had come into view. Lucy recalled an extra parking lot at the top and feared the same outcome, for all this bother.

"Understood. I'm not, either," Lucy agreed, mostly because she knew she couldn't race up the steps in her state. Even she would admit that would be a very risky and an extremely stupid thing to do.

She felt a sudden wave of remorse, thinking of how upset Matt would be if he knew what she was up to.

This was worse than a wild-goose chase. It was a wild . . . turkey chase or some bird with even less brains. Or rather, it would turn out to be if Kiera Nesbit left the beach before they could speak to her.

They were a few yards from the group when the class began to break up. The students relaxed from their final pose and stretched, then headed in all directions to retrieve their water containers and bags piled at the bottom of the wooden steps.

A few gathered around their teacher, and she answered their questions as she packed her supplies into a purple duffel bag.

Lucy glanced at Maggie. "It's now or never."

Without waiting for Maggie to answer, she walked straight toward Kiera.

The last student had left and Kiera stood alone. She stared at Lucy with a questioning expression.

She was even more attractive at close range than Lucy had noticed at the memorial. She had high cheekbones, large blue eyes, and a full, pouting mouth. Her shiny blond hair was gathered in a long braid that swung down to her back. Of course, she was very fit, in black spandex shorts and a fuchsia sports bra.

"Can I help you?" Her gaze took Lucy in from head to toe, lingering on her baby bump.

"I hope so . . ." Lucy was still winded. She forced a smile, trying to catch her breath. "You're Kiera Nesbit, right?"

"That's right . . . Are you interested in the class? I think you'll have to wait until your baby comes. Though tai chi is an excellent way to get back in shape, postpregnancy."

"It looks fun. But I'm not here about that," Lucy admitted, taking a few steps closer. "I saw you on Saturday, at the memorial for Colin Hurley."

Kiera's graceful, relaxed pose stiffened. She tugged the strap of her bag over her arm. "You're mistaking me for someone else. I have no idea who you're talking about."

"I know it was you. Hazel Huebner pointed you out."

Lucy's insistence was met by another puzzled stare. "I don't know anyone by that name, either. Sorry . . . I have to go now."

Kiera Nesbit—or whoever she was?—strode toward the stairs. Lucy trailed after her, wondering if she was mistaken.

She'd caught only a fleeting glimpse of the woman in black, across a crowded room. All she knew was that her first name was Kiera and she'd worked in the same office as Colin. Could her internet research have led her this far off track?

Wouldn't *that* be dumb and embarrassing?

"Wait . . . I'm sorry. Please, give me just a moment," Lucy stumbled along, trying to catch the tai chi teacher's glance.

If she could just look her in the eye, Lucy thought she could tell if the blonde was bluffing.

Her prey marched on, her gaze fixed straight ahead. Lucy quickened her pace and sensed Maggie trudging along, not far behind.

"Oh my gosh . . . Ow . . . ow . . . ow . . . Ouch!" Lucy felt a sharp edge jab in the sole of her foot, and her ankle twisted to one side with a burning pain.

She sat down abruptly on the sand. She tried to rub her ankle, but her belly was in the way. She gritted her teeth to keep from groaning and leaned back on her arms.

"Lucy . . . what happened?" Maggie was at her side instantly, her eyes wide with concern. "You're not going into labor . . . are you?"

"Not unless it starts in your ankle," she managed. "I stepped on something sharp and tripped."

She tried to straighten her foot, but the pain was too intense. Eyes squeezed shut, she gritted her teeth. When she opened them, Kiera Nesbit . . . or whoever she was . . . was crouched at her side along with Maggie.

"Can I help you? I know first aid."

Lucy nodded like a bobblehead doll. "Please."

The tai chi instructor gently massaged Lucy's ankle and calf. "Can you flex your foot?" Lucy tried and the joint seemed to work without much discomfort. "Good, it's probably just a sprain."

Lucy sighed. "I hope so."

"Don't move yet," her rescuer instructed. She reached into her purple bag and slipped a little blue pack from a box, then scrunched it in her hands as it made a crunching sound.

"Just an instant ice pack. It should help in a minute or two." She gently laid the packet on Lucy's ankle. "I think I have a compression wrap in here if you want me to put it on?"

"Would you?" Lucy felt very foolish and embarrassed.

"You've been very kind," Maggie said. "Somehow, she forgets she's pregnant and overdoes it."

"I'm sorry I bothered you. It's just that the husband of a very close friend died recently and—it sounds crazy, I know," Lucy explained between sips of a water bottle Maggie had handed her, "but the police think my friend did it. They're not even looking at other possibilities. I know she's totally innocent. It's so frustrating," Lucy rambled on, trying to explain the mixup. "I did some research online and confused you with a woman the guy used to work with, someone who might know who really killed him. Or at least, why he was killed."

The tai chi instructor stood up and tossed her braid over one shoulder. She took a breath, shoulders back, reminding Lucy of the groups' final, calming pose.

"You didn't make a mistake. I knew Colin Hurley. As much as anyone did," she qualified. "I am Kiera Nesbit."

Chapter 20

Lucy was struck dumb by the admission. Fortunately, Maggie was not. "Would you mind if we asked you a few questions? We won't take much more of your time."

Kiera crossed her arms over her chest. "What do you want to know?"

"Was Colin involved in any shady business? Any relationships or deals he needed to keep secret?" Lucy stared up at her, suddenly unaware of any discomfort. "He told his coworkers he'd inherited money, and he told his wife that a book he'd been writing was optioned for a movie."

"Neither story seems to be true," Maggie added.

Kiera tilted her head to the side. "I'm not surprised. That was Colin, though you'd never suspect it. Not at first. He was sort of a math nerd. A cute, geeky type, I guess you'd say. Hardly the type you'd think would lie so much." She sighed. "I knew his cover story about an inheritance was baloney. But he never told me where the money came from. Our relationship was unraveling by then."

"What sort of relationship was it? Were you having an affair?" Lucy had to summon up her inner-Suzanne to be so blunt, but also knew there was no time to be more diplomatic.

Kiera seemed surprised but nodded. "We were. For a brief time."

"Why did it unravel?" Maggie asked. "If you don't mind telling us."

"Everyone in the department was under tremendous stress. We were all working very long hours. There were a lot of big projects going on—road work, bridge repairs, the wind farm on the bay. Problems seemed to be cropping up every day. It was like playing Whac-A-Mole. On top of that, a few months earlier, an overpass on Route 1 collapsed. A car dropped into the Essex River and we were still dealing with the blowback from that tragedy."

Lucy recalled that event all over the local news at the time, but not the details. "So that's when you two broke up?"

"Yes, right around that time. The event had been investigated by a team of engineers and there was going to be a hearing at the state capitol to present the findings," Kiera recalled. "That's when I left my job at the department. I could see I wasn't getting anywhere. Our boss, George Wexler, favored the men and gave them all the best assignments. He had very old fashioned ideas about women in the workplace."

"That sounds frustrating," Maggie said.

"Frustrating is one word for it," Kiera's tone was bitter.

"It sounds as if you didn't like your boss much," Lucy said.

"Worse than that, I didn't respect him. It's hard to work for a person that you don't respect. I tried my best, but I was never one of his insiders, not like Colin."

"Did the office politics affect your relationship?"

"It didn't help. Colin was very involved in the report about the bridge collapse. He was in charge of the group that did the investigation and in charge of writing up their findings, which was a huge responsibility. But it wasn't just that. His feelings had cooled and I got the message.

The truth was, I already had second thoughts about him," she confessed. "Colin was easy to be with at first. He could be charming in his way, and flattered me to no end. But there was another side to his personality. He grew moody and distant, and always avoided talking about the future. I want marriage and a family someday, and finally realized I'd never have that with Colin, no matter what he said about leaving his wife."

"Colin did plan to divorce his wife right before he died. But he was also about to leave the country, and very abruptly," Lucy told her. "It looked like he was running away from something. Or someone?"

"I don't know anything about that. We weren't in touch after I quit that job. I wanted to move past that entire episode of my life and wasn't in touch with anyone in the department after I left," she stated flatly. "But I felt bad when I heard that Colin died. Maybe I had no right, but I wanted to pay my last respects."

Lucy wasn't sure if she believed all of Kiera's story but didn't want to badger her. Not any more than she had already.

"I don't know what else I can tell you. Colin wasn't the nicest person, but I cared for him. I don't think he ever really cared for me. He was very much in his own head, in his own world. He liked the idea of being with someone attractive. He wanted other men to feel envious. Not that I'm some airhead," she insisted. "I was also a senior engineer. But I knew that was the way he thought of our relationship."

She didn't seem like an airhead. Anything but, Lucy thought. And she had a kind heart.

"Can you make it back to your car?" Kiera asked.

"I was just about to ask her the same question," Maggie said. "I think our best bet is for me to bring the car around to the lot at the top of that staircase. And you can wiggle up, one step at a time, Lucy." She paused. "On your bottom."

The idea of wiggling up the long flight of steps on derriere was daunting but Lucy didn't complain. "I can do that. Good plan," Lucy squeaked.

She could tell that Maggie was peeved and she didn't dare argue.

With Kiera and Maggie's help, Lucy came to her feet. Maggie's concerned look made Lucy feel foolish for persuading her to come along. For thinking of this scheme at all.

With support on each side she made it to the steps and sat down with a long sigh.

"I'll go get the car," Maggie said. "I'll get you out of here somehow. Maybe a helicopter airlift."

"It won't come to that, don't worry." Lucy was determined to make it up the steps and to the car. If her ankle hurt, she'd wince and bear it. Good practice for labor pains, she decided.

Lucy somehow made it to the car, then handed Maggie the keys without comment. Seated on the passenger's side, she reapplied the ice pack, which still had some chill left.

"How does your ankle feel now?"

"Not as bad as my bottom," she reported.

"You did give me a scare. Thank goodness you didn't have an awkward fall," Maggie said as she steered the Jeep out of the parking lot. "I love you to pieces, but sorry to say, I'm not going anywhere with you until that baby comes."

Lucy could tell she meant it this time, too. "I understand. I won't even ask."

"If I was Matt, I'd take away your car keys . . . and your computer and cell phone. Especially after what just happened out there. You could have delivered your baby in a sand dune, with a volleyball team coaching you to push.

That would have made a humorous anecdote for a baby book."

Lucy wanted to laugh but knew Maggie was serious. "It would have. But I'll just have the usual boring story."

"I sincerely hope so." Maggie decided not to go the scenic way and turned on to the road that led to Route 1A. The sun had not quite set but the light was fading. Lucy felt sticky and sandy and very tired and hungry.

"I'm sorry I put you to all this trouble. You could have had a nice, relaxing evening home with Charles. I'm not sure we even learned anything."

Maggie ignored her apology. Lucy could tell she was still upset. "You need a bath and a big glass of milk tonight. Dairy relaxes your muscles."

"How about ice cream?"

"That works, too. Though I don't think you deserve any treats, miss. I know it's not entirely your fault, but I feel we narrowly escaped disaster. I know you're worried about Rebecca, but you've done all you can to help. You need to think about yourself and your baby."

"I know I do," Lucy agreed contritely. "From now until game day, I'll be totally focused on myself and the baby."

Maggie glanced at her and sighed again. She didn't seem to be buying it. "I know we get frustrated with the police. Believe me. But they always get it right in the end."

"With a little help from their friends," Lucy reminded her.

"Tell Rebecca whatever you've discovered and let her take it from there. She'll bring the information to her attorney and that's that. I don't think we can do anything more. We certainly can't drive around the countryside, cornering everyone who was close to Colin."

"There's no one else to corner. He was a real loner." Colin's retired supervisor, George Wexler, came to mind, but Hazel had mentioned he'd moved to Mexico. Of course, people in foreign countries still had email and phones.

Maggie had turned on to the main road. There was little traffic and they made good time returning to Plum Harbor. They were heading down Main Street so Maggie could pick up her car at the shop when a text message buzzed on Lucy's phone.

"Oh drat . . . Matt's home early. I bet he's wondering where I am." Lucy felt a new ache, in her stomach this time. Just nerves, she knew.

"You're a sight. I think you have seaweed in your hair," Maggie fretted. Lucy thought she was exaggerating, then recalled laying prone on the sand to stretch out her aching leg. Seaweed was definitely a possibility.

"What will you tell him?" Maggie asked.

She smoothed her hand over her ponytail. "You held a knitting class on the beach?"

Maggie closed her eyes and shook her head. Then whizzed past the shop and her Subaru. "If that's the best you can do, I'd better come in for backup."

Lucy was relieved and grateful. She reached across the seat and squeezed Maggie's hand. "You're a real pal, Mag. I'd name the baby after you, but everyone else will get jealous," she added in a whisper.

"Don't try to butter me up. The damage is done." Maggie tried to sound annoyed while holding back a laugh. "Margaret would be an odd name if it's a boy. Though . . . maybe not these days."

The dogs bounded to the door to greet them when Lucy led Maggie into the living room. "Hi, honey, I'm home," Lucy called out.

"Back here," Matt called from the kitchen.

The table was set for two and they found him at the stove, heating the chicken and white bean chili Lucy had made that afternoon and left in the fridge.

"What's up, you guys? Were you at the beach?"

"It was such a beautiful night, Maggie held a knitting class out there. It was great."

Matt looked confused. "Nobody minded getting sand in their yarn?"

"Maybe a little." Maggie shrugged. "Just an idea I wanted to try. It's so hard to keep customers knitting in the warm weather."

Matt couldn't argue with that. "Would you like to stay for dinner, Mag? There's plenty."

"Thanks, but I need to get home. I just wanted to say hello. Your garden looks great. Lucy said you've been working hard this year."

"I'm gardening for two these days," Matt said, his attention shifting from Maggie to his wife. "Lucy, what's wrong with your foot? Why are you limping?"

Lucy was headed for the bathroom. Her ankle still ached, and it was hard to put weight on it. She tried to hide her limp, but there was no sneaking past her husband.

"Oh, it's nothing. I stepped on something sharp at the beach, a broken shell probably, and I twisted my ankle a little. It'll be fine by tomorrow."

"Sit down, let me see, please."

Lucy sighed but did as she was told. Matt was in full doctor mode, even if his patients usually had four legs and a tail.

"She just twisted it a bit. She didn't fall," Maggie assured him. "We put an ice pack on at the beach. She could probably use more of that."

"Good idea, there's one in the freezer," Lucy said. Maggie walked to the fridge to fetch it while Matt washed his hands.

He returned to Lucy, lifted her foot and looked it over. "There's a cut on the sole of your foot, too. I'll get the first aid kit upstairs."

Lucy didn't answer. She didn't like the way he was staring at her. When he put his hands on his hips, she braced herself.

"I don't like this, Lucy," he said in a low tone. "Why do you take chances like this and make me worry?"

"It's partly my fault," Maggie piped up loyally. "I shouldn't have let her come."

"It's not Maggie's fault. I insisted." Lucy glanced at Maggie, silently thanking her. She was such a stalwart friend to take the blame. "I'm so sorry, Matt. I know it was very stupid and irresponsible. I don't know what I was thinking."

Maggie's scolding was one thing, but Matt's displeasure and worry hit harder. She had taken a foolish chance tonight, and he didn't even know the half of it.

Matt shook his head. "I'd never blame you, Maggie. I know how hardheaded she is, believe me."

"I am," Lucy agreed, the tears that had been brewing suddenly gushed out in a big, ugly cry. "I'm such a bad mom already . . . and I haven't even gotten started . . . I don't deserve to have a baby . . ."

Matt and Maggie exchanged glances. "Now, now. Don't say that. No harm done. You just sprained your ankle a bit," Maggie said as Matt rushed forward to comfort her.

"I didn't mean to make you cry, honey. You're going to be a great mom. Honestly."

Lucy sniffed and wiped her eyes with her orange smock top. Tink came over and licked her bare leg, which no doubt tasted salty from the beach.

"I'm a complete idiot. I don't know how you put up with me. I'll do better from now on, I promise."

Maggie had found the ice pack and pressed it to Lucy's ankle. "Maybe this little injury is just your guardian angel's way of slowing you down. Since you wouldn't stay put on your own."

Matt crossed his arms over his chest. "That's one way to look at it. You are grounded again, you know, for the duration."

Lucy nodded contritely and sniffed. "That goes without saying. I totally get it this time. Honest."

Lucy's gaze shifted from Matt to Maggie, who also stood with her arms crossed over her chest. Neither of them replied, which made her feel even worse.

Tink nuzzled her head in Lucy's lap and sighed in sympathy. At least somebody wasn't mad at her.

Chapter 21

Matt didn't talk much during dinner. She knew he had a perfect right to his reticence, so she didn't make a fuss, or object to the TV tuned to the Red Sox game. The murmuring commentary of the announcers offset his silent treatment.

She felt exhausted and went upstairs right after they ate, then took a bath and climbed into bed early.

With her sore ankle propped on a pillow and covered by a fresh ice pack, she tried to read more of Colin's manuscript, but her eyes drifted closed after a few pages. She was beat from her misadventure, and the gnarly narrative didn't help, either.

Lucy woke the next morning to find Tink staring at her. They were practically nose to nose, the dog's big golden head resting on the edge of the mattress.

Once Tink saw that Lucy was awake, she licked her face, then sat back in her "I am such a good dog" pose, which she usually reserved to beg for treats. Bright sunlight slipped through the crack between the curtain and the windowsill and Lucy knew she'd seriously overslept.

"Hi, sweetie," Lucy greeted her. "You let me sleep so late. Matt let you out, right?"

Tink wagged her tail and watched her mistress trudge to the bathroom, and Lucy had her answer. If the dog had any urgent needs she would have been dancing a jig by now.

Lucy splashed her face and combed her hair, then headed downstairs. Her ankle still ached and she was careful not to put much weight on it. She felt so dumb for bringing such a silly injury on herself and at this crucial time.

Maybe Maggie was right. Maybe it had been her guardian angel or some invisible protector of moms-to-be who decided to give her a major "time out." It helped to think of it that way.

She found a sweet note from Matt on the kitchen table and a smoothie for her breakfast, already blended, in the refrigerator.

She carried the glass to the umbrella table in the backyard, the dogs trailing behind her. Pale-pink roses and a bank of Russian sage had begun to bloom. Lucy thought she'd cut some flowers for the house later but couldn't think of anything to do after that. She didn't even have any projects left in her office, with everything on hold now until the baby arrived.

There was probably some new baby gadget left to assemble. Matt had done the furniture and bookcase. But Lucy took on smaller projects, like lamps and room décor.

She usually had to take the entire thing apart midway through because she had reversed, or completely forgotten, some essential part.

There was knitting, of course, but the baby argyle was turning out to be a small but complicated mess and not at all relaxing to work on. And there was always Colin's manuscript to wade through. She hadn't even finished chapter one but was already doubting her pregnant-lady intuition that the answers to her questions were tucked between the pages.

The phone rang and she found Maggie's name on the screen.

"Just checking in," Maggie greeted her. "How's your ankle?"

"Still hurts a bit, but I'll survive."

"Keep applying ice and stay off of it as much as you can."

"I can't get very far in a prison cell." Lucy couldn't hide her glum tone.

"Oh my . . . Save the drama for the grand finale, Lucy. We're not there yet," Maggie advised. "You sound a bit cranky."

"I am, a little," she admitted. "Maybe just foggy-headed from sleeping so much." It was already past eleven. Lucy could hardly believe she'd slept so late.

"Dana and Suzanne were here this morning. I gave them a condensed version of last's night fiasco. They agree you need to nest and rest."

"So, you were all talking about me this morning?"

"We were," Maggie admitted. "But with love and concern, so it wasn't actually gossip."

Lucy accepted that reasoning, though they'd doubtless gotten a good laugh out of the story. She was sorry she missed the morning chat and wasn't there to defend herself.

"Did Dana hear anything from Jack about the break-in at Rebecca's house?" she asked.

"Not much. None of the neighbors spotted anyone suspicious. The police are checking home security video on the street. But no strange cars or questionable strangers have been spotted yet." Maggie paused, then said, "You're not going to like this. Detective Reyes hasn't given up the theory that Rebecca possibly staged it to deflect the investigation. And arranged the motorcycle incident right before the memorial, too."

"—And arranged for her father, who has a critically weak heart, to be taken by surprise and struck on the head? You're right, I don't like hearing that." Lucy felt angry and frustrated. "It's utterly absurd. It's so clear that Rebecca is blameless. Why can't the police eliminate her and move on?"

"I don't understand why, either. Are you going to tell Rebecca that we spoke to Kiera Nesbit?"

Lucy had been mulling that question over. "I don't think so. Rebecca said she suspected that Colin got involved with other women, but it would be painful to learn that for certain. Maybe even more so now that he's gone."

"I agree; there isn't any reason to tell her that I can see. Kiera didn't disclose any information that can put the police on a new trail."

"Unfortunately not. I might try to find an email address for Colin's former boss, George Wexler, but I doubt he'll give up any good info about Colin, either. He'll probably respond with a short and polite message and claim he has no idea what I'm talking about, even if he knows something. It will be easy to brush me off at such a great distance."

"Kiera nearly got away with that ploy, even face to face. Except for your tumble. It served some purpose, I guess. Oh, hold on . . ."

Lucy heard Maggie speaking to a customer. "Yes, all the yarn in that bin is thirty percent off. There are more sale items in the back, too. Clearance specials."

"I have to go," she said, coming back on the line. "Even selling from the bargain bin helps."

Lucy doubted the shop's accounts were in such dire straits. Maggie said the same thing every summer and tended to exaggerate.

"Maybe 'Black Sheep on the Beach' *would* be a good promotion," Lucy replied.

"I had the same crazy thought this morning. But don't mention it to Phoebe. She'll drag me out there in my bathing suit tomorrow." Maggie said goodbye and hung up.

Lucy decided to head inside to the air-conditioning and called the dogs. Walley had been resting in the shade under the table. He was eager to go back into the air conditioning.

As usual, Tink was harder to find. Lucy finally spotted her tucked into a shady patch of dirt under a hydrangea bush. It was hard to believe the big dog could compact herself into the small space, but she looked very cool and comfortable—and dirty—when Lucy discovered her.

"Tink!? What are you doing under there? Come on out, you silly girl." Lucy gave her a firm look and Tink finally trotted to the patio. She waited until she was right next to Lucy to shake off the mud and leaves and probably a few bugs that had stuck to her thick fur.

"Ugh . . . you're all dirty now, too." Lucy brushed the dog's fur with her hand. "You can't pull these silly stunts once the baby comes. You know that, don't you?"

Tink answered with an adoring stare, enjoying the rubdown and attention. She panted with a doggy smile and licked Lucy's hand.

Lucy's mother had been concerned about how Tink and Walley would react to a baby. The dogs were so attached to Lucy and Matt, Isabel was afraid they might feel displaced and jealous. But Lucy had no doubt they would both be gentle guardians of a tiny new human. The dogs had often been around children, even very little ones, and had shown only calm, positive interest.

With his knowledge of animal behavior, Matt knew how to properly introduce the dogs to the new family member and felt sure they would easily blend into one big, happy pack.

Tink nudged Lucy's leg with her big head and Lucy grinned. "Right, time for a biscuit break. I didn't realize it was so late."

She led Tink and Walley inside with her stilted gait, glad for their company.

Lucy was well accustomed to being alone all day. She worked at home and had been single a while after her divorce before she found Matt.

But for some reason, being forced to stay in the house made her restless. Or maybe it was the anticipation of the baby coming. She was so well prepared, there were not many feathering the nest tasks left to distract her.

She decided to rearrange the piles of tiny clothing in the drawers of the new baby chest, switching the onesies, undershirts and pajamas to the top drawer, and crib sheets, mattress covers, and blankets to the bottom. Since they didn't know the baby's sex all the infant wear was in neutral colors, like yellow, white, and oatmeal. Lucy had been given a lot of gift certificates to buy the rest, when the time came.

The room still had a big blank spot saved for the crib. They'd ordered the piece in plenty of time, but the wrong model arrived. They'd promptly returned it and now waited anxiously, assured by tracking emails almost every day that their baby's crib was on the way.

"Don't worry, sweetheart. If the crib isn't there by the time you bring the baby home, the little one can sleep in a dresser drawer," her mother advised. "That's what folks did in the old days."

Lucy didn't feel comfortable with that idea, though the image was quaint and cozy, and reminded her of *The Little House On the Prairie* books she'd read as a girl. But she didn't live out on the prairie and hoped the right crib would soon appear.

After lunch, Lucy called Maggie, hoping to catch up on any news she had missed at the shop. But Maggie was about to start a class and couldn't talk for long.

"That's okay, I'll let you get back to work. It's just that I'm so bored I want to cry," Lucy confessed.

Maggie laughed. "Cry if you want to. It won't change a thing. I think you made this bed for yourself, Lucy. Why don't you just give up and take a nap in it?"

Lucy felt too sulky to laugh at Maggie's tart reply but finally, couldn't help it.

Rebecca had happily agreed to bring Dara home from school, but at half past two, Lucy saw Leo's old green van pull up. Dara and Sophie raced to the house, while Leo followed at a far slower pace.

Dara greeted Lucy with a hug and stared up. "Can Sophie have a snack here?"

"If her grandpa says it's okay." Lucy glanced at Leo.

"Fine with me if you make it quick. I have to get you over to get to dance class in a little while."

The two girls ran inside, the dogs chasing after them. Leo shook his head and smiled. "If anybody could bottle their energy, I'd pay a fortune for it."

"Me too," Lucy agreed, though she knew he was referring to the illness that sucked his vitality and strength. "Thanks for picking Dara up."

"No problem. Rebecca would have come, but the police released the café as a crime scene and she had to sign some papers at the station. A cleaning crew was on the way, too. I told her I'd deal with that, but she wanted to do it herself." He sighed heavily. "She's bound to get upset going back in there, poor girl."

Leo seemed upset relating the situation.

"Rebecca thought she might not reopen the café," Lucy replied. "How does she feel about it now?"

Leo shrugged his thin shoulders. "Everything's up in the air until the police find out who killed Colin. It sure wasn't my daughter. I'd stake my life on it," he insisted. His watery blue gaze met Lucy's. "I worry about her," he said quietly.

Lucy did, too, but she didn't think echoing his concern would help.

"The police have no solid evidence to hold against her. Only the video of her car at the café that night. It's not enough to charge someone with murder," Lucy assured him, though she wasn't entirely sure of that.

"I keep telling myself that, but they don't give up. And they're not looking any farther than their noses. She's run off the road and the house gets ransacked. What do the police do? Nothing, as far as I can see. I've been sleeping on the couch like a guard dog. More like an old, toothless hound who wouldn't scare a fly."

He laughed at his own joke but seemed short of breath, gasping on his words. Lucy wasn't sure what to say to calm him.

"The detectives play their cards close. We wouldn't necessarily know if they were looking into other leads, Leo. After the break-in, they must be."

Leo nodded but didn't answer, his gaze downcast, his beard brushing his chest.

Lucy didn't want to raise false hopes, but her heart ached to see him so disheartened. "My friends and I are trying to figure out who killed Colin, too. We'll give any information we dig up to Helen Forbes and to the police."

Leo looked up, clearly encouraged. "Rebecca didn't mention that. Have you found out anything yet?"

"Nothing substantial, but we've talked to a few people Colin knew and have some ideas."

Leo's expression brightened. "I'll hold a good thought. You're a true friend, Lucy. And with all you've got on your plate right now besides."

"Oh, I'm not very busy. It's just a lot of waiting now."

"It's worth the wait. Believe me." Leo met her gaze, his expression pensive. "I haven't always been a good father to Rebecca. You probably know that," he said quietly. "But she's always been the queen of my heart. Near or far. She and Sophie are everything to me."

Before Lucy could reply, he'd glanced at his watch and seemed alarmed. "I've got to get Sophie to ballet or I'll be in trouble with her teacher."

"Sure," Lucy said. She stepped inside and called the girls. They came to the door and hugged goodbye. Leo took Sophie's hand as they walked to the van.

When Lucy suggested that Dara start her homework, she made a face. "Want to help me in the baby's room?" Lucy suggested. "I have to put the mobile together and it has a hundred parts."

Dara liked that idea much better and they went upstairs together. Dara had Matt's patience for reading directions and his logical, right brain approach to such tasks. Lucy let her lead the process and did whatever she said.

The mobile's center looked like an old-fashioned carousel. Zoo animals hung from the strings around the rim. A tiny music box in the middle played "Rock-a-Bye Baby."

"What do you think?" It was only half-assembled, but Lucy picked it up so they could appreciate their handi-work. Lucy admired the plush zebra, giraffe, elephant, lion, and sloth as they dangled.

"It's cute. But why are the animals white and black?"

"The baby can't see colors right away, only white, black, and red. They can't see that well at all for a while. They recognize people by their smells."

"Like dogs?"

"Yes, I guess so." Lucy hadn't thought of babies that way, but it was true.

"Do you think the dogs are going to feel bad when the baby comes? They might feel like no one is paying attention to them anymore."

Lucy got the strong sense that Dara was thinking about herself, though she probably didn't realize it.

"You and Dad had Walley before Tink came along. Do you love Tink more? Is she your favorite now?"

Dara looked appalled by the question. "Of course not. I love them both a lot."

"I know. Because love is limitless. You can't run out of love, the more you give, the more you have. Dad and I will always 'love you to the moon and back.' And so will your mom and Tom," she added, mentioning Dara's mother and stepfather. "You're going to be a great big sister. I know that already. For one thing, I couldn't have put this thing together without you."

"Sure you could have. But it probably would have turned out a little lopsided," Dara teased her. "It's really cute. I can't wait to watch the baby try to grab it."

"Now that you mention it, I can't, either." Lucy smoothed Dara's hair with her hand and kissed her cheek.

Chapter 22

By Wednesday afternoon there was nothing left for Lucy to do but lay on the couch and read Colin's novel.

Colin had taken the prevailing advice to "write what you know" to heart. His protagonist was a civil engineer working for a small, fictional city in New England. He was far more intelligent than his peers, but a humble man whose talent and intellect went unnoticed. Basically, a nerd like Colin had been in real life.

Like many newbie novelists, Colin spent a long time describing the main character's early life before anything much happened. Lucy did her best to plow through. The writing made her eyes cross, rife with adjectives, melodrama, and stilted dialogue. It was so poorly written it was like reading a parody of an action thriller. Before she'd gotten too far into it, she fell asleep.

The next thing she knew, Matt was home with takeout.

By Thursday, Lucy was feeling bored and blue, but so was her ankle—blue, purple, and an icky shade of greenish yellow. She insisted the rainbow meant it was healing and she was ready to leave the house, but Matt remained unconvinced. Even if she took only a short drive to Maggie's shop.

"I won't stay long! I won't even take the dogs," she promised.

The last few days, she had been concerned that the dogs might make her twist her ankle again, or even pull her down, because she was so off-balance.

Matt walked them when he could, and Lucy gave them breaks during the day in a fenced space of the yard. It wasn't ideal, but they needed to get used to a new routine when the baby came. At least for a little while.

Lucy could easily see herself pushing a stroller with a dog leashed to each side, but it might take time to master that setup.

"Do you really have to go out, honey?" Matt said. "It's your right ankle. You shouldn't drive. I'll be at the office late on Thursday so I won't be around to take you."

"Suzanne will pick me up and drive me home. She won't mind at all."

"Will she carry you up the stairs to the porch?"

She hadn't thought about the stairs. She'd have to go up on her bottom, the way she did the stairway in the house to get to her bedroom, which was carpeted. There was a side door to the shop, she recalled, but before she could point that out, Matt continued.

"You're sound asleep on the couch by eight. I bet your gang is just warming up by then. All that snoring will distract them from their knitting."

"I don't snore, it's allergies. I can't take medication right now."

"Whatever it is, I think it's adorable." Matt raised his hands in a gesture of surrender. "I'm just saying, why go out at all? You're barely able to get around the house without tipping over. You promised the other night you wouldn't get overtired and take chances with our baby."

Lucy had made that promise and had meant it. Still, she

couldn't help answering him. "I don't see how knitting possibly falls into the category of reckless behavior."

"It wouldn't, under the usual circumstances. But your friends are an unusual group of women."

He left it at that. Lucy heaved a sigh but didn't reply.

"Why don't you use that meeting app on your computer? It works fine with clients," Matt suggested.

"That's not a bad idea." Lucy wondered why she hadn't thought of it herself. "Maggie is so hopeless with computers, she might not be able to get it running."

"Phoebe will help her. She'll know what to do." Matt smiled and kissed her forehead.

Lucy knew that tuning in on her computer wouldn't be as much fun as being there, but she also knew when she was beat.

A short time later, with Lucy on the phone, Phoebe talked Maggie through the steps of connecting her laptop to Lucy's.

Phoebe and Maggie suddenly filled Lucy's computer screen, waving at her from the worktable. Lucy waved back, her spirits lifting. It had been only a few days, but she really missed her pals.

She was alone in the house. Matt was working and Dara was with her mother and stepfather. There wasn't much to eat in the fridge. Lucy found some semi-acceptable lettuce in the spinner and tossed a salad together, throwing in a hard-boiled egg and half an avocado for protein. It wasn't very appetizing and easy to resist as she waited to eat with her friends. She had no doubt that their dinner would probably make her weep with envy. It was Suzanne's night to bring the entree and she was a fabulous cook.

She set her laptop on the kitchen table with her knitting tote nearby, then clicked on the meeting app at six thirty, as they'd planned. The screen remained blank. Maggie and company were late. She called Maggie's cell phone and was connected to voice mail.

"Hey, I'm at our virtual knitting meeting, but nobody else came. Did you forget to turn on your computer?" She paused, hoping Maggie would pick up. "Call me, okay?"

She put her phone down and stared at her static computer again. She felt like she'd been stood up for a date. Was she going to sit here all night, eating a wilted salad and knitting on her own? It was starting to look like it.

The doorbell rang, setting off the dogs. They stampeded into the living room, barking. Lucy shushed them as she hobbled to the foyer. At this time of the day, she expected a neighbor asking to borrow a lawn tool or returning one.

She pulled the door open and stood back in shock. "Surprise!" Her friends called out in a loud chorus.

"Matt told us you were still on house arrest and asked if we could bring the party here," Dana said.

"So, we did." Suzanne sailed in with her big red Dutch oven. That was always a good sign.

"He should have warned me . . . I would have picked up a little."

"That's why we surprised you. We didn't want you to go to any trouble," Maggie said as she walked past. "You need to get used to things being a little messy, Lucy—"

"When the baby comes?" Lucy finished for her.

Maggie laughed. "Only for about eighteen years."

She knew her friends were not the Martha Stewart police, but she still felt embarrassed by the piles of newspapers and magazines, random shoes, dog toys, and baskets of laundry waiting to be folded that littered the rooms.

The parade ended in the kitchen. Suzanne whisked an apron out of her tote and settled her pot on Lucy's stove.

Lucy longed to see what was inside. Before she could

peek under the lid, Suzanne gently slapped her hand. "Not yet. It's a surprise and it needs to warm up awhile. Why don't you give us the grand tour of the baby's room?"

The suggestion was unanimously passed. "Can we see it, Lucy, please?" Phoebe begged.

"Of course. I'm just warning you, the crib didn't come yet, so there's a big blank spot. But the rest is very much in order," she noted, leading the way upstairs.

"Not so fast. The experienced mothers in this group will let you know how organized you are," Suzanne corrected her. Lucy knew she was only teasing.

The room was a good size for a baby, but Lucy decided to stay in the hallway as her friends slowly walked in and gazed around. There was a chorus of oohs and aahs as they admired the pale-yellow walls and a cream-colored area rug covered with colorful flowers.

Then they noticed the wallpaper border Lucy had chosen that circled the room, just above white wainscotting.

"Where did you find this amazing wallpaper?" Dana asked with delight. "It looks like an illustration from a book by Beatrix Potter."

"A bunny family on a picnic? That's totally adorable," Maggie said, after she'd slipped on reading glasses to check the print closer.

"It's so sweet, I could cry." Phoebe stared around as if in a spell. "I love the mobile and the little books," she added, crouching down to check the titles on the rows of boards with books Lucy had already set up for the baby. "*Goodnight Moon*! My favorite." She held up the classic bedtime story by Margaret Wise Brown. "I'm going to put a copy on my nightstand. It will help me fall asleep."

"And have sweet dreams," Dana predicted. She picked up a giant stuffed bear Lucy had positioned on a rocking chair. "The baby will love this. It's so huge and huggable."

"My dad sent that one. I thought you'd all guess."

Lucy's father was a retired attorney who lived with Lucy's stepmother in Arizona, where they enjoyed playing golf together almost every day and sipping dry martinis as they watched the evening news. She loved her father, but he and her mother were so completely different from each other, she often wondered why they'd ever married.

Suzanne stood by the baby chest that doubled as a changing station. "Nice arrangement of the diapers, wipes, and butt cream," she said in an approving tone as she surveyed the nearby shelves. "Can we see the tiny clothes? It's always a highlight."

"My pleasure." Lucy walked up to the chest and opened the drawers. Then absorbed another wave of oohs and aahs as she lifted the onesies, pajamas, hats and socks. "I had the blankets and crib sheets in the top drawer for a while, but I decided that was dumb and rearranged the whole chest the other day."

"You'll do that a few more times in the next . . . How much time is left, two weeks?" Dana asked.

Lucy nodded solemnly and before anyone could comment, she changed the conversation. "We already have a nice rubber duck collection," she noted, pointing out the ducks lined on a shelf above the chest.

"You can never have too many of those," Phoebe agreed.

"Well, what do you think, ladies? Does this baby room pass inspection?" Maggie asked.

"With flying colors." Dana cast Lucy a wide smile. "I give it high marks for the bunny picnic alone."

"It's well equipped, neatly organized, and so cute you could die. So yes, I give it my highest rating," Suzanne agreed,

"I'm not an experienced mom," Phoebe began, "but I can't see how it could be any sweeter. The baby is going to be so cozy and happy here."

Lucy hoped so, and it felt good to hear that her friends thought so, too.

Suzanne sniffed the air like a hound dog. "I think dinner is ready. Let's go down and eat."

Back in the kitchen, Lucy headed for the dish cupboard. "Let me get some plates out and we can set the table."

"No need." Phoebe dug into a shopping bag. "We brought everything."

"It can all be recycled for a guilt-free cleanup." Maggie spread out paper plates, cups, and utensils, while Phoebe opened a bottle of wine and one of sparkling water.

"How long have you had this planned?" Lucy stood by the counter, marveling as the pop-up dinner party bloomed around her.

"Since Tuesday, when you called and told Maggie you were so bored you wanted to cry." Dana uncovered a platter of exotic-looking cheese, olives, and interesting crackers. "We knew Matt was going to keep you on lockdown all week and decided that a surprise would lift your spirits."

The sneak attack had definitely brightened her mood, but she still had questions. "So my sweet but sneaky husband was in on this, too?"

Maggie nodded. "He loved the idea. And he cooked up that computer meeting to placate you."

"I fell for that pretty easily," she admitted. "So all that computer stuff today was an act? You knew we weren't going to have a virtual knitting night?"

"Sort of," Phoebe admitted. But now Maggie knows how to get the meeting application going."

"With some help," Maggie qualified. "There will be plenty of cold, dark Thursday nights this winter when you won't want to leave the baby, even to be with us," Maggie predicted. "You'll be happy to tune in to the shop from home."

Lucy knew that was true. She felt fortunate to have the whole summer with the baby before the cold forced them to hibernate.

"You tricked me, but with good intention," she concluded.

"With the best intentions," Dana assured her.

Lucy had drifted to the stove, drawn by the savory aroma of Suzanne's dinner warming in the oven. "What did you make, Suzanne?"

"What's your favorite recipe of mine? Besides my chocolate cake."

Lucy thought for a moment. She didn't dare to hope. "Your mac and cheese?"

Suzanne nodded with a satisfied grin. "You guessed it."

"Did you really? I've been craving that for months."

"You did mention it once or twice." Suzanne gave her a look. Lucy knew she'd hinted about her pregnancy craving many more times than that.

Lucy hugged her, then turned to face the rest of her friends. "You guys are the best. Five minutes ago, I was staring at a wilted salad and a blank computer screen, feeling very sorry for myself."

Suzanne crinkled her nose. "You weren't really going to eat that, were you?"

Lucy ignored her. "The point is, I'm so lucky to have all of you in my life. Especially right now. Promise me nothing will change that?"

"*When the baby comes*, you mean?" Maggie finished for her.

Everyone laughed, especially Lucy, though she started to feel a bit weepy, as well. "Go ahead, tease me. I really mean it."

Dana handed Lucy a tissue and slipped her arm around

Lucy's shoulder. "Your whole life will change. But that's okay. We'll still love you and be here for you. And for your little one, too."

"And for each other," Maggie added.

Suzanne lifted her wineglass. "Well said. I'll drink to that."

"To Lucy and Baby Binger-MacDougal," Phoebe added. "Health and happiness always. We can't wait for the big day."

They brought their glasses together and beamed at her. Lucy replied with a shaky grin, not knowing whether to laugh or cry. She did know she'd rarely felt more grateful.

After enjoying their delicious dinner and also taking pleasure in tossing all the dishes in the trash, everyone pulled out their knitting. Dana made tea and coffee, and Maggie passed around a container of chocolate chip cookies that Lucy thought were just right. Crisp on the edges and gooey in the middle.

"It's official. I'm giving up on my argyle project," Suzanne announced between bites of a cookie. She waved her frazzled project like a flag of surrender.

Maggie held out her hand. "Give it here. I can fix it."

"Thanks, Mag, but no point in prolonging the agony. Consider this a mercy killing," Suzanne said, stuffing the project to the bottom of her knitting bag.

"I've been thrown off the horse. I need to build my confidence back. I think I'll do some finger knitting."

Maggie's eyes grew wide above the rim of her reading glasses. Lucy's reaction was not nearly as extreme, but she did chuckle at the mention of a knitting technique Maggie taught to her youngest students. The ones too little to handle knitting needles.

Maggie's gaze remained focused on her own project. She'd made quick work of the vest for Charles and was on to a short, summer-weight shrug. "In that case, you're probably up well past your bedtime. Did you finish your homework?" she teased.

"You're the one who told me to try that darned argyle stitch again. This setback is not entirely my fault," Suzanne countered.

"She has a point, Mag," Phoebe said quietly. "You always say, 'Knitting is not a race.' "

"Just do you, Suzanne," Dana encouraged. "If you feel like finger knitting, that's what you should do."

"See? Even my therapist approves. This defeat has been a blow. I have to find my way back, one stitch at a time," Suzanne muttered. She dug through her bag for a ball of yarn.

"Sorry to judge," Maggie said. "I should have been more understanding. I know you, Suzanne. You'll get bored with that baby stitch in no time. Your competitive streak will win out."

Lucy thought so, too, but didn't want to get involved in the debate.

"How's Rebecca doing?" Maggie asked. "Have you seen her since the memorial?"

"We've only chatted on the phone a few times. Mostly about the girls. She's been very busy with the café the past two days. The police released the crime scene and she's had a special cleaning crew there."

Lucy recalled her conversation with Leo after he brought Dara home, remembering his worry and concern.

"That's a good sign, don't you think?" Suzanne's upbeat tone interrupted her thoughts. "Maybe the police are opening the crime scene because they don't think Rebecca is guilty anymore."

"If they've eliminated her as a person of interest, they probably would have told her," Lucy pointed out.

Suzanne had found a ball of thick, soft white yarn and

was carefully winding the strand around her fingers. She thought Suzanne had been joking about the finger knitting, but she was really going through with it.

"It's impossible to say, one way or the other," Dana replied. "Jack hasn't heard anything new about the case. The police are still testing the theory that Rebecca staged the break-in at her house. Or she had help from someone."

"Like Nick the delicious-looking cook?" Suzanne asked.

"Something like that," Dana agreed with a wry smile. "The problem is, they don't have any witnesses or video that back up her story—that she never got out of her car that night."

"It still doesn't prove she was involved," Lucy reminded her friends. "But it doesn't put her in the clear, either."

"I hate to recall that ill-advised visit to Crane's Beach," Suzanne began. "But did that woman you tracked down tell you anything that could help Rebecca? She was Colin's secret squeeze. She must know some bit of helpful dirt."

"She suspected he was up to something but insisted she didn't know what," Maggie replied. "I believed her."

"I did, too," Lucy said. "She mentioned the department head, George Wexler. Hazel Huebner mentioned him, too. He didn't come to the memorial. Hazel said he took early retirement and moved to Mexico. I thought that was a red flag."

"Not necessarily." Dana clipped a few strands of yarn from the back of a button she'd just sewn on her project. "A lot of seniors relocate there. It's the new Florida. The cost of living is much cheaper than most anywhere in the U.S. With a pension from his county job, he's probably found a good retirement there."

"And he doesn't get buried by piles of snow all winter." Suzanne shivered with an imaginary chill. "I don't think it's a bad place to retire at all. I love Mexican food."

"Okay, maybe that move isn't suspicious. I still wonder if he knew what Colin was involved in." She shrugged. "I'm still working my way through the novel. It's tough going."

"I wonder if Detective Reyes took any notice of Colin's hobby. There must have been a copy on his laptop and maybe they even found one in his office. I wonder if anyone on her team was assigned to read it?" Maggie said.

"Good question, Mag," Dana said. "I'll ask Jack to find out. I'm curious, too, now that you mentioned it."

"It is the sort of thing investigators would do in a TV show," Suzanne noted.

"Right, they would assign the newbie to read it," Phoebe said. "The character who's always getting everyone coffee? And every time he or she would try to talk about it, the lead investigator would brush them off. Until finally, the rookie gets some great insight from the book that blows the case wide open."

"That is the way it goes, Phoebe. Ready to blow the case wide open, Lucy?" Suzanne asked.

Lucy laughed. "I'm a few chapters in, but Colin is a very slow storyteller. I haven't hit any major plot points yet."

"So his action-thriller doesn't have much action and isn't very thrilling either?" Maggie asked. "I understand now why Judith Esterhauzy wasn't impressed."

"And Graham Paxton," Lucy noted. "So far, he's got a main character named—are you ready?—Rick Stone."

Suzanne glanced at Dana. "Is that name macho enough for you?"

"More than enough," Dana agreed. "Go on, Lucy. Sorry to interrupt."

"I automatically think of Rick as Colin. His alter ego, or secret self. Rick is also an engineer working for a county public works department. Brilliant, but modest, and totally unappreciated by his boss, coworkers, and girlfriend," she added. "He's actually quite amazing, but no-body gives him any credit. He blends into the wallpaper."

"So far, I get why it's boring," Phoebe muttered.

"Until he turns into Super Geek. I cheated last night and skipped ahead," she admitted, "to a major disaster that should be in chapter one or two. Of course, Rick does some very heroic stuff."

"Wait, his superhero costume is baggy khakis, Top-Siders, and a buttoned-down shirt." Suzanne imagined the scene. "His pen protector has magical powers."

"His special calculator," Lucy corrected. "You were close."

"What's the title of this masterpiece?" Dana looked up from her work with a grin.

"The Sink Hole." Lucy could hardly say the title with a serious face.

Maggie had been counting stitches and marking the rows. Her head popped up like a meerkat. *"Stink Hole?* What kind of a title is that?"

Lucy giggled. "I said *sink*. As in kitchen?"

"I thought you said *stink*, too," Suzanne admitted. "I don't get it."

"A gigantic sinkhole opens up in the middle of a brand-new stretch of highway. Cars are crashing together and some fall right in. Trucks pile up and explode, and a brush fire starts. People in houses near the highway run for their lives. A zookeeper lets all the animals loose from their cages so they can run to safety. Oh, and crocodiles come up from the sewer."

"Nice touch. You gotta have a few crocs." Suzanne made a thumbs-up sign.

"Rick is running around trying to save people. He and this gorgeous woman he rescued from a burning car are cornered by a hungry tiger."

Maggie looked up from her knitting again. "I thought you said it was boring?"

"It's one of those books that sounds exciting when you explain the plot, but it's actually . . . well, bad writing."

Dana was quietly laughing. "I can see why he thought he'd get a movie option. But it's so over the top, it seems like a parody of the genre."

"No earthquake or volcano?" Maggie noted.

"Not yet. But he's hinting that a tsunami is building."

Phoebe stared at her. "Could that really happen?"

"I wondered, too, and checked online. Sinkholes are dangerous and they're no joke if you're driving near one, but it can't end civilization as we know it."

"What a relief. You had me worried for a minute there," Suzanne teased.

"You're a good sport to slog through that storyline, Lucy," Dana said. "Any ideas how it might connect to Colin's murder?"

"I think the question is, *Does* it connect?" Maggie murmured.

"So far, I don't see how," Lucy admitted. "But it gives me insight into the way his mind works."

"You're turning into an FBI profiler on us, Lucy." Phoebe's tone was a mixture of teasing and admiration.

"And that guy's mind is a scary neighborhood," Suzanne noted. "I think you've hung around there enough."

"I'll stick with it a while longer. I'm curious to see what happens," Lucy admitted. "And it helps me fall asleep."

"I know we're getting a laugh out of *Stink Hole*," Maggie said, purposely mangling the title, Lucy thought. "But I'm sorry you haven't found anything in the story that illuminates why Colin was killed or any clue that helps Rebecca."

"I'm disappointed, too," Lucy said quietly. "There must be something we're missing. I feel like time is running out."

"Because the baby is coming?" Phoebe asked.

Lucy nodded and forced a smile.

She really meant because the police were moving in on Rebecca, day by day, getting closer and closer to charging her with Colin's murder.

But she couldn't dare say it out loud.

Chapter 23

The surprise visit from her friends had refreshed Lucy's spirits. She woke up early Friday feeling energized and content and was the first one downstairs. She let the dogs out and started Matt's coffee, then stood at the counter, inhaling the scent of the forbidden brew.

Just two more weeks and she could have caffeine again. It was worth going through labor pains to have that particular privilege back.

Her husband found her sipping a smoothie and checking email on her phone. He kissed the top of her head. "Good morning, early bird. How's the ankle?"

"I'm ready to come off the bench, coach. But I won't make a big thing about it. I'm sorry I was such a grouch. It was silly to be in a snit because I had to stay off my feet for a few days."

"Apology accepted." Matt gave her a curious glance, before he opened the newspaper. She could tell he suspected this remorseful attitude was just a trick.

Tink had snuck into the laundry basket and stolen a pair of socks; her favorite chew toy. Lucy jumped up and snatched the socks away, sighing when saw the ragged hole in one toe. Head down, Tink stared up with an apologetic expression, then wagged her tail.

"Tink . . . No socks. You know that by now, sweetie."

"Smooth move," Matt said. "The Red Sox could use you at shortstop."

"Maybe next season." Lucy rubbed her belly. "Are you convinced now that my ankle is okay?"

"If you insist. But I'll still pick you up for our doctor's appointment today."

Lucy was always a little anxious visiting the doctor, especially as the pregnancy got further and further along. As usual, the waiting room was filled with pregnant moms and expectant dads. She'd already read most of the magazines but started an article on making homemade baby food just for a distraction.

A nurse soon called Lucy's name. She and Matt followed her to the exam room. "How are you feeling, Lucy?" the nurse asked as Lucy put on the paper gown.

"Great," Lucy answered with a smile.

"She sprained her ankle," Matt reported.

"I just twisted it a bit walking on the beach. I didn't fall," Lucy clarified.

The nurse made a note and took her vital signs—pulse, blood pressure, and blood sugar. Then helped Lucy step up on the scale. Digital numbers appeared that seemed astronomical, though the nurse assured her she wasn't gaining an unusual amount of weight.

Lucy hoped so. She'd read it took two years for a woman's body to recover from pregnancy. She'd initially thought the estimate must be an exaggeration, but now wondered if it would take even longer. Say, when her son or daughter moved up to middle school she might be back to her pre-pregnancy weight?

Her friends kept reminding her that her figure was the last thing she should worry about. She was relatively young and fit. "Everything will spring back into place.

Eventually," they promised. "Especially once the baby starts walking."

"Don't be one of those women who stroll out of the maternity ward in skinny jeans. We'll hate you," Suzanne promised.

Her OB/GYN, Dr. Avni Gupta, walked in and greeted Lucy and Matt with a smile. Lucy liked her doctor a lot and more than that, trusted her. The mother of three, Dr. Gupta had also given birth to a baby in her late thirties, just like Lucy, and knew about the special issues of later pregnancies firsthand.

She greeted Lucy and Matt and looked over the chart, then washed her hands, put on gloves, and began the exam. "Vital signs look good. So is your blood sugar. How do you feel, Lucy?"

"Tired, excited . . . hungry?"

Dr. Gupta smiled. "That sounds about right. What happened here?" She was checking Lucy's ankles for water retention and noticed the bruise.

"A little sprain."

"A big sprain," Matt corrected.

"It doesn't hurt at all. Matt made me stay off my feet a few days and do ice and all that."

Dr. Gupta glanced at him. "Good call. But you should be moving around as much as you're able. Walking is excellent exercise for you right now. Sturdy shoes, of course. On the sidewalk or a flat path. Drink plenty of water before and after. It will help keep things on track."

Lucy cast her husband a victorious look. "I'll keep moving, Doctor. Don't worry."

Matt crossed his arms over his chest but didn't say anything. The doctor listened to Lucy's heart and then searched Lucy's stomach with the stethoscope until she found the baby. She listened with serious focus, which always made Lucy nervous. Then smiled. "The heartbeat is strong. Just right."

She felt Lucy's belly and seemed satisfied by that, too. "The baby's getting big. They gain the most at the end. I'd say he or she is at least seven pounds now."

Matt looked pleased at the news. "That's a nice, healthy size. I was almost ten pounds when I was born," he said proudly.

Lucy's eyes grew wide. Had she heard that information before and purposely blocked it from her mind? "I hope our baby doesn't get that big before it's born."

The doctor smiled. "Unlikely at this point."

Matt left the room a moment while Lucy put her feet in stirrups and Dr. Gupta continued the exam.

She let Lucy put her feet down and glanced over Lucy's chart as Matt joined them again. "Everything looks good. You're due in two weeks, so I'll see you again next week for a sonogram. Call me with any questions," she added. "Or if any labor symptoms begin, of course."

"Of course," Lucy and Matt replied together, a small note of alarm in their voices.

Dr. Gupta squeezed Lucy's shoulder with a reassuring touch. "Last lap, Lucy. Your little one will be in your arms sooner than you think."

Lucy liked hearing that. Sometimes if felt as if her pregnancy would never end.

"Thank you, Doctor. See you next week."

Matt thanked the doctor and gave Lucy a hug. "You're a champ. It won't be long now, honey."

"I hope the end goes quicker than the last eight months. I'm so tired of waiting."

"I know." He brought Lucy her sundress and other clothes, and she slipped everything on. "Just remember what the doctor said. We'll have our little one in our arms very soon."

He smiled at the thought and Lucy did, too.

Lucy and Rebecca had planned to bring the girls to the park by the harbor after school for a playdate. Or rather, Dara and Sophie planned the outing and got their moms to agree. Rebecca insisted on picking them up.

"I can take them on my own, if you're tired or have things to do," Rebecca offered over the phone.

"Are you kidding? I've been cooped up in the house the whole week. I need some fresh air and maybe an ice cream cone. I'll meet you there when school gets out."

Lucy was the first to arrive at the park but waited only a few minutes before Rebecca pulled up.

"How did the visit with the doctor go?" Rebecca asked as the girls ran off to play.

"Everything is right on schedule. I've officially hit the weight of a pregnant Beluga. I guess when I'm ready to go back to work, I can find a job at an aquarium."

Rebecca laughed. "It's totally normal. I'm glad everything is going so well."

Rebecca had told her she'd really wanted children of her own, but she wasn't able to get pregnant, and Colin didn't want to pursue any special fertility options. Lucy knew it must seem ungrateful to be complaining so much about such an amazing blessing.

"I should be relieved, but I still feel stressed," she confessed.

"That's normal, too. People talk a lot about maternal instinct, but it's not automatic. You'll make some mistakes learning to be Mom. I know I did with Sophie. But it's all right."

Lucy had an instant rapport with Dara when they'd

met, but there had been a learning curve in becoming a good stepmother. Still, that was different from having a baby.

"It was easy with Dara, she was about six or so when we met. I'm not sure why, but the thought of caring for a tiny baby scares me. Isn't that awful to admit at this stage of the game?" She stared down at her burgeoning tummy. "Babies are so fragile and dependent and can't communicate at all."

"The baby will communicate, loud and clear, don't worry. Usually in the middle of the night. You'll learn to translate quickly."

Lucy and Rebecca chose a bench along the harbor where they could keep the girls in view.

Lucy took a deep breath of the fresh air as she settled herself in the shade. The sky was a clear blue with high, puffy clouds. The sunlight sparkled off the water. It was high tide and sea birds swooped and dipped over the waves, calling out noisily, while others quietly hopped along the rocks near the pier.

"We picked the perfect day," Lucy said. "I was at Crane's Beach on Monday, but it feels like a month ago."

She stopped herself, hoping Rebecca wouldn't ask what she was doing there. She wished she could tell Rebecca about Kiera Nesbit, if only to let Rebecca know that she was trying hard to find information that would put her in the clear.

"I've been stuck inside all week, too, at the café. It's great to be out in the fresh air." The breeze lifted Rebecca's long hair and she pushed it all to one side. "The crime scene cleaners are very thorough, but I still had to decide what to save or trash. And clean out the food cases."

"Sounds like a huge job," Lucy sympathized.

"My dad and his friend Alfie helped a lot. And Nick," she added. Had she averted her gaze when she said Nick's name? Lucy thought she had, then wondered if she'd just turned away because the sun was in her eyes. "If the place isn't spotless when I vacate, the landlord won't return the security deposit."

The word "vacate" sounded so final. "Are you closing the Happy Hands for good?"

Rebecca nodded. "I wasn't sure until I went back. I just can't . . . be there without thinking of Colin." Her voice got thick and quiet. "Customers will think about him, too and feel too creepy to come back. People in town are still talking about the murder."

Lucy knew that was true. The gossip would continue until the police solved the crime.

Rebecca glanced at her. "I have to be honest. I'm afraid that there are a lot of people in town who believe that I killed my husband. I'm the only name that comes up in the news reports about the investigation, 'the suspect's wife, Rebecca Hurley, a person of interest,' " she said in a tart tone. "That's another reason I decided closing the café would be the smartest thing to do right now. Instead of sitting there, paying rent and salaries and the cost of supplies without any customers."

"People don't think you're guilty, Rebecca. Okay, maybe some do," Lucy had to amend. "But they don't know you and are too easily influenced by news reports that are totally unfair. Those people are going to see that they're wrong."

"I hope so. But that day might take a while to arrive. I had to decide. I feel bad for the staff. A lot of them couldn't wait to see if the café would reopen and found other jobs, which was fine with me. Some were loyal and waited." Like Nick Russo, Lucy thought, but didn't say. "I've paid everyone's salary the past two weeks, but money's getting tight. Not an unfamiliar situation, actually," she noted in a wry tone.

"Matt and I can help. We'd be happy to," Lucy offered. She knew Matt wouldn't mind giving Rebecca a loan under the circumstances, even though he was more budget conscious with the baby coming.

"That's so sweet. I'll be fine. My dad has a little set aside and insisted that I take it. I'll pay him back with the insurance payment when it comes. But I need to find a job soon."

Lucy felt sad to hear that Rebecca was giving up her business. She'd worked hard to open her own restaurant and make it so successful.

Lucy thought Rebecca could get a bank loan to keep the café open, or even open a new place. But she guessed Rebecca had considered those solutions and ruled them out. Maybe she didn't have the enthusiasm anymore to run a café like The Happy Hands—more collateral damage of Colin's murder and another great loss for her.

"It is ironic that I'm strapped for money since Detective Reyes is still convinced I know the password to Colin's cyber account but won't tell them. They had me back in the station and pressed me for an hour about the code or the key, or whatever . . ." Rebecca took a breath. "Good thing Helen was there. I'd still be answering questions." Lucy was glad to hear that. "I have no idea what the password is, or where Colin hid the information. The police are getting help from a unit in Boston that specializes in investigating cyber crime, but I understand it's difficult, if not impossible, to figure out that sort of password."

"That's what I've learned, too. Which is one of the reasons criminals like those accounts so much," Lucy said. "Why won't the police see that the mere fact the account exists is a major clue that Colin was into something shady?"

Lucy continued, drawing on what she'd recently read. "It's used on the dark web, a part of the internet you can't

access with Google or Safari. You need special search en-
gines. There's one called Onion, I think. It can reach sites
where guns, drugs, and a lot of illegal merchandise are for
sale. The anonymous aspect of cyber coin makes it ideal
for that sort of shopping."

"I've heard that, too. But a lot of honest people invest in
cyber currency or use it just because they like the idea,"
Rebecca reminded her. "Colin was very high tech and futuristic. He had a strong antiauthority streak, too, though
it wasn't obvious at first. I can see how the concept attracted him. Maybe he wanted to deal in cryptocurrency
for fun, or to be on the cutting edge. Maybe the police will
get into the account and there won't be much there."

"Could be," Lucy offered, though she doubted it.

Sophie waved to Rebecca from the top of the climbing
bars. "Watch this, Mom. I'm going to swing all the way
down without stopping," she shouted.

"I'm watching, honey. Be careful," Rebecca called back.

With her eyes on Sophie and an encouraging smile fixed
on her pretty face, Rebecca said, "I guess I don't want to
think badly of him or find out he was in trouble with criminals."

"Of course, you don't." Lucy understood Rebecca's reaction. Even though the relationship wasn't perfect, Colin
had been Rebecca's husband. They'd shared a life together.

But Lucy still doubted that Colin's cyber account was
an innocent, fun, futuristic savings plan.

Sophie reached the bottom of the bars with quick, nim-
ble movements, then threw her arms up in a victory pose,
like an Olympic gymnast.

"Wow, you're like a silly sloth up there, swinging from
branch to branch." Rebecca's compliment made her stepdaughter giggle. "I couldn't do that in a million years."

"I know." Sophie ran to the other side to start again and
Dara followed.

"Colin wasn't a drug dealer, or anything like that. I think I would have noticed," Rebecca insisted. "But this virtual money thing has stirred up the pot. Helen said it gives the police another motive they can assign to me. They can speculate that I was after Colin's secret stash of money, assuming I knew of the account and where to find the password."

Lucy had already thought of that. But it wouldn't do any good to reinforce Rebecca's anxiety. "It also gives the police a reason to look for new suspects," Lucy offered. "Let's assume he didn't have it for innocent, honest use, but to hide money he'd received for some illegal purpose. That opens a world of possibilities. It should turn this investigation in a whole new direction."

And create reasonable doubt for a jury, if Rebecca ever faced a trial. But Lucy thought that point was better left unsaid.

"We'll have to see about that, won't we?" Rebecca glanced at her and then back at the playground. "I do worry that—" Rebecca paused and shook her head. "Forget it. I'm not even going to say it."

"What is it?" Lucy coaxed. "What are you thinking?"

"I worry that the police will confirm Colin was involved in some illicit scheme, but it won't make any difference for me. They'll still think I killed him, because he was going to take Sophie . . . and now, because he may have hidden a lot of money and they think I know how to get it. Or, already have it."

Rebecca turned to Lucy, her eyes glassy with tears. "I'm sorry, Lucy. I wish this part of the puzzle cleared me of suspicion. But it seems to weigh against me instead."

It was hard to hear her friend sound so bleak. Lucy searched for a few encouraging words and when she couldn't find any, changed the subject.

"I've been reading Colin's novel. It's very"—Lucy searched

for the right words to describe it—"interesting," she said finally. "When it's not putting me to sleep. I fall out so easily these days, I can't blame that entirely on his writing," she added, trying to be fair.

"I asked him a few times if I could read it, but he always told me it wasn't finished yet."

"It does seem like a rough draft," Lucy replied.

"I'll read it in time," she promised quietly. Lucy knew Rebecca's feelings were too raw right now for that endeavor. "Colin was very proud of it. Is it any good?"

"There's a lot going on—a disaster story, a mystery, a thriller. A little bit of romance, too. He's covered all the bases."

A nice way of saying he'd tossed in everything but the kitchen sink, but there was no need to be snarky.

"Any mention of cyber currency?" Rebecca asked.

"Good question. Not yet, but something in this"—she nearly said "mess"—"plot might shed a light on Colin's secrets. It's funny how people reveal themselves without realizing it."

"That's probably true for most people. But not Colin. He was very guarded. His emotions were vacuum packed. I doubt he let any secrets slip out, even in his writing."

Lucy hoped Rebecca was wrong about that, for her own sake, if for no other reason.

Dara and Sophie had moved on to the swings, their legs pumping them higher and higher. At the baby swings, Lucy watched a mom carefully secure a little one in an orange plastic seat, then gently push, chatting and cooing at her baby nonstop.

Rebecca caught Lucy watching the routine. "That will be you in a few months. Sophie and Dara will have a new playmate out here."

Lucy smiled, imagining the scene. Until her imagination

took a dark turn, wondering if Rebecca would be with them, or would she be behind bars, waiting for a trial?

Heaven forbid. What would become of Sophie? Rebecca was her stepmother and Leo her stepgrandfather. They might not be considered legal guardians, and Sophie might be placed in foster care.

She shook her head to chase away the frightening thought, even more determined to prove Rebecca had nothing to do with Colin's death.

As Lucy guessed, the girls could not be parted and persuaded Lucy and Rebecca to let them have a sleepover at Rebecca's house.

Her own house seemed quiet after dinner without Dara. Matt fell asleep on the couch watching a baseball game, and Lucy used the time to read more of Colin's novel. There was a fine line between pushing through it and reading so quickly she'd miss something.

Feeling as if she were back in school preparing for a quiz, she even took notes. She found no mention of cryptocurrency, but the plot took a few interesting turns—in between truckloads of adjectives, sentence fragments, and non sequiturs.

At the end of the night, she checked the page number to see how much she had left to read. Plenty.

She sighed, then recalled her worrisome conversation at the park with Rebecca and set a goal of finishing the book on the weekend.

In the dark, silent house, she heard the clock ticking, counting down the hours of her pregnancy and it seemed, of Rebecca's freedom as well.

Chapter 24

"She's back! Or *they're* back, I should say." Maggie stood at the top of the shop's porch steps and welcomed Lucy and her panting dogs on Monday morning.

"It hasn't been that long. Only a week." Lucy dropped the leashes and found the collapsible dog water bowl in her tote bag.

Suzanne sat in a shady corner, sipping iced coffee and nibbling a croissant. "It felt longer. Even though we saw you Thursday night."

"No limping, I see." Maggie looked over her ankle.

"Fully recovered. Even my doctor said I should walk a lot. Matt sort of gritted his teeth. If it was up to him, I'd be locked in a padded room until Baby Day."

"It would get messy slipping all the mac and cheese under the door," Suzanne said.

"You're a free woman until then. But don't tempt fate," Maggie warned.

"I've been very careful. A couch potato this weekend, to tell the truth. I set myself an assignment of finishing Colin's book."

Suzanne sat up with interest and put her phone aside. "Do you want your gold star now, or after you give the book report?"

"The report is ready. But first, some news from Rebecca. The police are hounding her for the password to get into Colin's cyber account. They had her in for questioning again last week. Detective Reyes is convinced she knows it. They've enlisted a special unit in Boston that deals in cybercrime to help."

"Reyes has to put up a strong front, even if she's not one hundred percent sure," Maggie reminded them.

"Whether she's bluffing or not, it's still a bad development for Rebecca," Suzanne said bluntly.

"Isn't it? These accounts are so anonymous and secure, a person could die and no one would ever know it was there. It's highly likely Colin didn't even put his real name on the account."

"You can do that? The bank always asks for a photo ID," Maggie noted.

"That's the idea of virtual currency, Mag. There's no bank or regulated institution controlling the transactions," Suzanne explained. "People who use it want to fly under the radar. To avoid taxes and all kinds of legal scrutiny. Remember what Lucy told us?"

"Not everyone who uses cyber currency is hiding something," Lucy pointed out. "But it is likely Colin was. The police won't say if the information has opened up new leads, but it must have, don't you think?"

"That seems logical to us. But only because we believe Rebecca is innocent," Maggie reminded her.

"Rebecca isn't seeing any positive side to this, either, unfortunately," Lucy told them. "I really hoped to find some mention of cyber currency in Colin's story, but that would have been too easy, right?"

"Any more crocodiles? I loved that touch." Suzanne returned to scrolling on her phone.

"It was clever," Maggie agreed. "We really believed that tall tale when I was a kid."

"Understandably. The dinosaurs had just left Main Street," Suzanne teased.

Maggie glared at her, then laughed. "There were a few pterodactyls lingering on the village green, now that you mention it."

"Do you want to hear what happened in the book or not?" Lucy asked.

"Of course we do . . . proceed, please." Maggie cast her a contrite look and returned to her knitting. She'd almost completed the shrug and was working on the border.

"The giant sinkhole caused car crashes, a forest fire, a blackout, and general pandemonium," Suzanne recalled.

"And Colin . . . I mean, his character, Rick Stone, had just rescued a beautiful woman and faced down a hungry tiger," Maggie added. "Catch us up from there."

"Good recall, Mag." Lucy was impressed.

"I've been taking my brain vitamins," Maggie replied without looking up from her work. Lucy wasn't sure if she was being sarcastic or not but did notice a small smile.

Lucy summarized the rest of the story, hitting the high points. "The beautiful woman dies in his arms and Rick vows to hunt down whoever is responsible for the catastrophe. As an engineer, he knows it shouldn't have happened on the spanking-new highway."

"Classic storyline. Some famous writer said there are only three plots. Seeking revenge is one of them," Maggie noted.

"My favorite, now that you mention it," Suzanne mumbled around a bite of pastry.

"The next three hundred pages are a bit dense and could use some heavy editing. A lot of car chases and computer hacking. He's shot at a few times, and tied up and left in a warehouse full of rats . . ."

"Ugh." Suzanne covered her mouth with a napkin just in time. "Spare me the creepy details . . . and the rodents."

"The bottom line is, Rick discovers that the county employee in charge of awarding contracts took a bribe from a shady construction company and—"

"You get what you pay for." Suzanne tossed her hands in the air. "It's the same old story."

"Rick becomes a whistleblower and takes on the entire corrupt system and then he's *really* in danger. But he finally prevails and the bad guys go to jail," Lucy concluded. "Oh, he meets another sexy woman along the way, a clever secretary who's always been underestimated because she's so gorgeous. She steals some confidential files so he can bring the evildoers to justice."

Suzanne sat back and clapped. "Well done, Lucy. I give you an A-plus."

Maggie snipped a strand of yarn. "I'm not surprised that Colin's alter ego is a super-macho, action hero engineer. But I can't see any connection to his murder. Do you?" she asked Lucy.

"No, I can't," Lucy admitted. "But I'm still working on it. That nice woman I met at the memorial, Hazel Huebner, said that there was a lot going on in the department right before Colin quit. There was a lot of pressure and some problems with projects. Keira Nesbit told us the same thing, too. I want to find out if there was any special project Colin was working on. I might even call Hazel Huebner. I think she'll remember me."

"If a giant sinkhole opened up around here, I think we'd remember," Suzanne noted quietly.

Lucy shrugged. "Maybe his masterpiece doesn't relate at all to his death and I'm spinning my wheels. I've gone this far. Investing a little more time won't make much difference, and it will satisfy my curiosity."

She watched Maggie count the stitches on the last row of her work, squinting through her reading glasses. She glanced at Lucy with a mild smile but didn't comment.

Lucy had the distinct feeling Maggie thought she *was* wasting her time but didn't want to say.

Suzanne stood up and brushed some crumbs off her smart linen dress; white on top and dark blue on the bottom, a design that was quite flattering to Suzanne's curvy figure.

"Got to run, ladies. I'm off to show a waterfront condo. I can't understand why the big fish aren't biting. It's so pristine, I think my clients are intimidated. Is there such a thing as too luxurious?"

"Fun to visit, but you wouldn't want to live there?" Lucy asked.

"Exactly—I'm thinking of tossing around some sneakers and schoolbooks. Maybe a few dirty coffee mugs? Just to make it feel homier."

"I've heard the scent of baking bread can help sell a house. Never sneakers," Maggie mused.

Suzanne laughed. "I'll skip the footwear, good advice."

"I'd better head home, too. It's starting to get warmer." When Lucy stood up the dogs automatically stood up, too.

"I can give you a ride, it's no trouble. Phoebe can watch over things for a while . . . if she ever comes down." Maggie glanced at her watch, but Lucy knew she never bothered Phoebe about keeping strict hours, especially in the summer when Phoebe worked her stall at the Farmers' Market a few days a week.

"I'll stick to the shady streets. I need to keep moving if I want this baby to arrive on time. Doctor's orders."

"I won't interfere, then. Call if you need anything," Maggie added.

"I'll be fine, thanks." With a cheerful wave, Lucy headed home to get on with her day.

The second crib was finally delivered on Tuesday morning. It came in a big, flat box. The delivery men carried it up to the baby's room and set it on the floor. Lucy called Matt before she dared to open it. She was eager to see what was inside, but also worried she'd find the wrong model again. All she could picture was her newborn baby sleeping in a dresser drawer.

"So? Does it look okay?" Matt asked on the other end of the phone call.

Lucy pulled back more cardboard to make sure. "Yes, thank goodness. They finally got it right."

"Great. I'll get home early and put it together. The last task on our baby to-do list."

Except for me going into labor, Lucy nearly added. But she restrained herself.

"Yup, that's it," she agreed.

True to his word, Matt got to work on the project minutes after he came through the door. The first phase was carrying up the big pieces. Lucy was in charge of a million little plastic bags with bolts, screws, and metal pieces needed to assemble the legs and rails and frame. She searched the entire box but found hardly any instructions. There was a video online, but that wasn't much help, either.

Matt sorted everything into neat piles on the floor of the baby's room. "The important thing is not to panic," he said quietly.

"I'll call the store tomorrow. They can probably send someone to put it together. Or recommend a service?" Lucy asked.

"I can do it. It's just going to take a while. I don't want to make any mistakes."

"Of course you can," she said quickly.

She felt guilty for doubting him. Matt prided himself on being handy and usually loved projects like this. Everything about the baby made them both a little nervous, she realized.

"You put the chest together really quickly. Even the drawers," she reminded him. "You'll breeze right through this job, honey."

He smiled and pushed the box to one side. "It will be up in time. Let's just say that."

On Wednesday night they went straight upstairs after dinner to work on the crib. Lucy sat in the nursing rocker with the directions and sometimes found the correct screwdriver Matt needed or a ratchet wrench, but mostly just watched.

"I know you want to help, honey, but you're making me nervous." He was kneeling on the floor, screwing metal brackets into the headboard.

"Sorry. I'll go make a cup of ginger tea." She was having heartburn lately, no matter how carefully she ate. "Do you want anything?"

"No thanks. I'll be down in a little while," he promised.

Lucy took that to mean, "Please don't come back up with your tea." So she didn't.

Later that night, she peeked in the room to check his progress. He would be done by the time the baby came. But just under the wire. She really thought they should call a furniture assembly service, who would swarm around the crib with their power drills and have it put together in no time flat. But it seemed important to Matt to do it himself, so she didn't mention it again.

It was Lucy's turn to bring the entrée for the meeting Thursday night, but her friends would not allow her to do any cooking. The debate raged over text messages for at least half an hour Thursday morning.

Suzanne was the first to object:

Are you crazy? You shouldn't be anywhere near a stove in this weather. I vote for take out.

Lucy quickly texted back:

I'll bring something cold. I'll surprise you.

Dana replied next:

Please don't go to any trouble for us. You have a pass until the baby comes.

Lucy texted back:

From what I hear, I'll need the pass #whenthebabycomes. Punch my ticket for tonight, please.

Phoebe jumped in:

I'll bring dessert.

Maggie liked Phoebe's note, then added:

I'm already signed up for the starter, so we're covered. See you later, ladies.

Lucy texted again:

Rebecca might come. Hope nobody minds that I invited her?

Everyone responded at once, assuring Lucy they would love to see Rebecca. Lucy knew they'd all be welcoming but guessed it would still be hard for Rebecca. She was avoiding almost everyone right now, feeling that most people suspected she'd killed Colin, even if they didn't show it.

Chapter 25

"So, what's this cold, noncooked dinner you made for us, Lucy?" Suzanne called out from the back of the shop as Lucy walked in with a platter covered with foil. "My guess is you picked up some sushi."

"Wrong, but that will be a good solution for another time."

The table was already set and her friends were a step ahead, sharing a platter of cold shrimp and cocktail sauce Maggie had put together.

"My guess is a special salad. Spinach with blue cheese and hard-boiled eggs?" Dana said.

"And bacon," Suzanne added, then noticed Dana's expression. "Whoops, sorry to ruin your food fantasy. Bacon on the side," she said quietly.

"You're getting closer, roughage is involved." Lucy lifted the cover to reveal a poached salmon, decorated with super-thin slices of lemon and springs of fresh dill. It rested on a bed of greens, with a bowl of cold cucumber yogurt sauce alongside. She'd also brought a bowl of quinoa salad.

Phoebe stepped closer for a better look. "Awesome salmon. It looks like a photo in a cookbook."

"Not quite, Pheebs, but thanks. It was fun to decorate it."

"It's beautiful, but we said no cooking," Maggie reminded Lucy.

"I promised I'd bring something cold. I never said I wouldn't turn the stove on. Poaching doesn't count as cooking, does it?"

"That's debatable." Suzanne had spread her napkin on her lap and sat poised to begin the meal. "Let's eat, I'm starving and that looks delish."

"Wait, what about Rebecca? Isn't she joining us?" Maggie glanced at Lucy.

"I thought so but . . ." Before Lucy could make excuses, they heard the shop door open and Rebecca appeared.

"Sorry I'm late. I hope I didn't hold anything up. I had to wait for my dad to come home. He's watching Sophie."

"We're just admiring Lucy's poached salmon. You haven't missed a thing." Maggie ushered Rebecca to the table, where she found an empty chair.

Everyone greeted her warmly. Lucy was happy to see that.

Maggie handed Lucy a cake lifter. "You ought to do the honors. I'd feel awful cutting into that masterpiece."

"Wait! I need to take a picture for Lucy's Instagram." Phoebe leaned forward and took several photos of the platter.

"I don't post food on social media, Pheebs. But thanks."

"If you don't, I will," Phoebe said with a tone of disbelief.

Lucy grinned and began to serve portions of the fish with a dollop of dill sauce on the side. Rebecca was first to receive a plate.

"This looks delicious. And very professional." Rebecca's compliment almost made Lucy blush.

"Maybe I *should* post a photo. It's probably the fanciest dish I'll cook for a while," Lucy mused.

"I'm so tired of those people who are always taking photos of their food. But I'd make an exception for this." Suzanne gratefully took her dish and Lucy began to serve Phoebe.

Dana poured Rebecca a glass of white wine. "We told her explicitly not to cook, but she surprised us."

"I have a few more surprises up my pot holder," Lucy promised. "I found some interesting information online about the Department of Public Works and what they were focused on right before Colin quit." She glanced at Rebecca. "I'm glad you're here. You may be able to fill in some of the blanks."

"I'll try my best." Rebecca sounded curious and even encouraged, which Lucy hoped was justified.

After everyone was served, Lucy sat at her place. The salmon had been tricky to cook, but it had turned out well. Her friends were not just being kind with their compliments.

They ate quietly for a few minutes before peppering her with questions.

"So, what's this clickbait you just dangled? What did you find out?" Suzanne asked.

"Spill it, pal," Phoebe said bluntly.

"I was disappointed when nothing in Colin's novel seemed linked to his death. I decided to look in the direction of his work. It doesn't seem that a civil servant's job could have any dangerous connections, but you can't rule anything out, right?"

"Absolutely," Suzanne agreed.

"Hazel Huebner had told me that she wasn't surprised when Colin left his job. She said there was a lot of pressure in the department, there were new projects starting up and big problems with some old ones," Lucy recalled. "I searched for any mention of the Department of Public Works in the local news archives to see what she meant. I found some small articles about new projects, a county office building going up, and a road repair plan."

Lucy turned, reached into her knitting bag, and took out a file folder. "There was one news story that jumped out. About two years ago, an overpass that spanned the Essex River collapsed. It was late at night, so there was hardly any traffic. But, very unfortunately, a nurse coming home from a late shift at the hospital was caught in the collapse. Her car fell into the river and she drowned."

Kiera Nesbit had mentioned that event causing lasting fallout, too. But Lucy didn't want to bring her name up in front of Rebecca and then be in the position of explaining the woman's connection to Colin.

Maggie gasped and covered her mouth with her hand. "I remember that, now that you mention it. A real tragedy."

"I remember that, too," Rebecca said. "There was a lot of finger-pointing in county government. Colin's department was held responsible. But he hadn't been there very long, at that time, so he was not on the staff when the overpass was built."

"It was about ten years old, I think," Lucy said, checking one of the articles she'd printed out. "Did he ever talk about the incident with you?"

"Not much. It was in the news a day or two when it happened. Of course I asked him about it. But he never gave me more than a brief answer. Bridges and buildings aren't supposed to collapse. No engineer likes to hear something like that. But he rarely spoke about his work and this situation was no exception." Rebecca paused a moment. "I think there was an investigation and that made everyone in the department nervous."

"There was an investigation. The state demanded it and politicians did, too, trying to show that they were looking out for the public's welfare."

Lucy sifted through the sheets in the folder and pulled another one out. "Here's an article about the report and the findings, which were delivered at a public hearing three or four months after the incident. The investigating team found that the bridge's supports, buried in the river bed, eroded due to highly-accelerated environmental impact," she explained, then read the article verbatim. " 'Which was not foreseen—and could not have been—at the time it was built. Massive storms and strong river currents. Super-high tides and flooding. Record-breaking summer and winter temperatures.' " Lucy looked up at her friends. "We hear it every night on the news. I don't have to read the entire list, right?"

"Unfortunately, we know the signs of climate change by heart," Dana sighed in agreement.

Lucy read the rest. " 'The committee strongly recommended revising building codes and standards, to not only keep current with climate change but also to anticipate a worst-case model of its progress.' "

"Well, at least they admit their mistake and offered a solution to prevent other bridges from falling apart. You can't put spilt milk back in the bottle, or something like that," Maggie said, unable to recall the exact words of the motto.

"I think there's no crying over the spilt milk, but you can't put a genie back in the bottle. Or a horse back in the barn?" Suzanne ventured.

"You can't get a horse in a bottle in the first place," Phoebe cut in, sounding frustrated. "Can we let Lucy finish, please?"

"Did you know that Colin was on the team that investigated the bridge failure and wrote the report?" Lucy asked Rebecca.

The blood drained from her face and her eyes grew wide. "No, I didn't. I suppose he could have mentioned it and I didn't understand the significance. He certainly didn't talk about it at home."

"Actually, he was the head of the team and wrote the report," Lucy told her. "That wasn't in any of the news articles, but I found out with a little more digging. Since it was a public hearing, all the documents go into the record and you can find them if you call the right people and ask a lot of questions. Oh, and pay seven dollars for the copying and mailing fee," she added, making her friends laugh.

Rebecca shook her head, she seemed confused and a little upset. "Colin never told me he was involved in such an important project. When was that hearing again?"

Lucy checked the news article and told her the date. "I checked with the department secretary, too. Hazel confirmed that was the time period all of this went on."

Hazel was curious to know why Lucy was interested in the event, but she made up some excuse about Rebecca making a scrapbook for Sophie and noting it had been an honor that Colin was tasked with the job of heading such an important investigation.

Rebecca was silent a moment, with a thoughtful expression. "I'm trying to remember what was going on with us. We hadn't moved to Plum Harbor yet. We were still in Peabody and I was working at Country Kitchen during Sophie's school hours and some weeknights and I was thinking of opening my own place. I guess I was in my own head a lot. Colin was short-tempered and seemed worn-out when he got home from work, but I never thought much of it."

"Were the building codes ever revised to adapt to climate change?" Dana asked.

Lucy met her glance. "I didn't have time to research that strand of the story, but from what I gleaned by chance, the recommendation is still being debated, between people who believe climate change is real and those who don't."

"People who don't believe in science, you mean?" Dana asked.

"Figures." Phoebe sounded angry. "Can we not talk about that part anymore? It just makes me think of polar bear mothers, who swim hundreds of miles with their cubs clinging to their back, while they look for a little chunk of ice to rest on."

Maggie sat back, moved by Phoebe's words. "When you put it like that, Phoebe, I want to leave my estate to the humane society."

"I already plan to," Phoebe said very seriously.

"I totally believe in climate change," Lucy cut in, "but there is another explanation for the bridge failure. One that was offered by expert witnesses, a team of engineers who testified for the plaintiff in a civil case that was filed against the state, the county, and the construction company who won the contract to build the bridge. The suit was brought by Connie Delgado's family."

"The poor woman who perished in the bridge failure?" Maggie asked.

"That's right," Lucy replied.

"What did those engineers say caused it?" Rebecca asked quietly.

Chapter 26

"They said the bridge was built with inferior building materials—cheap steel and cement—that did not meet the state's acceptable grade and standards, but certainly padded the construction company's profits."

"That's outrageous. A total abuse of the public trust." Suzanne was beside herself. "I hope those crooked builders were put out of business."

"The trial went on for about a week but was settled out of court," Lucy reported.

"How do you know all this?" Phoebe stared at her curiously. "Do you wave your hands over a magic ball or something?"

"Trial transcripts are easy to get your hands on, too. You just fill out a form . . . and pay a few bucks for the copying costs," she repeated with a grin. "I did need some specific information that was a little harder to pin down, like the exact title of the lawsuit, the name of the judge, the courtroom, and the docket number. Stuff like that."

Maggie tiled her head to one side. "It doesn't sound so easy to me."

"I found the name of the law firm from the newspaper articles that followed the story. So I had a friend of mine on the *Plum Harbor Times* call the firm and say that she was writing a follow-up piece."

Dana met Lucy's glance across the table. "Is that true?"

"It will be when I give Emily Creeder this information," Lucy replied, mentioning a friend who was a local reporter. "She was grateful to have me do the legwork," Lucy said, defending herself.

"I bet, especially in your condition," Maggie murmured. "I give you A for research and resourcefulness, and A-plus for rationalizing," Maggie said.

"That is an amazing pile of research, Lucy," Rebecca said. "But how does it connect to Colin? I still don't get it."

Lucy met her gaze and released a slow breath. She didn't want to upset Rebecca, but she had to be honest about her conclusions. "I know this will be hard for you to hear. I think Colin knew that environmental impact had not brought the bridge down, but he knew it was a plausible explanation and used it in the report to cover up the real reason."

"He knowingly lied about it, you mean." Rebecca seemed upset. "Maybe to protect his department? Or maybe someone forced him to do it?" Rebecca speculated.

"Maybe." Lucy nodded, marveling at her loyalty to a man who by all accounts had never treated her that well. "I thought of that. But in Colin's novel, his hero, Rick Stone, finds out the cause of the sinkhole was also the use of inferior building materials. A construction company tied to organized crime won the contract to build the road by paying off a lot of bureaucrats, including Rick's boss. Rick exposes the whole scheme, all the crooked officials and the mob-owned construction company. When the book ends, he's a regular hometown hero."

"I bet Colin planned a sequel, with Rick Stone, Geek of Action," Suzanne said.

"That's hard to say," Lucy replied, trying not get too far

off track. "The thing is, when I charted all this out—Rick's story and Colin's—here's what I saw." She showed them a handwritten sheet with two lists, side by side. "Rick was exposing the corruption. But Colin was covering it up. Rick was calling out the bribery." She paused. "But Colin had a hidden stash of money, in a cyber currency account. He also had extra money to buy a fancy bike and help with bills here and there. He told you that his novel had been optioned to be a film, which accounted for the extra cash. But that seems unlikely now."

Before she could say more, Phoebe cut in. "So Colin was in on the scheme. He was paid off to write the report that blamed the bridge collapse on climate change."

"I think so." Lucy glanced at Rebecca. "I'm sorry to accuse him. He's not around to defend himself. But it would explain a few things. More than a few, I think."

"I'm not arguing with you. It's just that . . ." Rebecca looked shaken. "This is a lot to take in. I had no idea Colin was involved so deeply in any of this—the report, the trial . . . It's mind-boggling."

"But it does make sense in a crazy, fun house mirror way," Suzanne said.

"It was a fun house mirror. Good analogy, Suzanne," Dana said. "In his novel, Colin had a chance to go back and do the right thing. To make a moral, ethical choice, instead of a dishonest one. He turns his story inside out, so that he wasn't part of the cover-up, he was the hero bringing the crooks to justice. Perhaps losing himself in the fictional version relieved his guilt."

"Sort of a 'Colin in Crook Land' thing," Phoebe offered. "Like *Alice in Wonderland*?"

Lucy recalled how Hazel Huebner had reminded her of the Red Queen. Strange coincidence. "We can stretch this analogy too far," she warned. "But Colin's boss, George Wexler, did retire about the same time Colin left the department, and quietly hopped off to Mexico like the March Hare. Late for an important date."

"He must have been involved even deeper than Colin," Maggie speculated.

"It may have gone even higher than that, but Wexler was definitely the domino above Colin. He was there when the bridge was built and long before that, as well. He had the authority to award contracts of fifty thousand dollars and under without much scrutiny. There was a competitive bid process for big projects like that bridge. But that wasn't too hard to sidestep. He probably gave the company of his choice inside information so that their bid would fit the budget and look like the best value for the taxpayers' dollars." Lucy glanced at Rebecca. "Did Colin talk about his boss much?"

"No more than you'd expect." Rebecca shrugged. "Now that you mention it, I always got the feeling Colin was George's favorite on the staff, the teacher's pet. Now I know why."

Maggie looked up from her needles. "Colin could blow the lid off a big can of worms otherwise."

"Worms again? Let's not go there, please." Suzanne looked at Phoebe. "Getting back to Colin, George might have been taking kickbacks from contractors for years. But after the bridge failed, he pulled Colin down the rabbit hole with him."

"Exactly," Lucy nodded.

"But if this incident is connected, why was Colin murdered now?" Rebecca asked. "He must have been given the money to write the false report about six months ago, right before he left his job."

"Maybe he asked for more and made some threats if he didn't get it. So he wasn't trusted to keep his silence," Lucy speculated. "Think about it, Rebecca. A few days after the motorcycle pushed his bike off the road, he packed up and grabbed his passport."

"We suspected from the start that Colin was running from a dangerous situation," Suzanne noted before Rebecca could reply. "Now we know what it was about."

"I think you did figure it out, Lucy. I'm sorry to sound as if I don't believe you." Rebecca seemed stunned and even ashamed. "Colin had an entire secret life going on right under my nose. Why didn't I see what was going on? I feel like a complete fool."

"You can't blame yourself. He was very good at dissembling," Lucy said quickly, though she knew the police would ask the same question.

"Like a talented magician, who makes the audience focus on one hand while the other is slipping a card up a sleeve. He knew how to distract you from what was really going on," Maggie added in a comforting tone.

"Thanks but I still feel as if I should have noticed or even sensed something was wrong. Maybe I did, but I brushed it aside. I didn't want to rock the boat. Now my cowardice has come home to roost. Colin might be alive if I hadn't ignored little signals and had persuaded him to confide in me." Rebecca dropped her gaze and sighed.

Lucy's heart went out to her. "You can't blame yourself for Colin keeping secrets and making bad choices. If he had been honest and open with you, I'm sure you would have tried to help him turn things around . . . and act more like his fictional hero. But he never gave you the chance."

Lucy wasn't sure if her words had helped. It was going to take time for Rebecca to accept the truth about Colin's double life.

Dana put her knitting aside and gave Rebecca her full attention. "Marriages are complicated. We strike unconscious bargains with each other, and it's only natural to protect the status quo. It's going to take time to sort all this out, Rebecca. And to understand your part in it. But I will say that it sounds like Colin got involved with criminals and he must have understood there could be dangerous consequences. That was his choice and his alone."

Rebecca nodded but didn't reply right away. "I guess that's true," she said finally. She turned to Lucy. "I don't mean to seem ungrateful. It took so much time and effort to dig all this up. What should I do now? Tell the police what you've found out?"

"It's better if Helen Forbes presents the information. The sooner the better."

"I'll call her tonight. She'll probably want to meet. Will you come with me? I'll never be able to explain it all the way you did, Lucy."

Lucy had expected Rebecca to ask her that. "Of course I will. I'll be interested to hear what she thinks about my theory."

Suzanne waved her hand. "She's going to love it. It covers all the bases. Even the way you were harassed on the road and your house was broken into, Rebecca. Whoever silenced Colin must think you know more than you do. The police should be protecting you instead of interrogating you."

"Very true, Suzanne," Phoebe said. "But doesn't that mean, since we now all know about this dirty dealing, we're in danger, too?"

Lucy hadn't thought of that. She exchanged glances with her friends. "What happens at the Black Sheep knitting shop stays at the Black Sheep knitting shop." She tried to strike a light tone. "At least until this is all figured out and Detective Reyes catches the bad guys."

"Agreed," Maggie nodded, staring down at her knitting. Lucy could tell the topic made her nervous.

"That's a wise suggestion," Dana said. "Just to be on the safe side."

Suzanne waved her hand, dismissing their concerns. "Don't worry, ladies. The police will be in the hot seat, not us. They'll take all the credit for figuring this out, just like they've always done when we do their heavy lifting. Helen should send them Lucy's file with a box of donuts. It's one long coffee break over there, if you ask me."

Ever since Suzanne had been pinned as the prime suspect in a murder investigation, she had no great love for the local police. Lucy thought far better of their work ethic. They had a hard job and did it well. Though it was clear the investigating teams needed assistance from time to time. She could also understand why it was hard, if not impossible, for them to admit that a knitting group had cracked their case.

Rebecca checked her phone. "I'd better go, I promised my dad I'd be back by nine." She looked at Lucy as she stood and gathered her things. "I'll get in touch with Helen tonight and let you know if she can see us."

"I have no plans," Lucy replied.

"Except for having a baby," Phoebe muttered.

Lucy laughed but didn't reply. She was getting close, but tomorrow seemed unlikely to be Baby Day. She didn't feel a single symptom of labor coming on.

Rebecca thanked everyone and said good night. After she left, the group sat in silence, working on their knitting, and the dessert Phoebe had made for them, a lovely peach pie.

"That was a masterful job of research, Lucy," Suzanne said, spooning up a last bite of peaches. "Your best yet."

"It was indeed," Maggie agreed. "I'm sure Helen Forbes will be impressed."

Lucy glowed under the praise. "I just hope it will convince Detective Reyes that Rebecca is not her target."

"I do wonder how Rebecca didn't know Colin was up to all this nasty stuff. Don't you think the police will find that suspicious?" Suzanne said.

Lucy felt a prickle of concern. "You sound as if you're suspicious, too."

"Of course not. I'm just thinking how this might look to the police. Once they've pegged you as a person of interest, they push the evidence around like letters on a Scrabble board until it spells out the words they want to see."

Maggie frowned. "I'm not sure I get your meaning. And you know how I love to play Scrabble."

"All this hidden dirt about Colin is probably true. But if Reyes thinks Rebecca was aware of it, the detectives might also think Rebecca took advantage of that to kill Colin and blame it on these dangerous connections. This mob-owned construction company, or whoever was behind bribing the Department of Public Works."

"That's possible, I suppose." Maggie pulled a length of yarn from the ball in her yarn holder and turned her work to the other side. "Especially since Rebecca will be the one to bring the information forward."

"And even though her house was broken into, and she also had an incident on the road, no one was really hurt. The police might still think it was all staged," Suzanne added.

"I'm the one bringing the new info forward," Lucy corrected, feeling frustrated by the direction of the conversation. "The police will realize that they should have put these dots together a while ago."

"I'm sorry, Lucy. I didn't mean to get you upset," Suzanne apologized. "Don't pay any attention to me."

"Apology accepted. You don't want a pregnant woman mad at you. It's not a pretty sight."

Suzanne offered a sweet smile. "Nonsense. You're the prettiest mom-to-be for miles. Even when you get all huffy."

Lucy smiled back and felt the rough patch was smoothed over. She tried not to let Suzanne's doubts get under her skin. The saucy brunette didn't have much of a filter on her mouth at times and would be the first to admit it.

Lucy noticed how her other friends had not rushed forward to defend Rebecca, but decided not to dwell on that, either.

She worked on her knitting awhile longer, another blanket for the baby, then felt a wave of fatigue crash over her and could barely stifle a yawn. She hated to be the first to go, but these days she was usually asleep by now on the sofa, as Matt often noted. The snoring part, debatable.

Lucy said good night to her friends and Maggie walked her to the door. "Good luck with Helen Forbes tomorrow. Let us know how it goes." Maggie gave her shoulder a reassuring pat. "She's a very sharp attorney. She'll know how to make the most of what you've uncovered."

"That's what I'm counting on," Lucy said.

Chapter 27

The dogs ran to greet her when she walked in, tails wagging. They knew she gave way more biscuits and treats at night than Matt ever did. But she still believed they loved her, too.

She went straight to the treat jar. Walley circled, like a shark with a wagging tail. Tink sat in her "good dog" pose, squirming for Lucy's attention.

Matt was watching a nature show. Penguins sat on giant eggs in the rough, cold tundra, shifting and fluffing their feathers. They looked very uncomfortable. "The dads sit on the eggs while the mothers forage for food," Matt reported in a serious tone.

"There's a good idea. Remind me to come back as a penguin in my next life . . . actually, if we decide to have more children in this one."

He chuckled and lowered the volume on the TV. "You're home early. Feeling okay?"

She knew he was going to ask her that. She poured some water into the electric kettle and set up a mug for tea. "I'm a little tired. I think I'll just go up to sleep. Rebecca asked me to visit Helen Forbes with her tomorrow morning."

Just after leaving the knitting shop, Lucy had found a text from Rebecca. Helen wanted to see them tomorrow morning, at half past nine. Lucy quickly confirmed it was a good time.

Matt strolled over to the counter and looked over the fruit bowl, then picked out a big orange. "Why is that?"

"I did a little research about what was going on at the Department of Public Works just before Colin left. He may have been involved in a cover-up and graft, which is probably the reason he was murdered."

Matt frowned. She could tell he was a bit confused.

"I know it sounds far-fetched, but the pieces fit. Even Emily Creeder agrees with me."

"It sounds like more than a *little* research, Lucy. That sounds like . . . a thesis."

Lucy felt color rise in her cheeks and tried to hide behind the big mug of tea. "I love poking around on the internet, you know that."

"I think you were a research librarian in another life. I'm just surprised you were poking around about the Essex County Department of Public Works, not about breastfeeding or teething or diaper rash."

Feeling accused of neglecting her maternal duties already, she tried not to be defensive. "I've thoroughly studied those topics. Quiz me, if you like. I even know about colic and thrush. Rebecca really needs help right now. It's urgent."

He sighed and put his arm around her shoulder. "I'm sorry. I know you've memorized those baby books front to back. And I know what a loyal friend you are. I hope Rebecca realizes how lucky she is to have you in her corner."

"She absolutely does." Lucy sipped her tea and frowned. "After Rebecca left the shop, Suzanne seemed to doubt some of Rebecca's story. It made me upset."

"You know Suzanne. She says the first thing that comes into her head."

"I don't mind most of the time. It just got under my skin. She apologized right away, too. It was nothing."

"I'm glad you made up. I've never heard of any of your friends getting into a tiff that lasted more than five minutes." He squeezed her shoulder. "I have to admit, I hope the visit to Rebecca's attorney is the last of it. Let Helen Forbes take over now. I don't want to watch you wheeled into the delivery room searching Google on your laptop."

Lucy wanted to laugh at the suggestion, but his expression was too serious. "Helen is the last stop. I'm only googling baby topics from now on. At least, until my water breaks."

He hugged her tight and kissed her forehead. "Just what I wanted to hear. I'm beat. Let's get up to bed."

Lucy agreed with that suggestion.

The next morning, Lucy didn't have time to give the dogs a long walk. Just a quick loop around the block. Rebecca's Volvo appeared in the driveway a few minutes after nine, and Lucy waved from the window.

Just as she picked up her purse and keys off the kitchen counter, Tink trotted over and butted Lucy's leg with her muzzle, her signal that she wanted to go out again.

"Sorry, honey. You got shortchanged this morning with that skimpy walk, didn't you? Want to go out in the yard?"

Lucy went to the back door and Tink followed, tail wagging, then followed Lucy into the fenced-off section Matt had built as a dog run. Lucy latched the gate securely. She'd only be gone an hour or so. Tink might need a good brushing later, but she'd be fine.

Lucy had heard a lot about Helen Forbes but they had never met. It would have been hard for anyone to live up to Helen's acclaim, but as soon as Helen spun around in her big chair and popped up to shake hands, Lucy felt certain the attorney deserved the high praises and more.

She was not tall, her build almost birdlike, and Lucy guessed her age to be in the early sixties, though her smile and lively manner subtracted years from that number. Her deep voice and confident tone was arresting and a great asset in a courtroom, Lucy imagined. As well as her bold style—her shock of thick white hair, in a short, stylish cut; large, square glasses with a shiny black frame; and a slash of bright red lipstick her only cosmetic.

"Sit down, sit down. Now what is this urgent information you've found?" Helen's tone was that of a person who rarely wastes a minute with small talk.

"Lucy did some research about the Department of Public Works and what was going on there right before Colin left his job," Rebecca explained. "And she's also read Colin's novel."

"The one he was working on when he died?"

"That's right." Rebecca paused and glanced at Lucy. "It's complicated. She needs to explain it."

Lucy took her folder from the canvas tote bag she'd carried in with all her documents. She was suddenly nervous. It was one thing to "report" to her knitting gang, but something altogether different to show and explain what she discovered to an attorney, especially one like Helen Forbes. She suddenly felt like a silly, meddling, bored pregnant woman who had nothing better to do than dream up a kooky, complicated theory about a government coverup. Would Helen laugh at her? Of course not, but she might brush her off in a kind but condescending way. That would be embarrassing enough.

Rebecca leaned over and touched her arm. "Lucy, are you all right? Would you like some water?"

Rebecca and Helen stared at her, waiting. "I'm fine. I just needed a minute to put my thoughts in order," Lucy murmured.

Without glancing up at her audience, she began, focused on the information she'd found and the conclusions she'd arrived at, just as she'd outlined her theory about Colin's actions and the consequences, to her friends the night before.

As she spoke, she passed Helen each of the newspaper articles about the bridge collapse and the investigation and state hearing, and the transcript of the court case brought by the victim's family, and finally, even Colin's manuscript. By the end of her recitation, the pile of paper on Helen's desk was so high, Lucy could barely see the diminutive attorney behind it.

But she could easily hear her. "What a mother lode of research. If you'll excuse the pun, Lucy. I could say a gold mine. But I don't want to get ahead of myself. Truth be told, people who hold political office, even the district attorney, who should be above the fray, find it hard to point a finger at a colleague, even one as crooked as a dog's hind leg. But first things first. I think this is more than enough information to inspire and even oblige Detective Reyes to investigate new leads."

"I hope so," Rebecca said quietly. "I really do."

"I've told you before, dear. If this ever goes to trial— I'm not saying it *ever* will," Helen quickly clarified, "—the prosecution has no chance if the investigating team ignored evidence and viable leads. Whether they like it or not, they're required to follow up."

Helen stood up and rested a manicured hand on the stack of documents. "You leave this to me now." She patted the mother lode. "It's in good hands."

Lucy thought it was, too. She had one more item to pass on and reached into her handbag. Then set a plastic sandwich bag with a thumb drive on top of the printout of Colin's manuscript. "The manuscript was on this thumb drive. The police will probably want that, too, right?"

"Definitely." Helen picked up the bag and looked it over. "Where did you get this?"

"I found it in Colin's bike bag," Rebecca told her. "In the fanny pack he used to carry tools and snacks when he was cycling."

Helen put the little bag down on her desk top. "Interesting." She looked back at Lucy and Rebecca. "I'll call Detective Reyes right away and send this over. I doubt we'll hear anything for a while. I'll keep you posted, Rebecca."

"I'll be waiting. Thank you, Helen." Rebecca rose from her chair.

"Nonsense, I should be thanking you. Especially you, Lucy. Brilliant work," Helen stated flatly. "It was a pleasure to meet you. Good luck with the baby."

Lucy smiled in answer, and nearly laughed out loud, recalling her stage fright. She thanked the attorney for her good wishes and said good-bye, beaming at the compliment as she and Rebecca left Helen's office.

Lucy returned home a few minutes after eleven. The house seemed quiet. Walley trotted toward her, whining, then ran to the back door. Lucy followed at a quick pace. "Need to go out, pal? Don't worry. Here you go . . ." She opened the door, led him to the dog run, and unlatched the gate.

He kept looking back at her, as if trying to tell her something. When the gate was open, he trotted in, barked with alarm and turned to look back at her. "Don't you get it yet?!" his expression seemed to say.

A cold hand gripped her heart. The dog run was empty. Tink was gone.

Lucy felt the world spin around her, her vision hazy. She ran around the yard, peering under bushes even though it was perfectly obvious that Tink was not there.

She looked for holes in the fence, or places where Tink may have dug out, even though she wasn't much of a digger and had never done that before. And how would that help now anyway? Tink was gone!

She marched out into the yard, calling for her. "Tink! Tink? Where are you, you silly girl. Tinnnnkkkk?"

She checked all the golden retriever's hiding places, under the hydrangea and rose of Sharon, even the narrow space behind the shed. She stood in the middle of the yard, short of breath, pulse racing. Tink was gone. Well and truly gone.

She herded Walley back into the house and locked the back door, then grabbed her purse and keys. She dialed Matt as she ran to her car and slipped behind the wheel.

"Matt? . . . It's me . . ."

He was instantly alarmed at her tone. "Is it time? Did your labor start, honey?"

"It's Tink . . ." She tried to keep calm but could barely hold herself together. "I put her in the dog run, just for an hour while I went to town. When I got back, she was gone. I locked the gate. I'm positive."

"All right. I believe you." Matt didn't sound as if he entirely believed her but wasn't going to challenge the story. "And you checked the yard? Under the bushes and behind the shed?"

"I checked everywhere. Honest. I'm going to drive around the neighborhood and look for her. Can you please come home and help me?"

She knew it was next to impossible for her husband to leave his practice most days. The appointments were back-to-back, and his patients needed his attention as much as any human patient needed a doctor, sometimes even more.

"I'm sure that old girl didn't get far. Deep breaths, honey. Try to stay calm. I'll be home in a minute. We'll find her. I promise."

His calm words and knowing he'd soon be back made Lucy feel loads better. "Thank you," she said quietly. "You're right. She can't be far."

After Matt hung up, Lucy steadied herself, then carefully backed the car out of the driveway. Matt was right. They would find Tink soon. She couldn't have gotten far. In fact, she might be on her way home already.

The neighborhood was a grid of streets with beachy-sounding names, like Gull Drive and Shore Road. Lucy started down her street, Pebble Lane, driving slowly so she wouldn't miss spotting her dog.

Tink had never left their property before, even when she wasn't confined in the dog run. Lucy was sure she had locked the gate securely. She had no doubt. She found the whole situation perplexing.

Hours later, she was even more confused. Her slow search of the nearby streets proved fruitless. When she saw anyone walking on the street, or outside their house, she stopped to ask if they'd spotted a golden retriever running loose in the neighborhood. No one recalled seeing Tink. Matt came home and drove around more while Lucy called her friends to report the crisis.

Suzanne, Dana, Maggie, and even Rebecca joined the search, while Phoebe watched the shop. Maggie's husband, Charles, went out to look as well and after six, Phoebe joined, too.

Lucy put notices on Facebook and the neighborhood's

online bulletin board—Our Town. She'd seen loads of posts there for lost pets and, with few exceptions, the dogs, cats, and even birds and guinea pigs were soon found.

Lucy kept checking the notifications. There was much sympathy but no sightings of a golden retriever roaming in the Marshes, or any neighborhood nearby. She wondered how that could possibly be?

Tink was a big dog, as obvious as a big, golden bear. Friendly, with few doggy manners. The merest scent of food would mesmerize her. If she was running through backyards, she'd doubtlessly turn over a few trash pails to search for snacks. Or crash a few family barbeques.

While Matt and her friends searched in their cars, Lucy made a flyer and printed out a stack. Tink's photo was in the middle with Lucy's phone number and the words, "LOST DOG—REWARD!" in big red letters across the top.

She'd added the usual information: Tink's description, her friendly personality, and how she'd do anything for a treat. She and Matt cruised in Matt's truck for another two hours, taping the posters to telephone poles and anywhere else they could think of.

They ate a late dinner of takeout pizza. Lucy could hardly swallow a bite. The sight of pizza crust made her weepy. Tink loved the leftover treat so much, Lucy would stuff the crunchy bits into her chew toy so she couldn't gobble them too quickly.

It was hard to go up to bed, knowing Tink was still out there, but Matt coaxed her up the stairs. "Someone probably took her in to their house and is spoiling her rotten. Someone who hasn't seen our posters or called the police about her."

"Our phone number is right on her name tag. If she was

found, someone would call. She has a microchip. They'd take her to a vet, and we'd be contacted."

"Maybe her collar fell off," Matt speculated. "As for the chip, some people don't think of that right away. Come on, honey. You need your rest." He waited for her to follow him upstairs, but she still resisted. "We'll look again tomorrow, bright and early. I set my alarm for five thirty."

Now he looked worried about her and the baby. He'd worked so hard all day trying to find Tink, she didn't want to stress him about her well-being, too.

Lucy reluctantly went upstairs, got in bed, and shut off the light. Matt was breathing deeply, fast asleep minutes later, but she lay there staring into the dark. She'd close her eyes and see images of poor Tink, wandering in the dark, hungry and cold . . . even though it was at least seventy-five or even eighty degrees out.

She rolled on one side and then the other. Then finally, she slipped out of bed, grabbed her robe, and headed downstairs with a light tread that she hoped would not wake her husband.

She searched her phone for any new responses to her post, but found only more sympathetic dog lovers commiserating and wishing her luck in the search.

Walley had followed her. The chocolate Lab seemed sad and missed his buddy, too. He laid down next to her chair with a grunt, his big head resting on his paws. She leaned over and scratched between his ears, his favorite spot, but he didn't stir.

"She'll come back, Walley. That silly girl will come home. I don't even know how she got out. She has to be some sort of Houdini-dog to unlatch that gate. Unless someone came into the yard and took her out?"

The thought was jarring but totally illogical. Lucy dismissed it. Why would anyone do something that malicious? The notion made her uneasy. Lucy pulled her bathrobe closer around her body, warding off a chill as she pictured Tink led away by a stranger. The sweet dog was so easily won over. All it took was a few biscuits and kind words, and she'd go with anyone.

The disturbing image was the last thing she remembered before she fell asleep in the chair.

Chapter 28

Walley was whining and pawing the front door, no small feat for a dog missing a back leg. Somehow, he kept his balance, yipping with excitement when Lucy woke and opened her eyes.

She sat up slowly. Sleeping in the armchair had left all sorts of kinks in her neck and back. Walley trotted over and poked her with his muzzle, then sat back and barked.

"What is it, pal? Do you have to go out?"

A small lamp on the side table cast a low light, most of the room left in shadow. It was still pitch-black outside, Lucy had no idea of the hour. The dogs rarely bothered her in the middle of the night, unless they were sick.

Panting with excitement, Walley trotted back to the door and Lucy roused herself to help him. Then she heard another bark, this time from out on the porch. She stumbled the last few steps and pulled open the door.

Tink stood staring at her and wagged her tail. She was tied to the porch rail with a strand of nylon cord looped through her collar. She jumped up happily when she saw Lucy and ran to her. Lucy crouched and opened her arms.

"Tink . . . My sweet girl. You're back . . ."

Tink covered Lucy's face with licks, her tail wagging furiously. Lucy wrapped her arms around the big dog and buried her face in Tink's fur, crying with happiness and relief.

Walley had run outside and joined the lovefest, snuffling both of them.

"Lucy? You found Tink?" Lucy turned to find Matt in the doorway, blinking sleep from his eyes. He walked over to pet Tink and was rewarded with more dog kisses.

"Walley woke me up and I found her out here. Someone must have seen our signs and brought her back."

Matt helped Lucy up, then untied the cord from the dog's collar. Tink happily ran inside and Walley followed.

"There's a note attached," Matt said, as he untied the other end from the porch railing.

"I hope they left a phone number. I'd like to thank whoever brought her back." Lucy walked closer to read it with him. "We did promise a reward."

"I don't think that will be necessary." Matt's tone was grim as he held the note out for her to see.

Written on a plain sheet of white paper in black block letters it read:

GOT THE MESSAGE? STAY OUT OF IT, LITTLE MAMA.
THE NEXT TIME YOU WON'T BE SO LUCKY.

Below the message, she found a crude drawing of a skull and crossbones.

She glanced at Matt, feeling a sense of dread. "This is so frightening. Thank goodness she wasn't hurt."

She stared out at the front yard and street, silent yet suddenly ominous. Someone could be out there, she realized, watching them right now.

Matt must have had the same thought. He slung his arm around her shoulder and rushed her through the front door. "Let's get inside. We need to call the police."

* * *

After a morning walk with Matt and Walley, Tink went back to her dog bed and fell into a deep sleep. Lucy watched her snooze as she sipped her breakfast smoothie. The poor girl was exhausted from her ordeal, Lucy thought. She felt tired, too, despite catching a few more hours of sleep after the police officers left. The sun was just coming up by then.

She'd put the word out first thing to her friends that Tink had been found, noting the strange circumstances.

Maggie answered first:

Thank goodness! So happy she's home and unharmed.

Then Dana:

That's the main thing.

Then Phoebe:

The rest is weird and scary!

And finally, Suzanne:

Meet at the Schooner for lunch, everyone? I want a full debrief.

The suggestion was quickly and unanimously approved except for Phoebe, who couldn't leave her market stall. Charles had agreed to watch the shop as long as Maggie closed early so they could go catch a late-afternoon sail.

Lucy was the last to reply:

Moving even slower than usual today, but I'll be there.

One would think that on a bright, summer day most people would be at the beach, golfing, sailing, or tending a garden. Generally doing anything but waiting in line, under the hot sun in front of the Schooner Diner. Lucy marveled how the homey, retro eatery attracted a crowd no matter the season.

Lucy knew that her friends were already inside at a table. Edie Steiber sat at her usual post behind the cash register, like a bouffant Buddha, surveying the wait list. Or maybe like the muscle-bound guy outside a nightclub who gets to decide who gets in and who doesn't? Maggie and her friends were always treated like red carpet VIPs.

Lucy spotted them quickly and made her way to the table. Suzanne jumped up and gave her a hug. "You poor thing! What a fright. I'm surprised the ordeal didn't bring on your labor."

Lucy laughed. "That was *all* we needed last night."

"Suzanne, what a thing to say." Maggie shook her head and held out Lucy's chair. "You do look tired. Sounds as if you hardly slept. You should take a long nap this afternoon."

The suggestion was a good one. Lucy guessed she'd feel extra sleepy after one the Schooner's meals. A waitress came by and delivered an iced coffee to Suzanne and a hot coffee to Maggie.

"Anything to drink, miss?" she asked.

"Just water, thanks," Lucy replied.

"Dana's running late. She said we should order and she'll catch up," Suzanne reported, glancing at her phone. She gave the waitress her order, and Maggie and Lucy did the same.

"What did the police say when you showed them the note?" Suzanne asked once the waitress left. "Have you heard from Detective Reyes yet?"

"The officers who came to the house were concerned. They asked if we had any friction with our neighbors, or any of Matt's patients. I tried to explain what I thought the note meant—whoever took Tink wants me to stop helping Rebecca. But they didn't show much reaction, just took down the information," Lucy recalled. "They did say they would pass our statement and the note to Detective Reyes's team. But I haven't heard anything."

"That's more than annoying." Suzanne seemed upset. "You're obviously being threatened. Just like Rebecca was. It's dangerous."

"I agree." Maggie's tone was quieter, but still concerned. "I think Detective Reyes will be in touch soon. She's probably digging her way through that stack of research you gave Helen Forbes yesterday. Maybe she wants to get a sense of that scenario before she questions you."

"Was that just yesterday?" Lucy shook her head. "It feels likes weeks ago to me."

Maggie smiled mildly and patted her hand. "You've been through a lot in the last twenty-four hours."

"It was awful. I'm just so grateful Tink was returned." Lucy didn't want to talk about Tink's disappearance anymore after her long night of fretting and waiting. But her friends were right. She had to take the message seriously.

Suzanne glanced at Lucy. "What I don't understand is how Tink's dognapper—or the person who hired the dognapper—knew what you'd been up to. Reading Colin's novel, researching his work, and digging up dirt on the Department of Public Works."

"I've wondered about that, too. I can't figure out the link, but I did speak to the department secretary, Hazel Huebner, and someone at the law firm that filed the suit against the county. I suppose someone involved in the cover-up could have a source at either of those places? Even Emily may have mentioned my theory to a colleague at the newspaper, or a friend, and somehow the wrong person got wind of it?"

"Six degrees of separation." Maggie sipped her coffee.

Even on the most scorching summer days, she preferred it hot, never iced.

"What does that mean?" Suzanne stared at her.

"It means that everyone is connected in some way by six other people. If Lucy's reporter friend mentioned her suspicions to a colleague, and they mentioned it to their friend, or romantic partner and so on, it could have reached someone who has an interest in keeping the information buried."

"I get it. But that seems too much of a coincidence." Suzanne met Lucy's glance. "You know that sweet old gal who gave you an earful at the memorial? I bet she knows exactly what went on with that cover-up, and is in it up to her hairpins. I bet she's the one who tipped someone off about you. Like her old boss, George What's-his-name . . ."

"Wexler," Lucy filled in for her.

"That's right, the guy who ran off to South America. I bet she told him, or someone behind the scenes, that you've been asking a lot of questions."

"It was Mexico, but you must be joking." The suggestion seemed laughable to Lucy. Until she gave it more consideration. Had the Red Queen told someone that Lucy was looking into the bridge collapse report and the hearing, a dark chapter for the Department of Public Works that some people might prefer stayed buried and forgotten?

Dana stood at the entrance gazing around and Maggie waved to her. Lucy watched their slim, blond friend weave between the tables, taking care that her rolled-up yoga matt didn't bump into anything.

"Sorry I'm late." She slipped into a chair and slid the matt under the table. "The class went a few minutes longer than usual and Jack called as I was driving over. He heard some news about the investigation."

Lucy sat up, eager to hear the news. "Did the police follow through on the information I found?"

"Yes, they have. In a way," Dana spoke quietly. At first Lucy thought she was just settling down after a rush to meet them. But her expression was somber. "I'm sorry to tell you this, Lucy. The police took Rebecca to the station for more questioning. Jack thinks they'll charge her this time."

Chapter 29

Lucy couldn't believe Dana's declaration. Dana couldn't possibly have the story right. Or maybe, for once, Jack's police station sources were mistaken.

"Charge her for Colin's death? I don't understand. All the information I found pointed in another direction."

Dana took a breath and met Lucy's gaze. "The passcode to Colin's cyber account was on the thumb drive. On the last page of the manuscript. Did you see it? You probably didn't recognize what you were looking at."

Lucy winced. She felt embarrassed. "I never read the last page. Not word for word. I just skimmed the last chapter. I feel terrible for getting Rebecca in trouble. If I'd seen the passcode, maybe Helen wouldn't have given the police the thumb drive."

"From what you told us, you can't be blamed for not reading every last word of that book," Maggie cut in quickly. "Maybe Colin realized how hard it would be for anyone to finish it and knew the last page was the perfect hiding spot."

"He sounds like too much of an egotist to me to be so clear eyed." Suzanne crunched on an ice cube. "I'd say, he didn't think anyone would get their hands on the thumb drive."

"Whether he was hiding it or not, you can't blame yourself for not finding it, Lucy," Dana said. "It's just a string of numbers and symbols and probably looked like a line of random typing that should have been deleted."

"Unless you're an investigator who specializes in cyber currency," Maggie filled in.

"And if you had noticed and realized what it was, you would have been obliged to pass it on to the police, or guilty of withholding evidence. Rebecca and Helen as well," Dana reminded her.

Lucy knew that was true. Was Detective Reyes going to call her in for questioning, too? Lucy didn't want to think about it. With her luck, her labor would start in the middle of the police station and Matt would lose his mind.

"Did the police get into the account?" Suzanne asked. "I'm dying to know how much was stashed away. Even if it is fake money."

Lucy was curious about that, too. Though she guessed the higher the figure, the worse it would be for Rebecca.

"That's just it. The investigators found the account empty. They traced the last transaction, a withdrawal that cleaned out several hundred thousand dollars. They can't tell yet whether the currency was moved to a new account or cashed in. But they do know that the transaction occurred after Colin's death."

Lucy felt her stomach drop, as if she were in an elevator that had skipped a few floors.

"Okay, so someone had the passcode and cleaned out the account," Maggie said quickly. "That still doesn't mean it was Rebecca."

Dana glanced at her. "I'm sure that's what Helen Forbes argued. The problem is the police figured out the IP address of the device that was used to make the last transaction and it was traced to Rebecca's house."

"Slow down, lady. You lost me with the techno-talk," Suzanne said. "What's an IP address?"

"It's like a phone number," Lucy explained. "It's the way devices connect to each other and connect to the internet. If you have a home Wi-Fi network, and practically everyone does these days, it has a specific IP address, and all the devices in your house—phones, computers, TVs, e-readers—have the same one." She glanced at Dana. "I didn't realize the police can narrow down an IP address to a specific house. I thought the closest they could get was a zip code, or even a neighborhood."

"That's the first step. They can get a specific location with more detailed information that can only be collected with a warrant issued by a judge. Which they acquired last night," Dana sighed.

"But Rebecca had no idea the account code was on the thumb drive," Lucy insisted. "I can be a witness to that. I can tell Detective Reyes. She told me she hadn't tried it in a computer and wasn't even sure it would work. The plastic bag only said, SINK HOLE–DRAFT 3."

"Jack said that's not the problem. The police believe she didn't know the code was on the thumb drive and if she had, she wouldn't have passed it to them. They think she already had the code and was lying when she claimed she couldn't find it."

Lucy's head was spinning. She felt frustrated and defeated. She didn't know what to say.

The waitress appeared with their orders and set a turkey BLT in front of Suzanne and a salad in front of Maggie. Lucy had ordered avocado toast but felt sure she couldn't eat a bite.

"Anything for you, ma'am?" the waitress asked Dana.

Before Dana could reply, Lucy said, "Let's share. I've lost my appetite."

Dana replied with a sympathetic look and patted her hand, then looked back at the waitress. "Just some iced tea, please."

"I thought all the information I gave Helen Forbes was going to put Rebecca in the clear. Not give the police the last bit of evidence they needed to charge her with Colin's murder." Lucy covered her face with her hands. "I feel so frustrated, I could cry."

"Oh, Lucy. I'm so sorry I told you all this." Dana gently rubbed Lucy's shoulder. "But I knew you'd find out sooner or later."

Lucy knew that was true. It was best to hear it now, with her friends, who understood what this drastic turn meant to her.

"Do you think Detective Reyes is paying any attention to the bridge failure and the report Colin wrote as a cover-up? And the very good chance that's why he was murdered? Helen Forbes believed me. She didn't say it," Lucy added. "But I can tell she took the information seriously and thought it would be a big help."

"It will help, Rebecca. You'll see," Suzanne encouraged her. "Even if Reyes can prove Rebecca had the code and cleaned out the account, that still doesn't prove she killed Colin. Only that she may have taken advantage of the situation after he died."

"Good point, Suzanne. The investigation must follow up on all these loose ends, Lucy. Or the prosecution's case won't hold up in court."

Lucy hated to hear the information she'd uncovered referred to as "loose ends" almost as much as she hated to imagine Rebecca on trial for this crime. But she held her tongue. Dana was only trying to make her feel better.

She nibbled on her half of the toast, hardly tasting it.

The long vigil of waiting for news about Tink and dozing most of the night in the armchair suddenly caught up. She felt exhausted and sat back with a sigh.

"Are you all right?" Maggie leaned forward with concern.

"I'm just tired. I should probably head home and take that nap you prescribed."

"I can take you," Dana offered. "You can come back to town later with Matt and pick up your car," she suggested.

Before Lucy could reply, Dana's phone buzzed with a text. She picked it up and checked the message.

"It's an update from Jack. He just heard that Nick Russo went down to the station and confessed to Colin's murder." Dana looked up at her friends, her complexion pale. "I have to admit, I didn't see that coming."

"Nick? The handsome, hot chef killed Colin? Geez." Suzanne sounded stunned. "I guess it makes sense in a way, but I hate to see him go down for the crime, even if he really did it."

"What do you think, Lucy?" Dana asked.

"I'm surprised, too. But when I think about it, not so surprised," she admitted. "I told you about the argument I saw the night we were at the café. A few hours before Colin was killed, it turned out. Little did we realize," she noted. "When Nick confronted Colin, he literally put himself between Rebecca and her angry husband. Like a wall," Lucy recalled. "Maybe he went back to the café that night to talk to Colin about the way he treated Rebecca and things got out of hand?"

"And a bookcase tipped over and crushed his romantic rival?" Suzanne finished for her. "Hmmm . . . not exactly self-defense. Or even a believable accident. As much as I like the guy."

"I guess I agree. It's going to be hard for the chivalrous

chef to convince the police Colin's death had been an accident. But perhaps he can convince them it wasn't intentional?"

Dana sighed and sat back. She hadn't eaten much of her half of the sandwich, either, Lucy noticed. "The question is, 'Can he convince the police he did it at all?' " She glanced at Lucy. "You've never said it out right, but I think you've hinted that there's an attraction, or affection of some kind, between Rebecca and Nick. And the police have a video of him comforting her behind the restaurant that very night," Dana recalled. "My feeling is that the police will speculate Nick is confessing to get Rebecca off the hook. Or, that they planned Colin's death together, but Nick is willing to take the blame."

Lucy hadn't thought of it that way. Mainly because she so sincerely trusted in Rebecca's innocence. She couldn't deny Dana's viewpoint made sense, but she refused to believe it was true.

"You'll probably read this in the newspaper tomorrow, so I guess it's no big deal if I tell you now." Her friends gave Lucy their full attention, eyes alight with curiosity. "Nick Russo was an accountant before he became a cook. He went to prison for falsifying financial records in order to plump up a firm's assets and make it look more attractive to a buyer."

"Interesting," Dana said. "The police will try to use that against him, but erasing some numbers in the loss column on a spreadsheet is hardly the same as murdering someone."

"That's what I thought, at first. But his defense was that a woman he was in love with persuaded him to do it, in order to help her family, who owned the company." Lucy paused. "Now, he's confessing to Colin's murder, and we think the only reason he may have done it is to protect Rebecca."

"I get your point." Suzanne had initially cut off the crusts from her sandwich, but now nibbled on them nervously. "Sounds like Nick's noble instincts keep getting him in trouble. And maybe even jail."

"I think he has a gallant streak, but I don't think he did it," Lucy said flatly. "I don't believe either Rebecca or Nick was involved in Colin's death."

Her friends replied with sympathetic glances, but none spoke up to agree, she noticed.

"Either way, his confession . . . or fake confession . . . is a game-changer," Maggie said. "What now?"

Lucy could tell by her tone the latest news had also shaken her.

"We can only wait and see. The police might hold Nick and release Rebecca," Dana suggested.

Or charge both of them, Lucy added silently. But she wouldn't voice that thought. The possibility was too chilling.

Chapter 30

Tink barked happily as Lucy walked through the front door. Lucy felt relieved at the sight of her, and then silly for the reaction. Thankfully, the big dog seemed untouched by her ordeal, though Lucy still felt a bit traumatized.

The house was quiet. Matt was at work, and Dara was with her mother and stepfather. Lucy didn't mind the solitude. She gave both dogs a break in their yard, then settled on the couch with a thick baby book.

She'd almost reached the end of the instructive tome and wanted to finish by the time the baby arrived. But she felt too distracted to focus on the text, worrying about what would happen to Rebecca.

Did the police really have enough evidence to charge her with Colin's death? It sounded as if they were getting dangerously close, but maybe, Lucy prayed, not there yet?

Her thoughts went back to Maggie's comment about six degrees of separation, and she wondered how the dots connected from Tink's dognapping and even the break-in at Rebecca's house, to the misdeeds at the Department of Public Works. Was Hazel Huebner a two-faced queen?

Keira Nesbit had convinced Lucy that she'd been both unaware and uninvolved with Colin's bad deeds and any wrongdoing at the department. But maybe that was not the case. She insisted that she had no contact with any of her former coworkers. But after their meeting on the beach maybe Keira had reported Lucy's fumbling inquiries to someone in the shadows.

Like George Wexler? He was the only figure in the fog Lucy's imagination could conjure. She felt foolishly remiss now for ignoring his part in the story. But he was a key player. At the very top of the food chain. He had given Colin the job of writing the report and drawn him into the cover-up, and long before that, Wexler had awarded the bridge contract to some shoddy construction firm in exchange for a payoff. Wexler could still have contacts in the area. Or could have even returned to the country without Hazel or Keira knowing. Or maybe they did know and hid that information as well?

Lucy opened her laptop and searched the internet and social media for any sign of him. She only found old references, from his tenure in county government, which was frustrating. Just before she was about to close the computer, she searched for Hazel Huebner. Her profile came up quickly on Facebook. She opened the list of Hazel's friends and looked them over carefully. Hazel had mentioned that George came back to New England for a visit in the early spring, when his daughter had a baby. Down at the bottom of the list of over a hundred of Hazel's "friends" Lucy found the photo of a smiling young woman named Jeanine Wexler-Ryan.

She quickly searched for Jeanine's page and looked over the posts and photos – about a million that featured a newborn baby, named Avery. Lucy felt vaguely annoyed at the name choice. Avery was one of her top three. Was it really so common?

Photos of little Avery with her Mom and Dad, with just her Mom . . . and just her Dad. Many of baby Avery alone,

looking cute in different outifts and with the family dog, a
Golden-Doodle named Dixie. A few with doting Grandma
Irene and Pappa Tom. And finally, Avery snuggled in the
arms of a man identified as "Grandpa George."

The photo with Grandpa George had been taken in
early May, weeks before Colin's death. Lucy was disappointed to see that the timing did not overlap. That would
have been too easy.

"George, did you sneak in and out of the country, flying
under the radar of your old aquaintances, is that it?" she
asked aloud. George Wexler did not answer, though after
she asked the question she knew that if she'd passed him
on the street, she would have never noticed or remembered. A benign looking man, he was tall and thin with a
long face, bald head, and thick wire rimmed glasses that
were hopelessly out of date. Hardly a murderer, or even a
corrupt county employee. Was George behind Colin's life
threatening bicycle accident and his gruesome death at the
café? And the break-in at Rebecca's house and her own
road rage incident?

Would the police take any stock in the accusation? Especially now, when they believed they had the goods on
Rebecca. Lucy felt deflated and frustrated.

She picked up her phone, wondering if Leo had any
news. But she didn't want to bother him. Considering his
illness and frailty, the pressure he was under right now
was practically life-threatening.

Instead of calling, she sent a text:

**Just wondering if there's any update about Rebecca, or
Nick? Call or text anytime. Please let me know if you need
help with Sophie. Home now and will be here all evening.**

As if sensing Lucy's distress, Tink trotted over and
rested her head in Lucy's lap. Lucy smiled and softly
stroked her head. "You're a regular therapy dog. We need
to get you certified."

Lucy's eyes closed, her hand resting in the dog's soft fur. A short nap was a good idea, she reasoned as she drifted off. Perhaps when she woke up there would be news about Rebecca.

Good news, she hoped.

Lucy woke to a sharp knock on the front door. The sound set both dogs into a barking fit and a race to the foyer. She pushed herself up off the couch and found her sandals. No small feat in her condition.

"Just a minute," she called out.

The house was filled with the golden light of late afternoon, and Lucy realized she'd slept a long time. Much longer than she'd intended.

Walley hung back as she opened the door, but Tink pushed forward and Lucy held fast to her collar. The golden retriever was usually too friendly for her own good, as proven yesterday when she allowed someone to take her from the backyard.

But lately, she'd become very protective, as if she knew that her mistress was in a vulnerable state. Especially when delivery or repair people came to the door; the dog not only barked but would even growl. Lucy doubted she'd ever hurt anyone, but never wanted to take that chance.

Lucy slowly opened the door to find Rebecca's father. She was glad to see him. "Leo, did you get my text?"

"I did." He nodded, his white beard brushing his T-shirt, one of the many he owned that was decorated with the faded logo of a 1970s rock band. "Can you watch Sophie awhile? I'm sorry, but I don't know how long it will be. I'm going down to the police station to see if I can help Rebecca. I'll sit there all night if I have to."

Tink tugged on Lucy's hold, trying to sniff Leo. Lucy pulled her back. "Have you heard anything? Are they charging Rebecca? How long can they keep her there if they don't have any evidence?"

"I'm not really sure. They think she knew the code to Colin's account and claim that she lied in her signed statements and obstructed the investigation. I don't know how they can prove it, but I'm worried. These things can snowball . . ."

He looked pale and distressed, glancing up at Lucy as he spoke, but seemed to be talking to himself in a way, too. Lucy's heart went out to him. She saw Sophie in the front seat of his van, using her cell phone. Dara would be home soon to keep her company. Perhaps they were already talking to each other.

"Sophie can stay for as long you need her to," Lucy said. "Dara will be home any minute and . . ."

Tink lunged forward and Leo stepped back, looking alarmed. Lucy wasn't sure what she was up to but didn't wait to find out.

But as Lucy pulled the dog back, Tink's tail wagged and she sat, in her "good dog" position. She stared up at Leo hopefully, waiting for a treat.

Leo stared back at her, then up at Lucy. "Dogs love me, I don't know what it is."

Tink pawed his leg and whined, then resumed her best begging pose.

Lucy remembered what Matt had said that morning, after she'd found the missing hound tied to the porch. "Too bad she can't tell us who took her. Or at least describe her dognapper."

Lucy had laughed at the time. But wasn't Tink telling her who it was right now?

"Of course Tink likes you, Leo . . . You fed her a lot of treats yesterday, didn't you?"

Wide-eyed with shock, he looked about to feign confusion, or deny the accusation. His gaze shifted from Lucy to the dog, and he sighed. He looked too tired to keep up the pretense.

"You're a smart woman. Rebecca always says that."

The compliment wasn't a comfort. She'd been partly shooting in the dark but had hit a bull's-eye.

"I think I know why you did it. The same reason you ransacked Rebecca's house, acting as if you were attacked, too, and even chased her car on a motorcycle. To convince the police that there's someone out there responsible for Colin's death. Someone who wants to keep your son-in-law's secrets buried."

Leo nodded and rubbed his beard. "Someone else *is* responsible. Rebecca is completely innocent," he insisted. "I knew Colin better than she did. I'd hear him on the phone when he thought no one was listening. I knew he was up to no good, lying to Rebecca, hiding money, disrespecting her and their marriage in just about every way a man could."

He looked back at Lucy. "I'm her father. Can you imagine what it was like for me to stand by and watch that? He didn't abuse her physically. But in every other way, I'd say."

His tone was low but vehement, the force of his words causing a sudden coughing fit. He leaned aside and covered his mouth with his hand.

It was the venom of his words that convinced her. But she waited until he'd caught his breath. "Can I get you some water, Leo? Maybe some hot tea?"

He shook his head and raised a large, callused hand. "I'll be fine. I just need to get my breath. I'd better get over to the station."

Lucy caught his gaze and held it. "To wait for Rebecca to be released? . . . Or tell the police something that will convince them to release her?"

She could hardly believe the question had left her lips, and watched his reaction.

"Who killed Colin, you mean? Gee whiz—if only I knew." He laughed nervously.

"But you won't let Rebecca or even Nick Russo be charged for the crime. That's why you'll stay in the station all night, waiting to hear what Detective Reyes and the DA decide to do, right?"

Leo stared into her eyes about to reply, then looked down at his boots.

"I might not wait that long, sitting on a hard bench for hours. I'm too old and weary for that routine. Besides, what's the point? It will be better for everyone if I go right in and say my piece." He looked back up at Lucy. "You know what I mean."

Lucy's mouth went dry, her pulse pounding. "Yes, I do," she said simply.

Leo covered his face with his hand, his expression suddenly crumpling. He tried to hide his tears but couldn't.

"I did it for Rebecca. My little girl. I never protected her when she was young. I took off and left her, like a real loser. She grew up so independent and strong. When I tracked her down she forgave me. I know I didn't deserve it, but that's who she is. I'm busting with pride every time I get to say she's my daughter, though I can't take a grain of credit for the way she turned out."

He pulled a bandana from his pocket and wiped his bloodshot eyes. Lucy didn't dare interrupt him.

"This was my chance to take care of her. My one chance. I did what I had to do. Colin was no good. A liar, a cheat. I knew what he was up to. I knew the whole deal. Overheard him on the phone late at night at the café, when I was cleaning up.

"I knew he was in trouble, right after that motorcycle nearly turned him into roadkill. I knew he was making plans to run, too. 'Good riddance to bad rubbish,' I said. 'Rebecca will be well rid of him. She'd find someone new, a man who really loves her and thanks his lucky stars that he has my daughter. Not like this self-centered bum.' Then Colin told Rebecca he was taking Sophie. No visiting, no contact. No nothing. The heartless SOB." Leo paused and took a deep, wheezing breath, squinting at her with small blue eyes. "That would have broken Rebecca's heart in a million pieces, and my granddaughter's heart, too. That little girl adores Rebecca. She's the only mother Sophie has ever known. It would have cast a shadow over their lives forever. How could either of them ever be truly happy after that? Something in me snapped. I couldn't let that happen. Not while I had breath left in this sorry sack of bones. I had to stop it. I had to protect Rebecca any way I could."

Lucy could not condone Leo's decision, but she couldn't argue with his conclusion, either. If Colin had carried out his plan to leave the country and taken Sophie with him on the run, he would have inflicted lifelong emotional pain on both his wife and daughter.

Before she could ask any more questions, Leo said, "I'm sorry that I scared you yesterday, Lucy. I know you went the limit to help Rebecca get out of this jam. That's on me. I thought I had it all figured out. I never guessed it would boomerang back on her the way it did. I had to keep creating diversions, not that the police took the bait much." Leo shook his head, his expression remorseful. "Why the heck did she go back to the café that night? That messed up everything."

Because he had planned an alibi for her, calling her to pick him up at the urgent care center far from the scene of Colin's murder, Lucy guessed he meant.

"I tried to do one fatherly deed, but I screwed that up,

too. I'll step up and take what's coming. It doesn't matter. You must have heard from Rebecca that I'm a dead man walking? I can't even stop sucking on these cancer sticks." He offered a brief tobacco-stained grin and patted the pack of cigarettes in his shirt pocket. "I'm just grateful I made it this far. Every day I open my eyes is gravy."

Lucy felt stunned. Before she could find the words to answer him, Matt's truck pulled up to the house. The side door flew open and Dara flew out. Sophie had spotted her from Leo's van and the two girls met on the front lawn in a smothering, BFF hug.

Leo's face softened in a smile as he looked on. "I'd better go. A task begun is half-done, and all that."

"My friend Maggie always says that."

"Because it's true." Leo took another long, steadying breath. "Thanks again for watching Sophie."

"She'll be fine. Please don't worry."

"You don't need to worry about Rebecca, either. Or Nick Russo," Leo promised. "It's going to be okay."

Not for Leo, Lucy knew. But he seemed at peace with the choices he'd made.

She watched Leo walk out to the front yard and he spoke to Sophie in a soft voice a few moments and then hugged her. His eyes were squeezed shut and he was crying again, but he forced a smile as they parted and headed for his van with a cheery wave.

"Catch you later, sunshine. Your mom will be back soon to pick you up. Don't worry."

Sophie stood next to Dara, a pink backpack dangling from one hand as she waved goodbye with the other. "Bye, Grandpa. See you later," Lucy heard her call out.

Lucy felt a lump in her throat. When would Sophie see her grandfather again? He wouldn't be back to Rebecca's tonight. Not ever again, most likely.

Matt came up the porch steps as Leo's van disappeared down the street. He kissed Lucy's cheek. "Hey, sweetie, how's it going? Any news about Rebecca?"

During the day, Lucy had told Matt that both Rebecca and Nick were being held for questioning at the police station and would possibly be charged.

"There's a lot to catch you up on. But it might have to wait. I don't want the girls to hear us," she said in a hushed tone.

Matt's brows jumped up. "Did the police figure out who killed Colin?" he whispered.

"Not yet. But . . . I just did."

Chapter 31

Lucy was in touch with her friends with text messages on Saturday night and into Sunday. Just as Leo predicted, Rebecca and Nick were soon released. Sophie had a sleepover with Dara, and Lucy saw Rebecca on Sunday. Rebecca couldn't speak at first and hugged Lucy for a long time. Rebecca was obviously relieved she'd been released. But even though one phase of her ordeal was over, another had just begun.

Lucy didn't ask questions or press Rebecca for anything more than she wanted to disclose. She knew that her friend would tell her everything when she was ready. All Rebecca needed now was sympathy and support. She was still reeling from her father's confession and could barely face what he would endure next.

Monday was the first chance Lucy and her friends could find to get together and they made a plan to meet early at Maggie's shop. Phoebe usually slept in on Monday after working hard at the market all weekend, but even she set an alarm so she'd be downstairs in time.

Suzanne and Dana were already sitting on the porch when Lucy arrived. Maggie was tending the flower boxes, deadheading the petunias, geraniums, and some small blue flowers that Lucy didn't know the name of.

"Hey, everybody. You beat me." Lucy climbed up on the porch. She held the handrail for balance and let her dogs pull her up that last few steps. Her body was so heavy and awkward, she felt like a round-bottom toy that keeps popping up when it's pushed down.

"Did you walk all the way from home this morning?" Maggie pulled off her garden gloves and rushed to meet her. "I'm not sure that was wise."

Lucy plopped into a wicker chair and Maggie handed her a glass of ice water. "I feel great. I slept like a rock. I went to bed at nine and woke up at seven."

"Better note that in your diary. It won't happen again for a long time," Suzanne warned.

"*Once the baby comes*, you mean?" Lucy said, beating her to the usual punch line.

Dana sat sipping a green smoothie as she worked on her knitting. She looked cool and professional, dressed for office hours in a tan linen skirt and a pale blue blouse. "You needed a good rest after everything you went through this weekend. First Tink, and then Leo. No wonder you were exhausted."

Before Lucy could reply, Phoebe stumbled out of the shop in her pajamas, a black tank top, and pink shorts covered with yellow smiley faces. Her dark hair was bunched to one side in a bun, the blue streak swirled all around.

Holding a big mug of coffee, she greeted Lucy with a sleepy smile. "Hey, Lucy. What did I miss?"

"Nothing juicy yet. I guess I'll start with Leo's visit."

Suzanne put her phone aside and gave Lucy her full attention. "How did you get him to spill his guts? That's what I want to hear."

"Tink gets most of the credit. She was the first to sniff him out."

The dog rested at Lucy's feet, working on a chew toy, but suddenly looked up, as if she knew that she was being discussed.

Lucy explained how Tink had become protective during her pregnancy but acted so familiar with Leo it was suspicious. To the point of going into her "See what a good dog I am?" position and pawing him for a treat.

"She only does that with me and Matt, and not even Matt so much. She never does it to a stranger."

Lucy paused, thinking back to her conversation with Leo. "Once I got him to admit that he'd taken Tink on Friday, the rest of the tale tumbled out."

"So, he planned Colin's murder. It wasn't an accident?" Maggie asked.

Lucy dipped a tissue into the cold water and patted her forehead. It was warmer out than she realized, and the walk to town was more exertion than she expected.

"He didn't go into specific details, but he did say he knew that Colin was in trouble and going on the run. Leo didn't mind that at all. But once Colin decided to take Sophie with him, Leo said he 'snapped.' He couldn't let him do that to Rebecca. He felt guilty for abandoning his family when Rebecca was a little girl and felt compelled to make it up to her."

"By killing his son-in-law?" Suzanne's dark eyes were wide. "I know a lot of fathers don't like the guy their daughter brings home, but this was . . . extreme."

Phoebe was curled in a big wicker chair, sipping her coffee. "I can hardly believe it, either. Leo looks like this sweet old hippie folk singer dude. With his Grateful Dead T-shirts and all that. What happened to peace, love, and understanding? Did he at least seem sorry about what he did?"

"I can't recall that he ever expressed remorse about killing Colin," Lucy said honestly. "He was only sorry that his plan hadn't worked out. He never intended for Rebecca to become a suspect. He never expected her to go back to the café. He'd worked out an alibi for her by pretending to have chest pains and checking into the urgent care that was up near Newburyport."

Maggie was working on the last flower box, picking off dead blossoms and carefully watering. She looked up with a curious expression. "I'm sorry, but I don't understand the timing. Had Leo already killed Colin when he went to the urgent care? How could that be?"

Lucy glanced at Dana. "Good point, I'm not sure. Did Jack hear how Leo explained the sequence of events to the police?"

"He did. It's rather clever, too." Dana sat back and put her knitting aside. "Leo never saw a doctor at the urgent care. It was his friend Alfie, his singing partner. They look so much alike it was easy for Alfie to use Leo's ID and feign chest pains while Leo was at the café. In and out quickly, tipping the bookcase. A security video from the urgent care—that police checked just this weekend—shows that Leo met Rebecca in the parking lot and never went inside."

"So, her alibi was meant to be that she was on the way to meet her father and couldn't have killed Colin," Suzanne said, working it out aloud. "Meanwhile, she'd gone to the café and may have even been sitting in her car when Leo was there, too. About to go in to kill her husband."

"That's right. Their paths may have crossed that night," Dana replied. "If she had worked up the nerve to go inside the café, she would have found Colin dead. Or maybe even found Leo there, in the act."

Maggie shuddered as she took a seat. "That's a shocking thought."

"Leo told the police he'd planned everything. Even

shutting off the security camera behind the café," Dana added. "The problem was that later, a video from that camera would have proven Rebecca never left her car."

"What about that break-in at her house?" Maggie asked.

"Another maddening glitch for Leo," Dana said. "He told the police he did stage the break-in as they'd suspected. Alfie helped again, striking Leo on the head and tying him up."

"Did Leo chase Rebecca off the road with the motorcycle?" she asked Dana.

"He claims that he did. He doesn't look fit enough, but it's amazing what the mind can make the body do, if the motive is urgent enough," Dana replied.

"I bet the police had their doubts when he walked in and told them he also wanted to confess to Colin's murder," Maggie said. "After Nick Russo had done the same thing."

"Right, take a number, fella." Phoebe rolled her eyes.

"I'm sure they did, but his confession must have been compelling. He knew so much about Colin's secret life, too," Lucy recalled. "And his plans to leave the country."

"He also knew about Colin's cyber currency account and where Colin had hidden the password, in addition to the last page of his novel," Dana added.

"*Where?*" her friends asked in a shocked chorus.

"In a cycling shoe, tucked under the foot bed pad. A slip of paper no larger than the message in a fortune cookie. Leo told the police that he withdrew everything after Colin died and hid it in another cyber account that he opened for that purpose" Dana continued. "He intended to give the money to Rebecca after the smoke cleared and truly believes it was small compensation for the pain Colin had put her through. He admitted he'd jumped the gun on that move but was worried someone in Colin's shadowy past knew about the stash and would beat him to it. He never expected the police to solve that part of the puzzle."

"But they did. Thanks to me," Lucy added. "Ironically, that turned out to be the piece that gave Detective Reyes enough evidence to charge Rebecca." Lucy was about to say more but paused to take a deep breath.

The glass of ice water she'd gulped down set off a flurry of baby kicks. She felt a cramp in her stomach and got up to walk it off.

Suzanne watched her curiously, but Lucy ignored her stare. Her back hurt a little and she rubbed it with her hand.

"Leo also came prepared to convince the police of his confession," Dana added, as she turned her work to start a new row. "He'd used the screwdriver on his Swiss Army knife to loosen the rusted bolts on the bookcase and had saved it in a plastic bag, in case he ever needed it as evidence to prove he was the culprit. Maybe he did consider that Rebecca might be accused and it was his insurance? The forensic lab easily matched the microscopic rusty bits on Leo's knife to the scratches in the bolts. And he gave them some other details of that night that only Colin's killer could have known."

"I guess he realized he might not get away with it. Despite the dirty deeds Colin had been up to. There was someone really after him, who chased him down on his bike, right?" Suzanne asked.

"That was real," Lucy nodded. "One can only guess that whoever was after Colin is still out there, too. Just before Leo dropped by, I had this sinking feeling that George Wexler was behind Colin's murder. If not personally, then definitely connected, and we'd totally overlooked him as a suspect. Even if that's not the case, Wexler may have been connected to the attempt on Colin's life. Or knows who wanted Colin out of the way. He may not be guilty of murder, but Wexler has plenty to account for.

"Even if he's not guilty of Colin's murder, he is probably responsible for the death of Connie Delgado, the woman who died in the bridge collapse," Suzanne reminded them. "So what the heck is happening with that? Isn't someone going to follow up on your amazing research?" she asked Lucy.

"It hasn't been officially announced but sounds like the county supervisor and DA will open an investigation of the Department of Public Works," Dana said.

"You heard it first right here, folks," Phoebe followed up in a news announcer's voice.

"And what about Leo?" Maggie asked. "Since he's made a full confession, he must be in jail, waiting to be sentenced."

"That's unclear," Dana replied. "He confessed but hasn't entered a plea. Helen Forbes is representing him, and Leo might plead that emotional distress due to his concern about Rebecca drove him to kill Colin. The charge could be lowered from first degree to manslaughter."

"It will still be years behind bars," Lucy said. "He told me he had nothing to lose because his days are numbered. Will they really toss a frail old man with heart failure in prison?"

"I've heard that there are nursing home facilities in the corrections system," Maggie said. "Maybe he'll end up somewhere like that, where he can get medical care."

"Speaking of silver is the new orange, what about Alfie?" Suzanne asked. "Was he charged with anything?"

"Only obstructing the investigation by helping Leo stage the break-in," Lucy replied. "Both he and Leo claimed that Alfie had no idea Leo was going to kill Colin that fateful night, when Alfie faked Leo's identity at the urgent care center. And the police couldn't prove that Alfie knew of Leo's plan. All Leo told him was that he needed a favor, so that he could help Rebecca."

"Will Alfie go to jail?" Phoebe asked. Lucy could tell she felt sorry for him.

"He's been put on house arrest due to his own health problems and the judge ordered him to do some community service."

Phoebe smiled, looking relieved. "That's not so bad."

"No, it's not. All things considered." Lucy tried to smile back but couldn't manage it. She'd paced the length of the porch, her hands pressing her sore back. She felt a stronger cramp and paused to suck in a breath.

"I'd never approve of what Leo did, but if you'd heard him explain what moved him to do it . . ." Lucy's voice trailed off. "I guess I feel sorry for him. Maybe I shouldn't."

"It sounds to me as if he was desperate to compensate for deserting Rebecca when she was a little girl," Dana offered. "That's a big bucket to fill. I'm not sure it's possible."

Lucy agreed with Dana's view. "The sad and ironic thing is, Rebecca forgave him and loved him anyway. She never needed him to make up for the past or prove he could be a good father. She was shocked and heartbroken when she heard what he done . . ."

Lucy meant to say more but had to suck in a breath as a sharp pain cut across her belly. She rested her hand on her baby bump and winced.

"Uh-oh . . . I've been watching you, Madam. Looks like something's cooking." Suzanne rose and placed a firm hand on Lucy's back to support her. "Want to sit down or walk? I suggest walking," she added before Lucy could reply. "It helps a lot when you're in labor."

Lucy met Suzanne's steady, dark gaze. "I am not—" Another twinge, not quite as bad, cut off her denial. She squeezed her eyes and let it break over her like an ocean wave.

"Oh dear . . . is anyone timing this?" Maggie jumped up and tried to find the timer on her cell phone, but dropped it on the floor.

Dana stood on Lucy's other side and checked her pulse. "How long have you been feeling the pains, Lucy?" she asked quietly.

Lucy shrugged. "Oh, I don't know. I woke up sort of crampy, but thought I'd slept in a funny position. And I felt a few pangs on the way here," she recalled. "But I was walking uphill and didn't pay much attention to it."

"Well, we need to pay attention to it now," Maggie said in a decisive tone. "I think you should call your doctor. See what she says, though I bet she tells you to get over to the hospital."

Despite the cramps that were lasting longer and feeling stronger, Lucy still couldn't get her mind around the reality of the moment.

"How can I be going into labor? Everyone says first babies are late."

Phoebe was upset, her eyes wide, her long hair falling loose from its clip. "I was, like, six weeks early and weighed less than a burrito. You need to get to a hospital, Lucy, or I'm going to boil hot water and gather up clean rags, like they do in the movies."

"Calm down, Phoebe. We're not quite at that stage," Maggie calmly admonished her. Then to Lucy she said, "I'm sure if we put our heads together, we could deliver your baby. But I doubt Matt would like that."

"No, he wouldn't," Lucy agreed.

Dana had found Lucy's phone and opened the list of her favorite contacts. She hit Matt's number and handed Lucy the phone.

He picked up on the first ring. "Hey, honey. What's up?"

"I'm at Maggie's shop," she managed. "I think . . . it's time."

He answered in a rush of questions. "Are you sure? Did you call Dr. Gupta? Did the pains start?"

"It's time!" her friends shouted behind her in a chorus.

Suzanne moved closer to the phone. "You'd better get over here pronto, buddy. This is not a dress rehearsal."

Matt replied in a mere squeak. "I'm on my way . . ."

Chapter 32

"She's perfect," Lucy's hushed words were edged with giddy excitement. "Look at those tiny fingers . . . and her little toes?" Lucy quickly tugged the edge of the flannel blanket over the baby's bare foot, though the hospital room was the perfect temperature. "I can't believe she's really here."

"Neither can I. I'm, like . . . dumfounded." Matt hovered over the bed as the baby slept soundly, snuggled across Lucy's chest. "Look at those eyelashes. And that tiny curl."

"It's not so tiny for a baby. It's enough for a little bow," Lucy murmured. She lifted her hand but dared not touch the soft honey-blond tuft that sprouted on the baby's downy head.

Matt smiled into her eyes and kissed her on the forehead. "You did a great job last night. I was sort of a mess. I forgot everything we learned in the class."

He had been sort of a mess, but Lucy had barely noticed. "You were there, cheering me on. We brought her into the world together, that's what counts."

Matt squeezed her hand but didn't reply. He wasn't the sort of man who was ashamed to cry, but his eyes had glazed over with tears more in the last twenty-four hours than all the time she'd known him.

"What should we call her?" he asked finally.

"Strawberry Crumpet. That's what she looks like to me," Lucy observed. "But I don't think that will work out for the long run. She doesn't look like any of our top three girls' names, either," Lucy mused, recalling the list. "Avery, Carrie, Serena?" She glanced at him. "What do you think?"

Matt shook his head and offered an indulgent smile. "You did all the hard work last night. You choose her name."

Having a baby had not been any picnic, but the most worthwhile effort she'd ever made, Lucy reflected. Despite the initial excitement, there had been no danger of giving birth in the knitting shop. Her labor had lasted several hours.

Long enough for her mother to fly in from Colorado and make it to the hospital just as Lucy was wheeled into the delivery room. Isabel had been allowed to visit Lucy in the recovery area, right after the baby was born, and greeted her daughter with tearful joy and a large stuffed dinosaur.

"I just met my new granddaughter. She's breathtaking. I love her to the moon and back already . . . just like I love you, sweetheart," she reminded Lucy with a hug.

Lucy had considered naming the baby after her mother, if they had a girl. But Isabel was not one of Matt's favorites. She thought it was sweet of him to let her decide, but she wouldn't pick a name he didn't care for.

"What about Charlotte? I've always liked that name."

He took a moment to consider it. "Charlotte, huh? I never thought of it . . . but it's interesting."

"And classic, in a way," Lucy pointed out. "And we can

call her Charlie as a nickname, if she likes, so it's not too formal or girlie?"

Matt leaned closer and gently touched the baby's index finger. "Hey, little one, what do you think of the name, Charlotte? Do you like that handle?"

The baby squirmed a bit, but with eyes still shut grabbed his finger.

He chuckled quietly. "I think that's a yes. What a grip! She's going to be a real athlete. Tennis, maybe? Or golf?"

Lucy had to smile at his excitement, a sudden vision of the years ahead unfurling before her like a long ribbon, a sunny road, that they'd travel together.

"Here she comes! Her royal babyness, Princess Charlotte!" Suzanne stood at the top of the porch steps, heralding the baby's arrival as she busily snapped photos with her cell phone. Or maybe she was taking a video? "Her first visit to the shop!" Suzanne said, meeting Lucy at the bottom of the steps.

Dana, Maggie, and Phoebe had been waving and calling out greetings from the porch. They quickly ran down the steps and surrounded the stroller.

Lucy wasn't sure how the baby would react to her enthusiastic fans. She peered over the edge of the stroller hood. Charlotte was so quiet, she guessed she was asleep. But the baby calmly stared back, sucking on her fist, unfazed by the reception.

Dana stared into the stroller, beaming. "She's completely adorable. I could eat her up."

"With a spoon," Maggie agreed.

"I love her outfit. I'd love to find some rompers printed with rubber ducks." Lucy thought Phoebe was joking, until she saw her serious expression. Phoebe glanced up at her. "Cute hairdo, too," she added.

Lucy smiled. "Her hair is growing like crazy. She was ready for a bow."

"I see Tink and Walley got dressed for the occasion as well," Maggie remarked, eyeing the dogs who stood calmly on either side of their new baby's chariot.

Lucy rolled her eyes and laughed. "Silly, right? I thought it would be fun to fuss them up a little."

She'd tied a big pink fabric flower to Tink's collar, one that she'd saved from Charlotte's many baby gifts. Walley wore a white shirt collar and bowtie, left over from a Halloween costume. She could never persuade him to keep the top hat on for long.

"How was the walk? Any unexpected speed bumps?" Maggie sounded as if she'd expected a call asking for help at any minute this morning.

"One surprise, but we handled it." Lucy had practiced wheeling the jogging stroller with the two dogs attached around her neighborhood for the past few weeks and had finally felt ready to venture all the way to town.

Tink did spot a cat, which pulled them off course with a surprising lurch, but Lucy managed to get them back on track quickly.

"Let's get that baby up on the porch," Dana suggested. "So we can fuss over her in the shade."

"Good idea." Lucy unstrapped the baby and slipped her into a fabric baby carrier she had already slung over her shoulders. Dana grabbed the baby bag, and Phoebe brought the dogs.

Everyone was soon settled in their usual places and Maggie served cold drinks from the tea cart and even gave the dogs water in plastic bowls.

Lucy held Charlotte sitting on her lap, facing out. The baby gazed around with wide eyes. Lucy's friends were mesmerized. They'd all visited her at Lucy's home the past few weeks and had even come to the hospital soon after she was born. But having Charlotte at the shop was different. Lucy felt it, too.

"This makes it official. Charlotte's one of the gang now," Suzanne said happily. "Maggie might even try to teach her baby knitting."

Maggie shook her head. "As if there's such a thing. She'll learn it all in due time."

"Including argyle?" Suzanne practically whispered.

"Even that," Maggie insisted, "which reminds me . . ." She reached into her knitting bag and pulled out a package wrapped in yellow tissue paper. She handed it to Lucy. "This is for Charlotte. I think it will fit by the time the weather gets cool."

"Maggie . . . you shouldn't have." Shifting the baby to one side of her lap, Lucy began to pull back the paper. Maggie had already given her so many beautiful gifts— sweaters, hats, mittens, booties, and blankets. Lucy guessed she'd gone to work the moment Lucy had announced she was pregnant.

Lucy unfolded the last layer and found a tiny hooded sweater inside, knit in a fine, super-soft pink yarn with a band of argyle, stitched in pale yellow and powder blue.

"Maggie, this is so beautiful! I absolutely love it." Lucy was flabbergasted. "You little sneak. When did you make this for her?"

"You and the baby have been bonding the past month. I had plenty of time." Lucy could tell she was proud and pleased at Lucy's reaction.

"It's exactly the sweater I imagined. But so much nicer than the one I started," Lucy recalled. "Those gender neutral colors looked like a bowl of lumpy granola by the time I gave up on it."

Maggie laughed. "No comment. At least you tried."

"I'll try again. Someday. Right now, it's hard to see how knitting will fit into my schedule," she admitted.

"It's tough to find time for a shower at first," Dana recalled. "Until the baby gets set in a routine. Is she sleeping much at night?"

"She wakes up a few times, but it's not so bad. I've mastered the art of breastfeeding in my sleep." The baby squirmed and Lucy checked her diaper. "My mom left on Sunday. It was great to have her with us. She was a big help."

"It's great that she was able to stay awhile," Maggie said. "Where was she headed? Some new exotic digging site?"

Lucy shook her head, smiling. "She found a summer gig practically in the neighborhood. Some shore town in Connecticut. Guilford, maybe? Or Niantic? An old house was knocked down and when the new owner started construction, artifacts turned up from the early settlers and Native Americans, dating back to the 1600s. She usually studies much older communities, but she wanted to be close enough to visit on weekends."

"You'll appreciate having her nearby," Maggie said. "You're still on the new baby high, but you'll need a break soon. Charles and I would be happy to babysit anytime. You and Matt can have a night out . . . or you can just take a long nap."

"Ditto for me and Jack," Dana said.

"Ditto for me, too," Suzanne added. "My gang would go gaga over that little doll."

"Don't forget me on the babysitter list, Lucy. I'm all in," Phoebe promised.

"Good to know, my friends. What an awesome lineup. I'm going to collect on those offers, too. Especially when I go back to work. Which won't be for at least six weeks," she clarified. "But I got a call from Helen Forbes that made me wonder if I should make a career change. She was impressed with the research I did for Rebecca. Even though I missed the cyber account password hidden in Colin's manuscript." Lucy still felt foolish about that and vowed to be more thorough the next times. "Helen wants to meet and talk about how I can help with her cases."

"That's big, Lucy! Good for you," Dana said with a happy laugh. "Your amazing talents are finally being recognized."

"I know you love your art and design business, but that could be fun, and a fresh direction," Maggie said thoughtfully.

"And probably very lucrative," Suzanne added. "And we can be backup if you get stuck. I'd love to stitch and dish about Helen's cases."

"There are probably confidentiality issues," Lucy reminded her. "But, before you know it, Maggie will be hanging an extra sign out front, 'Black Sheep Detective Agency.' "

Maggie shook her head. She'd been flitting around the porch, serving cold drinks and a plate of home-baked spice cookies.

"I wouldn't go that far. Though the name is catchy," she allowed. "You have the whole summer to enjoy the baby before you decide what to do. How's Dara been enjoying her new sib?"

"She adores having a baby sister. And I didn't realize how much a nine-year-old could help. She reads to her and plays with her and is the perfect backup at bath time. She told us that she doesn't want to go to camp this summer because she'll miss Charlotte too much. But we think when the time comes, she'll be ready to have fun with Sophie and her other friends."

"Speaking of Sophie, how's Rebecca doing?" Maggie asked.

"She's doing her best," Lucy reported. "Leo isn't well. He's in a prison hospital. Even if he rallies, Rebecca doesn't expect him to live much longer. He knew that he didn't have much time left. He told me that made his decision to take Colin's life easier," she recalled.

"Poor Rebecca, she hasn't caught a break lately, has she?" Suzanne said. "She doesn't even have the café to return to."

"She was looking for restaurant work. But now she and Nick decided to open a new café together. She won't get any of the money recovered from Colin's cyber account. It's been seized as evidence in the investigation of the Department of Public Works. But Rebecca and Nick are pooling their resources and looking for a location," Lucy explained. "Probably not in Plum Harbor. Rebecca is sensitive about all the negative publicity she's had here. But someplace nearby, like Newburyport or Gloucester."

"That's a bright spot for her. I'm glad she has something to look forward to." Dana was playing with the baby, waving a little bear-shaped rattle she'd found in Lucy's baby bag.

"I hope it works out for them, too," Maggie agreed.

"In every way that counts," Suzanne added.

Lucy caught her meaning. "Right now, Nick and Rebecca are just friends and possibly business partners. Rebecca said they're taking it slow in the relationship department."

"Please . . . the guy is crazy about her, anybody can see that," Suzanne insisted. "He even confessed to a murder he didn't commit so she'd be in the clear. He's a knight in a white apron."

"A lucky knight, too, since the police never charged him

for that gallant act," Dana noted. "Making a false confession is against the law. Noble reason, or not."

Dana sat back and tucked the baby toy into Charlotte's bag. But Suzanne leaned forward and gently smoothed a little pink sock that had almost slipped off.

"I just want to say one more thing," Suzanne began in a strangely serious tone. She glanced at Lucy, her gaze lowered. "I'm sorry that I ever doubted Rebecca, even for one millisecond. It wasn't very nice, even if she was unaware. I know it hurt your feelings. I know I shouldn't blurt out every thought that flits across my brain. But I can't seem to control it."

Suzanne's sincere words caught Lucy off-balance. "It did hurt my feelings," she admitted, "and it made me feel frustrated. I mean, if you didn't believe she was innocent, what chance did she have with the police?" Lucy recalled thinking back. "It's big of you to apologize, Suzanne. I admire someone who can admit when they've made a mistake."

"You know me. I'm a big person in a lot of ways," Suzanne returned to her usual jocular tone.

"So we've noticed," Maggie said. "And you are getting better with the blurting. We know you try."

"You do try," Lucy agreed. "As for Rebecca, you can be nice to her on Thursday. I invited her to knitting night."

Her friends looked pleased. "We'll all be happy to see her," Maggie said.

"It will be like a fresh start." Phoebe smiled at the baby. "Wouldn't it be cool if we could be babies again and start over with a completely clean slate?"

"Isn't that called amnesia?" Suzanne looked to Dana for an answer.

"I know what you mean," Lucy replied. "It's good to

put the past behind and start fresh. To see everything as if for the first time. The way I see the world now, because of my daughter."

Maggie smiled down at the little girl. "I agree. Babies are so inspiring. They give you hope for a better world. Three cheers for our new baby, Charlotte Binger-MacDougal, the next Black Sheep generation," Maggie declared. "I can't wait to watch her grow."

Notes from the Black Sheep & Company Bulletin Board

Dear Knitting Friends,

Is it already August? Where did the summer go? I know that most of you are busy soaking up the last weeks of summer sunshine and maybe even vacationing before school and office schedules pick up. I excuse your absence from the shop, but as I always say, the holiday gift list won't be filled if your needles are idle in the summer and fall.

The shop is quiet, but I don't mind at all. We've had some excitement here lately. As many of you know, Lucy Binger and Matt MacDougal have a beautiful baby girl who's about two months old. Charlotte visits often and brightens up the shop in a way nothing else can. It's an in-

describable thrill to watch a new generation of
our knitting circle arrive and thrive. We fuss
over Charlotte as if she's a princess. She is, to us.
I know she'll be swaddled in our handiwork and
our love for the rest of her days.

On a darker note, I'm sure you've all heard
about the dreadful and mysterious death of Colin
Hurley. I know that many in town quietly and
not so quietly suspected his wife, Rebecca. I suppose from a distance, without knowing her or
the facts of the case, I might have made the same
mistaken assumption. But my friends and I believed in her innocence from the start. Lucy
Binger in particular was committed to finding
proof of Rebecca's innocence and in the process
of that search, she uncovered graft and corruption in our county government. Due to Lucy's research, insight and hard work, an investigation
of Essex County's Department of Public Works
has been launched. Bravo! Not bad for a woman
who was over eight months pregnant, I must
say.

The irony is that while Rebecca's name is now
cleared, the identity of Colin's killer has been a
tragedy for her family. We continue to support
her and send all good wishes for the success of
her new restaurant in Rockport, which we hear
will open soon.

As always, in times that are joyful or challenging, the Black Sheep keep knitting. And you

should, too. This is an excellent time to take a class at the shop. You'll have our full attention. Or bring in a project that's misbehaving or even one you've given up on. I love solving stitching glitches.

For those who are well along the fiber road, I'll add that our group tried the argyle stitch this summer—with mixed results. The point is that we all tried and if you really want to earn your knitting stripes, you need to take a run at that pattern, too.

Since I believe in building on our knitting success stories, I'm posting links for two free patterns. The first is a classic pullover, a vintage all-over argyle pattern in a fine gauge. The second is also intermediate level, but a more contemporary take. It uses a larger-gauge needle and the simple argyle band makes it a bit easier.

Both can adapt to many stunning color combinations. Please drop by the shop if you'd like suggestions. Or, as noted above, if you hit some stitching speed bumps. Hate to brag, but I'm often called "The Yarn Whisperer."

Enjoy the rest of the summer and happy knitting!
Maggie

Lady's Argyle Pullover – A vintage pattern
https://freevintageknitting.com/free-sweater-pattern/cm736/ladys-argyle-pullover

Modern Pullover with Argyle Band
https://www.yarnspirations.com/bernat-argyle-sweater/BRK0129-006055M.html

Notes from the Black Sheep & Company Bulletin Board

Dear friends and fellow knitters,

First, Matt and I are so grateful for all of your good wishes and congratulations on the birth of our daughter, Charlotte. Everyone predicted my routine would be blown to bits "once the baby comes" and I must admit, they were right! But we're gradually finding a new schedule—me, Charlotte . . . and the dogs, of course. And it's all good. The bottom line is, I love being a mom even more than I ever expected, or imagined. Which was a high bar to meet.

Yes, there are some stressful moments, but my dear friends are only a text away. Just between us, they sometimes give me too much advice. I'm not complaining. Who needs baby books when you have a team of fairy godmothers hovering nearby?

I hear the little critter stirring in her crib so I'll keep this short. The entire village knows about my nine-month craving for Baked Mac & Cheese, and many have asked for my favorite recipe. Here it is, passed down from my dear Granny Binger. It's hardly a gourmet version, like my friend Suzanne prepares, but I love it. Maybe because of the happy memories?

I'll let you decide for yourself and make some happy memories around the dinner table with your own family. I wonder if Charlotte will like this dish as much as I do? When she's old enough to eat real food, I mean. So many adventures ahead! I can hardly wait.

With love and gratitude,
Lucy Binger

Granny Binger's Baked Mac & Cheese

Ingredients
8 oz elbow macaroni (about half a 16-oz box)
2 tbsp unsalted butter, plus a pat or two to coat the baking dish
16 oz cheddar cheese in blocks and good quality*
8 oz cream cheese (room temperature)
1 13-oz can evaporated milk
1½ cup whole milk
1 tsp salt
⅛ tsp ground nutmeg
1 large egg, beaten
Fresh ground pepper (to your taste)

*Note: This cheese can be all of one type: extra sharp, sharp, or mild, or a mixture. Or you can sub in 8 oz Monterey Jack or Gouda, depending on your preference. Do not use pregrated cheese since it tends to be dry and will make the dish far less creamy. Granny *always* grated the cheese herself and you should, too.

Instructions
Preheat oven to 350°F. Lightly coat a 3-quart casserole dish or 9 × 13 pan with a pat or more of butter or spray with cooking spray.

Cook macaroni according to package directions, adding at least 2 minutes to the maximum time listed on the package. The macaroni should be tender. This will make the dish creamier.

Drain macaroni and return to pot, making sure the pot is empty of all water.

Stir the butter into the macaroni until butter is melted, and leave macaroni in warm pot.

Shred cheese blocks using a box grater. Set aside about half of the shredded cheese mixture for later.

In a large bowl, blend the softened cream cheese with evaporated milk until mostly smooth (remaining lumps will dissolve in the oven).

Mix in the whole milk, followed by the salt and nutmeg. Stir in half of the shredded cheese.

Taste mixture to see if seasonings are to your preference and adjust if necessary.

Stir in the beaten egg.

Add buttered macaroni to milk/cheese/egg mixture and stir to combine.

Pour the mixture into the casserole dish or pan. Top with the remaining grated cheese.

Bake at 350 degrees for 50 minutes.

Enjoy!